GREEK ISLAND SUMMER

SUMMER READING COLLECTION

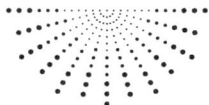

MELISSA HILL

ISLAND SUN

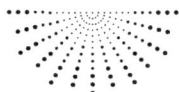

CHAPTER ONE

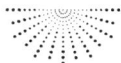

"To Ellie, my annoyingly lucky best friend," Maria toasted, with a bottle of beer, a grin on her face. "Congratulations for landing not just your dream job, but one with a guy who is probably the most talented, but *definitely* the hottest chef on TV."

Everyone on the roof terrace of the San Francisco town-house held up their drinks and hollered in unison. She blushed and raised her own glass in return as the night sky pulsed from the Golden Gate Bridge across the water.

It was chillier than usual in the city, even for summer and she zipped up her jacket to fight the shivers that were a combination of both cold and nerves.

She was excited but also more than a little overwhelmed about her new job, and there were a lot of things she had to do to get ready for her first day on Monday. Her best friend's party was a welcome distraction.

Zack Rose...

She was *actually* going to work for Zack Rose— internationally acclaimed chef, cookbook author and TV personality. A bona-fide international celebrity with over *twenty million* social media followers.

The thought that Ellie would share the same planet as the guy, let alone be one of his employees, seemed laughable, but it was true.

It had taken three rounds of interviews, but she had done it, knocking out a plethora of other applicants and landing a much sought-after marketing position with his media company.

"So what's he like?" Maria asked, beer in hand as she sat beside Ellie on the outdoor sofa.

"Who - Zack?"

Her friend nodded enthusiastically, but her eyes were slightly vacant, indicating she had already imbibed a few Bud Lights for the evening, which on her small frame would carry her well through the night.

Ellie shrugged. "I only met him briefly during the interview process and we haven't really talked."

"Never mind that - is he as hot as he looks on TV?"

Ellie didn't want to burst Maria's bubble, but she didn't want to lie to her best friend either.

"Yes and no. You know how he looks so tanned onscreen and has perfect white teeth? In reality, he looks a lot older, his skin is absurdly orange and his teeth look like they've been bleached white about five times too many. That alone you'd probably be able to get past, but he's also *super* skinny. On TV he looks normal and healthy, but in person... he's almost scrawny."

Maria nodded slowly as if she had just heard something deep and spiritual, but in actuality was just trying to not appear as drunk as she was.

"Is he seeing someone?" she asked, evidently unfazed by anything Ellie had just told her.

She laughed. "I don't know. I just got the job a couple of

weeks ago and I don't start until Monday. I know as much as you do about his personal life. Probably less, I expect."

Scott, a mutual friend, plopped down on the other side of her declaring, "Ellie's going to hook us up with all the celebs!" He gestured to everything on the roof. "And soon, instead of eating takeout Magiano's here, Zack Rose himself will be catering our little get-togethers."

He held out his fist for Maria to bump, but she didn't get it and left him hanging.

Ellie giggled and did it for her. "Um... don't get your hopes up guys," she said dubiously. "At most, maybe I'll be able to get you a signed cookbook for Christmas."

"You're in denial," Maria slurred. "You need to accept your own worth. You and I are not the same pimply-faced graduates in tens of thousands in debt anymore. You're shit-hot marketing guru Ellie Moore, and only... I don't know what your debt is anymore but I imagine it's much less now. You're moving on up sweetie, and now your world is about to look a whole lot different. Are you ready?"

"I think so," Ellie replied sheepishly, clinking glasses with her friends.

But was she?

CHAPTER TWO

THE FOLLOWING MONDAY, Ellie arrived at Zack Rose's media complex an hour early so she could have time to organise her desk and acclimate to her new surroundings.

The media offices/studio comprised a bland concrete building about fifteen minutes away from the city.

This had surprised her each time she went in for a follow-up interview. For an A-list celebrity/business tycoon, Zack Rose apparently had no problem working in a generic office building on a forgetful street.

Ellie never brought it up, but the guy himself did during the first interview:

"I'm a self-made man and as such, I understand the value of money," he said in his English accent, but with that faint Mediterranean twinge that belied his Greek roots.

"I could afford something ten times better than this place, but I'm not willing to spend the money on it, and I wouldn't be the man I am today if I did. So I think very carefully about what I consider necessary, and what I consider frivolous. I surround myself with the best people I can find, and I'm willing to pay top dollar for them because I know at this point in my life that if I didn't I'd be wasting my money— and I *hate*, notice I'm using the word *hate* - I *hate* wasting money. I tell you this so you know how important this is to me. Are you, Ellie, the best in your field? Will hiring you be the best use of my money? Or will I be flushing it down the toilet if I do?"

Ellie hadn't specifically prepared for this question during her practice interviews, but she knew right off the bat how she would handle it.

Without hesitation, she looked him confidently in the eye and said, "I am the best you'll find, and I'm the best investment of your money because—"

She believed how she handled that question is what landed her the job— in particular her use of the word *investment*.

In the marketing world, confidence, real or otherwise, was how you persuaded people, Ellie knew.

Whether what she said was true or not, well…

When she pulled into the attached parking garage she noticed that there was already a handful of cars present. Things were already in full swing at— she checked her watch— 6:55 am.

Inside the building, a small, bespectacled rat-like man appeared out of the shadows when she came through the door, and put a finger to his lips. He made circling motions in the air to indicate that they were recording in an adjoining studio.

Ellie nodded and proceeded to tiptoe past, but the small man stopped her again. He mimed to her that she needed to take off her heels before he would allow her to walk any further.

She slipped them off, and the unnamed sentry walked her to the media offices in the back.

Treading lightly, she got a glimpse of Zack Rose in-studio on the way. Spiky blond hair, artificially tanned skin, glowing white teeth, he was kneading dough and talking continuously as he did:

"I know it's a pain to work with, but we're not making pizza dough here. It's got to be a little sticky. Add too much flour to make it easier on yourself, and you will have botched the whole process. Your dough will be too thick for pasta. If that happens or has already happened, put it aside. You may as well make pizza with it later. Just hit pause, rewind, I'll still be here, smiling like this— " he walked up to the camera and gave an extra long, sarcastically wide smile and stopped still.

As he was pretending to be frozen, he caught a glimpse of Ellie looking at him when she walked by. It was only a moment, but she thought she saw a flicker of annoyance in his eyes. It quickly faded as he held up the dough one more time to the cameras.

The sentry opened a door for her and they both walked into the cubicled office.

The man eased the door closed behind them before turning around.

"I'm so sorry," Ellie blurted. "I didn't know he recorded this early. I thought I was going to be the first one in."

"Mr. Rose begins his days very early. Tomorrow, if you choose to arrive at the same time, I would ask that you walk around and enter from the street entrance. It's not convenient, but Mr. Rose hates to be distracted while he's recording." Then he bowed to her and added, "Good day, Miss Thomson, and good luck. I hope *you* last longer than the others."

He left, making sure he eased the door closed again with only a whisper.

Others? How many others have there been? Ellie wondered, gulping.

.   .   .

8

SHE FOUND her cubicle and unloaded her small bag of stuff on the desk. She booted up her laptop and as she was arranging her things, she heard someone else approach quietly.

They stepped slowly and softly as if they were afraid they might trip off an alarm.

A lean, muscular man peered at her and Ellie recognised him as the lead member of the existing marketing team Jeff Welch. He had been at all of her interviews.

"Oh *Ellie*," he whispered, smirking. "You didn't come in through the parking garage did you?" He seemed to think it was hilarious.

She nodded, gulping afresh.

Jeff scrunched up his face and shook his head dramatically. "Whatever you do, don't do *that* again. He'll probably let it fly today, but next time—"

"Walk around and come in through the front. Someone already told me."

Jeff relaxed a little. "It's not a big deal," he continued, flitting around her work area, picking up a picture of her and Maria and looking at it, before quickly losing interest and putting it back. "He just gets into his groove and doesn't like to be taken out of it." He smiled wide and asked, "So - excited for your first day?"

Ellie smiled back and said that she was.

"Good. Just a heads up; Z the great and powerful, has arranged something fun to start you off. Do you have a passport, by any chance?"

"I..." This took Ellie completely off guard. "Yes, but not with me. It's somewhere in my apartment. Why? Where am I going?"

"I'll let Big Z explain it to you. First, I've got to arrange some coffee. He should be done in a few minutes."

Ellie wanted to call Maria and sob that she'd messed up her

first day already, especially when she saw more staff start trickling in through the front entrance. No one at all came in via the door she had been escorted through.

They all knew better.

Just then, the boss himself barged in briskly with a towel wrapped around his neck. "Ellie. Ellie Thomson," Zack shouted. "My office - now."

Her heart stopped. Crap, I'm getting fired already.

CHAPTER THREE

ELLIE WALKED across the hall to Zack's office, certain she was about to be yelled at, berated and finally, fired. He motioned for her to close the door and sit down.

"You speak Greek, yes?" he barked without preamble, walking with the towel still around his neck.

"Yes," she said, afraid to add that she'd studied it years ago in college but wasn't exactly fluent.

"Still fluent?" her new boss asked as if reading her mind.

Ellie thought about fudging but decided against it. "No, not really. Not enough practice."

He shrugged. "It doesn't matter. Everyone speaks English over there anyway. Everyone relevant, anyway."

Over where?

"I'm sorry, I don't understand," she asked. "I thought I was on the marketing team to help expand your business?"

"Yes, that's right. *Which* is why you're going to Crete," he said theatrically, wiping his face with his towel. "As you know, I was raised in England," he continued, his voice muffled through the material, "and by all accounts I'm English— as you can no doubt tell from my accent. But my parents are Greek, and our family lived in Crete before my father got a job in London. As you also know, my book sales are astronomical around the globe, my show's TV ratings are sky-high, and last month I opened a restaurant in Mexico City against everyone's best advice— all thinking it was the most idiotic thing I'd ever done— and yet it's booked every night for the rest of the year! The third restaurant I opened up here on the West Coast is the same— solid bookings. By all accounts, I should be a happy man and *you*," he emphasised, "should have an easy job. But there's one place I'm not famous, Ellie. One place where my food is ignored, my books overlooked and my TV ratings non-existent. I'll give you a dime if you can guess where."

"Greece? Crete, even?"

Zack flicked an imaginary coin over to Ellie and she pretended to catch it, at which he smiled for a moment and she relaxed a little.

"The place of my forefathers couldn't care less about me. I want a piece of that market - a big piece. If anyone notices and decides to bring to attention that my own people think my food is crap, then my empire crumbles overnight." He snapped his fingers to emphasise. "And I need you to get over there and stop that from happening."

"There's no way they don't like your food," Ellie argued and shook her head. "I've always watched your show and ate at your restaurants every chance I could get. Your modern take on Mediterranean food is amazing. Nobody could ever say it's … crap."

Zack smiled wide— he apparently liked compliments, which Ellie realised was probably why the lack of attention in Greece wasn't so much a business gap, but a major blow to his ego.

"So you're going to Crete," he continued. "There's a restaurant in Hersonissos called Thasos. Every night it's packed just like my own, and people fly in from all over the world just to go to there. I need you to figure out why it's so popular because together..." he paused for dramatic effect, "we're going to take it down."

Ellie's eyes widened.

"People need to be flying to Crete to go to *my* place, not theirs. I'm going to open up a rival restaurant that will make everyone forget all about this Thasos, and you're going to lay the groundwork for that. Understood?"

Ellie nodded, understanding that her first task for Zack's company would be a form of corporate espionage.

She could do it though; a major part of her skills was zoning in on something successful, understanding exactly what made it so and then replicating the results.

Marketing 101.

"It's a big job," Zack continued. "And a bloody important one to me, but I trust you with it. I know you can do it. I had a feeling about you the first time I met you."

"I won't prove you wrong," Ellie said determinedly.

Zack nodded as if he already knew this. "Jeff will arrange your tickets and will be going along with you. I've already pulled a few strings and got you both a reservation at Thasos on Thursday night after you fly in."

"Thursday this ... week?" she clarified, taken aback.

Her boss looked up sharply. "Will that be a problem? Any family members you need to deal with or a boyfriend, perhaps?"

"No, there's no one like that. Won't be a problem."

Zack nodded and motioned that they were done. She was at the doorway of her office when she heard him add, "Welcome to the team."

Ellie beamed. A trip overseas to an idyllic island in the sun on her very first week?

Maybe working for Zack Rose wouldn't be so bad after all.

CHAPTER FOUR

SHE SPENT the rest of the day researching the Cretan restaurant scene and reviewing Thasos' menu.

The restaurant's offerings seemed pretty standard Mediterranean fare and the ingredients used were certainly nowhere near as innovative or imaginative as Zack's.

Yet reviews across the board were stellar, suggesting there was something more to this place than met the eye.

Many reviewers claimed it was the best dining experience of their lives, and a few even claimed to have had healing experiences there (whatever that meant).

And aesthetically Thasos was beautiful—no surprise if Zack considered it a serious rival. Judging from the pictures on its website, and its geographical position on Google Earth, the restaurant could not have been located at a better spot on the island.

Not only did the crystal clear Aegean waters glimmer on the horizon in a lot of the shots taken from customer tables, but it was also right in the heart of Hersonissos, a popular Cretan tourist town.

Whoever owned the place must be swimming in money, Ellie thought.

The exterior of the building was interesting in an avantgarde sort of way. It seemed to be paying homage to Greece's past with sandstone blocks and arm-wide columns and was either designed to incorporate an iconic Greek structure of the distant past or made to look as if it did.

Architecture aside though, whoever had decorated the interior had avoided the common pitfall most other clichéd Greek tavernas fell into: there was not a single statue anywhere in the restaurant.

Smart, Ellie thought.

Subconsciously the restaurant seemed to tell each of its customers that it was offering something different, something unexpected from other traditional Greek tourist eateries. That people shouldn't go to Thasos if they were looking for a shish kebab and a Corona. This place was authentic through and through, and despite herself, Ellie was already excited about eating there.

If Zack truly wanted to compete with Thasos on level terms, from what little she had already gathered, he would have his work cut out for him.

She leaned back in her chair. In truth, she didn't even need to visit in person to know that Thasos would be a seriously difficult rival to topple. She had enough experience in the business world to tell apart the barkers from the biters.

To compete with a restaurant of this calibre, one as popular and established with tourists and locals alike was going to require more than just skill.

Ellie sighed, understanding that her upcoming jaunt to Crete would certainly be no vacation.

CHAPTER FIVE

IT WOULD BE an overstatement to say that Ellie hated flying, but it did make her extremely uncomfortable because of her height — at six feet, there was just nowhere to put her feet.

The farthest she had ever flown was from San Francisco to New York City. It was roughly a six-hour flight, and she'd felt bruised and beaten afterwards.

Compare that to the coming trip to Athens, which including connections was estimated at sixteen and a half hours… and then onwards to Crete.

Sixteen and a half ever-loving hours. Maybe she could use the time to brush up on her Greek and re-read *The Stand*. Hell, she'd probably have time to finish the famously long Stephen King tome *and* be fluent in Greek by the time they landed.

So when the evening before they left, Jeff showed up at her desk with a pair of business class tickets, and she nearly wept with delight.

"Seriously?" she asked her new work colleague, not able to hide her awe and surprise.

"Honey, we're too tall to fly coach," he said theatrically,

then leaned in and whispered, "Zack would probably throw a hissy fit if he knew, but... I'm not going to tell if you don't." Then he winked and flounced back to his own office.

Ellie could have kissed him but doubted the guy would get anything out of it.

On Thursday afternoon - after a long, but surprisingly comfortable flight across the Atlantic, she and Jeff sat in the departure lounge at Athens airport, waiting to board their connecting flight to Crete.

Though she'd slept through much of it, Ellie was still fatigued and more than a little tipsy from the liberally poured alcohol in the business class cabin.

Still, her chatty new colleague was great fun to spend time with (not to mention wickedly indiscreet about their famous boss) and throughout the journey she and Jeff had become firm friends.

"You know, that hottie over there has been checking you out for the past five minutes," Jeff commented now, nodding across the departure lounge.

Ellie too had noticed a gorgeous guy throw a couple of appreciative glances her way. About early thirties, he had the look of a native, and 'hottie' was indeed an appropriate description.

But he'd obviously heard Jeff talking about him and just then quickly turned back to the book he was reading.

"And now you've scared him off," she muttered. "Great job, wingman."

Jeff shrugged. "He shouldn't be looking anyway. How does he know we're not together?"

Ellie chuckled. "Really? You honestly think we look like a couple?"

"Fair enough," Jeff said, feigning hurt.

People in the waiting area started to move about restlessly, and Ellie realised they were about to start boarding their flight.

"Where are you sitting on this one?" she asked, getting out her boarding pass. There was no business class option on the connecting flight to the island. Unfortunately.

But at least the trip was short.

"Across the aisle and one up from you, I think."

Out of the corner of her eye, Ellie saw the guy looking at her again across the waiting area. It was surprising, she thought as after such a long flight, she must look terrible.

She was wearing a pair of white jeans that emphasised her long legs and had paired it with an oversized black t-shirt that showed just the right amount of cleavage.

"Sexy without being slutty - nice," Jeff had described her upon meeting him at San Francisco airport earlier.

The hottie seemed to sense Ellie looking at him, but instead of acknowledging that she too was checking him out, he quickly went back to his book.

It was a shame because he truly was handsome as sin.

His eyes were deep brown, and though his black hair was a curly mass, it had gorgeous silkiness to it. Unlike most of their fellow travellers - mostly tourists who had dressed down for the coming flight - he was also meticulously well put together. Shiny brown shoes, dark-pressed pants, refined buttoned-up shirt with the sleeves folded up to his elbows.

She leaned over and whispered into Jeff's ear.

"Is he actually Greek or just of Greek descent do you think?"

Jeff scanned him and said, "Your observational skills are horrible. Greek, obviously."

"How do you know?"

"Other than the obvious— no tourist I've seen has ever worn anything other than sneakers on a flight— he's reading a translated Stephen King."

So he was. Ellie hadn't noticed that. And a nice coincidence that he was a King fan too.

"You should go talk to him," Jeff said. "You're probably not seated anywhere near him. It's now or never."

Ellie thought about it, but then the guy looked up at the airline stewardess as she announced boarding, and suddenly jumped up and walked away as if he'd realised he was sitting in the wrong waiting area.

Disappointed, she watched him leave.

CHAPTER SIX

YAWNING HARD as she trooped tiredly onboard, Ellie had the cold air blasting at full force and her little neck pillow wrapped around her as soon as she had stowed her carry-on bag.

She plopped down into her window seat and was asleep before the aircraft was even half-boarded.

"Wake up," she heard Jeff whisper in her ear, startling her. "Ellie!"

She snapped awake. "What? What's wrong?" she asked, groggily. "Are we landing already?"

Jeff pointed behind her. "In one minute that Greek hottie who ogled you in departures and who you in turn ogled back is going to come out of the bathroom and sit back down beside you. Try not to drool all over him this time."

Beside her?

Ellie caught sight of the Greek Stephen King book face down and open on the vacant seat alongside hers. The hot guy was actually sitting *beside* her; she must have been already asleep when he'd boarded...

"I didn't drool *that* much when I looked at him—" she argued.

"Nope, I mean *literally*." Jeff held up his phone and waggled it at her as he mouthed, "I'll show you later."

The Greek with the beautiful brown eyes was returning to his seat, and Ellie ripped her neck pillow off, shimmied her oversized top straight, and pretended to be looking out the window when he sat back down next to her.

Had she just drooled onto him in her sleep? *Please God, no.*

She discreetly glanced at his left shoulder. Oh hell … his dark shirt was blotted all over. Not only had Ellie apparently rested on him while asleep, but she had obviously cuddled right into him to find the most comfy spot too. Mortifying!

Ignoring her, he pulled out his Greek version of *Mr. Mercedes*. Ellie looked at her watch and saw that they still had a little while to go with the journey.

May as well get this over with, she thought.

"Erm …I've just been informed that I've been sleeping on you. I'm so sorry," Ellie said to him.

He chuckled and looked up from his book. "It's OK. It's part of the flying experience. Part of … how you would say … the package."

Ellie tried to smile, but what came out was more of a grimace than anything else.

"And I've also been told I drooled on you," she admitted.

"Did you? Hm, I didn't notice."

A lie, but a white one. The best kind.

"So," she said changing the subject. "Stephen King? Do you like him?"

"Very much," he said. "I just finished the JFK one, *11/22/63*. Have you read it?"

Ellie nodded. "I try to read widely, but every time I pick up a book for travel, it's a King one." She shrugged. "You know any book by him is going to be good. Did *11/22/63* break your heart as much as it broke mine?"

The man zeroed his gaze upon her and nodded devoutly. "The whole time I was reading it, I could have cared less about Jake going after Oswald. The real story was the love story."

"I know. I wept after I finished it. He could have been so happy. Why didn't he just stay? Why didn't he just teach?"

"I cried too," the man said.

Ellie's brain stopped. A man had just admitted to crying over a love story. The accent gave him away as not American, but admitting to crying cemented it.

"But part of it bothered me, though," she said. "So often in stories, the moral is that man should lay aside his own ambitions and be content with a simple life. Is it so wrong to want more out of life? To try and do something noteworthy? Can't you do both? Why does it have to be a choice."

"No, I don't think that's what Mr. King was saying. I think he was saying that love is just as historical as anything else. That *it is* the great thing in your life— not the other stuff you think is."

"Uh-oh, I think I'm sitting next to a romantic," Ellie joked.

"But the message is true, don't you think? It feels right. When you have true love you could not care less about everything else going on in the world. That you're not settling if you abandon your historical, grandiose notions because love is more powerful than anything you could imagine. It truly is something that deserves your complete, undivided attention, yes?"

Wow. Ellie swooned a little, wondering what kind of conversations this guy had with people he knew.

She decided then and there that she wanted to know.

"I'm Ellie. Ellie Moore." She held out her hand.

"Chris. Christos Katsaros."

They shook hands. His was strong and calloused but made a point to grip hers gently.

"So have you personally known that kind of love?" Ellie asked, not caring that it was her obvious way of asking if he had a girlfriend.

"Me? No. But I believe in it. And my parents, I believe they have it."

"That's nice."

They chatted for a little more until eventually she asked: "Are you from Crete, Chris?"

"Yes. I live in the town of Hersonnissos."

"Oh really? How strange! I'm going to Hersonnissos too."

As Ellie said this, a little voice in her head told her to back up a little and not come across as too eager or forward.

"Yes. My parents and I run a restaurant there," he continued. "It's a very popular place. Perhaps you've heard of it ..."

Ellie gasped. Cosmic synchronicity - or fate - was something she truly believed in. Like the pounding of a prescient drum in an Alfred Hitchcock movie, it comes and you can't do a damn thing about it.

Please don't say it, she begged, unable to believe this. For the love of God don't say—

"...it's called Thasos."

CHAPTER SEVEN

Soon after, the plane landed at Chania International Airport. It was early morning, judging by the light.

The sun was rising amidst glowing orange clouds, and the Aegean sea appeared darker than it probably would in an hour or two. Right then it was a rippling dark purple mass.

Ellie walked off the plane behind Chris. She had steered the conversation away from the restaurant as quickly as she could, but not before he'd invited her to visit there.

What could she do but say yes? She was not only going to go - this evening actually - but she *had* to go, and Chris was going to see her when he did, thinking she was there to see him.

And he'd be right, but not completely.

In the arrivals hall, he stopped amidst the busy crowd and, fished his wallet out. He handed her a business card with his phone number, email and address of the restaurant.

"Come and eat at our place, please" Chris reiterated. "Don't worry about reservations."

"I will," Ellie said, smiling. "I'd really like that."

"I must hurry now. I got a text while I was sleeping that I

needed to pick up some shipments of food on my way back. Our normal driver woke up sick. If I speed and ignore every traffic law, I won't be too late for the pickup time." He chuckled. "It is a relief. At least the place hasn't burned down in my absence."

Jeff was waiting for her in the carousel area and whipped out his phone as soon as Ellie appeared.

"I've been *dying* to catch up with you," he gasped, smiling. "I've wanted to show you these photos for so long I'm shaking in excitement."

"Go ahead," Ellie sighed. "Let's get it over with."

Jeff swiped his phone and showed her a picture of her sleeping on Chris's shoulder during the first half of the flight. Not only had Ellie found his shoulder to sleep and drool on, but she'd actually wrapped her hand around his right arm, hugging him to her.

"Oh my goodness. I'm all over him..." she said, mouth agape. Mortified, she sheepishly asked Jeff to delete it, but not before sending a copy to her. He nodded and did so there and then.

"That's not the only one I wanted to show you, though. See, check these out. In particular, this pic." He held up a picture of Ellie with her mouth open and drool running down her chin. "It's my favourite. You look like a zombie. I'm going to airbrush some blood on you and blow it up for *Walking Dead* nights. Want me to send this one to you, too?"

It was then that Ellie realised that Jeff truly *would* be a friend for life.

He already had too much on her.

. . .

IT TOOK another couple of hours for the two to reach Hersonissos from the airport, but it was a relaxed and easy drive in a transport shuttle.

The island of Crete was a lot more hilly than Ellie had imagined. Also less green than she thought it would be, she commented to Jeff.

"That's the West Coast," her colleague whom she knew had visited before, told her. "The east coast is a lot drier for some reason. Go west and you'll feel like you're in a rainforest."

There were some trees but they were mostly variations of pine or palm, and the few shrubs that grew from the white, parched earth were dry and dwarfed-looking. They made the whole East Coast look like one long extended dune.

Ellie rolled the window of the shuttle down and noted that even the air seemed dry. A digital thermometer on the dash blinked that it was in the upper eighties, but it didn't feel like it. The old saying *it's not the heat, it's the humidity* was true.

But Hersonissos itself was bustling with people and alive with dynamic architecture packed at every turn. Brightly coloured mopeds zoomed by, people walked and talked in steady streams, and the air smelled of a combination of fried food and salty air.

The shuttle dropped them off in front of their hotel, which Jeff had chosen wisely— the Aegean Sea crashed into the sand just a stone's throw away.

They tried to check in but were informed by a gorgeous but snotty receptionist with perfect hair, perfect skin, and perfect nails that they were much too early.

Ellie begged, but to no avail. "Please. It feels like we've been travelling for days - we can't just wander around for six more hours. You have to have something. I'll take anything."

"No, this cannot be done. It is against procedure. If you

want, you may leave your bags with us until your room is ready."

"But it's not about the bags ..." Ellie began.

Jeff pushed his way in and took over.

"Hey there," he said to the receptionist in a very low, deep voice. Then he leaned in, puffed his chest out, and complimented her hair before explaining that they had just been on an excruciatingly long flight with two connections, and the thought of waiting until three in the afternoon was simply inconceivable. Ignoring her weak protests to his compliments, he then idly asked what perfume she was wearing.

"It works well for you," he said, laying it on thick. "Always wear it. You smell... I can't even explain it. It's almost nostalgic for me..." He pretended to think, and said, "Oh, I know, don't take this the wrong way, but you smell just like the girl I took to my senior prom. The one who got away ..."

Ellie couldn't believe that any woman would actually believe an iota of this blatant nonsense, but incredibly Jeff's flirtations were working.

Blushing deeply, the receptionist eventually took their passport details and magically 'found' a room Jeff and Ellie could use to freshen up until theirs was ready. That was if they didn't mind sharing for the moment - whereupon she looked over at Ellie as if she were some kind of fungus.

"We'll phone when your rooms are ready," she said to Jeff, who took her hand and kissed it. The girl practically swooned.

In the elevator, Ellie said, "You sure know how to lay on the charm, Romeo."

He grinned. "I know how to get what I want if that's what you're saying."

They unloaded their luggage and Jeff said he was going to go for a walk, leaving with nothing but his wallet and his sunglasses.

Ellie stripped down and took a quick hot shower. It felt great to get out of her travelling clothes. During those last couple of hours in the shuttle, it felt like her jeans were trying to meld and become one with her skin.

She cranked the water as hot as it could go and was happy to find it could go quite high. When she finished showering, she went out to the balcony overlooking a quiet beach.

She hadn't even thought to bring a swimsuit, but now wished she had. Truth be told, she didn't like how she looked in swimsuits, be they one-pieces or bikinis.

She was too tall and felt like she looked like an Amazonian warrior enough as it was. Showing a lot of skin just seemed to make it worse. But she thought she could brave it here - especially in this heat.

She went in and collapsed onto the bed, thinking about meeting Chris on the plane. How typical was it that the one guy she had genuinely been attracted to in years was slated to be her first victim as Zack Rose's marketing person?

Talk about fate - not to mention bad timing.

She recalled his eyes— those beautiful, dark brown eyes— and remembered what he'd said about love.

"....more powerful than anything you could imagine. It truly is something that deserves your complete, undivided attention."

"I work for the devil," she moaned into her pillow.

Only Satan would have Ellie crush such a beautiful, sensitive man in the name of progress.

CHAPTER EIGHT

SHE WOKE up mid-afternoon and realised she should get up soon if she didn't want to be jet-lagged throughout the entire trip.

She turned on the TV in the background while she got ready, and it automatically came on to a cooking program.

Of course.

There was her boss— Mr. Zack Rose himself, smiling and looking straight at her. Ellie thought his presence - albeit on TV - was more than a little eerie as if he was keeping an eye on her through the screen.

Zack was telling a story about his Greek grandfather, but that's not what she found eerie. What got to her were his eyes. The rest of him seemed jovial and animated, but not his eyes. His gaze was cold and calculating as if communicating a different message— one solely intended for Ellie.

You better draw blood, they said. You are there to do my bidding. Don't forget it.

Ellie switched off the TV.

The sound of the ocean was better.

· · ·

"I'm so glad you're wearing heels," Jeff said to her later, while they were waiting for their taxi to come to the hotel. "It means you own your height which is sexy if you embrace it. And I never would have thought it, but white looks great on you, and it's just the right amount of tight."

"Thanks - I think."

The taxi driver who pulled up was an overweight, balding man badly in need of a shave. He looked back at them once they were seated and asked, in perfect English, where they wanted to go.

"Thasos - the restaurant? You know it?" Ellie asked, buckling herself in.

He blinked slowly and nodded. "Yes, I know it and can take you there. No problem. But you should know, this time of day the traffic is unpredictable. It can be rough, even outside of the tourist rush. If you want, we can agree on a fixed price or we can go by time. It's up to you."

"How long in good traffic would it take us to get there?" Jeff asked.

The man shrugged. "It's hard to say. Maybe a minute or two in perfect conditions. Twenty euros, though, and I'll take you there. It doesn't matter to me. I'm working either way."

Jeff and Ellie looked at each other and silently communicated that this seemed fair. This was a work trip after all.

"OK," her colleague said. "Works for us," and handed the driver the money.

The man pocketed it and shifted his taxi to first gear.

Ellie was about to ask Jeff if he had researched anything about Thasos when the car suddenly stopped.

"There," the driver said and pointed to the restaurant. He had driven them about four blocks away from the hotel.

Jeff bit the inside of his cheek and said, "The traffic conditions. They were good then?"

"Perfect," the driver said and chuckled.

Ellie was still shaking her head in disbelief as they got out, but Jeff shrugged as the taxi drove off.

"There's one of those guys in every city on this little planet. He got us. Just count your losses and move on."

"But I didn't pay. You did," she pointed out, trying to keep a straight face. She was amazed anyone could get one over on Jeff.

"All the more reason for you to keep on walking," her colleague said through gritted teeth and took her arm as they walked up to Thasos' front of house.

Over the roaring of the ocean surf, a young man asked if they had reservations. Ellie gave him the details as Zack had already arranged and he led them inside.

The first thing the two noticed about Thasos, other than the delicious scent of Mediterranean cooking, was a pianist in the back near the patio, playing soft, melodic music.

Ellie liked it, and so did Jeff, who stared at the pianist with intense curiosity.

"I think I know him," he whispered.

"Who?" she asked, looking around.

"The piano player. I've watched him on YouTube for years now. He doesn't upload much, but on occasion he does. His mic needs to be upgraded, the video quality looks like something from the mid-nineties, there's never any description below, but..." he trailed off and Ellie inwardly laughed at him for verbalising his YouTube pet peeves.

He turned to the maitre d' and asked, "He composed the music he's playing right now, didn't he?"

"Patrick? Yes, everything he plays he composes. He comes here to try out his new music. That and he seems to like the acoustics here."

The man led them to a table in a corner that gave Jeff an uninterrupted view of the pianist.

Ellie's seat allowed her to look out at the sea. The north side of the restaurant was one big wall of panelled glass that could be opened back in high summer. Instantly transfixed by the beautiful Aegean waters, she relaxed and took in the view.

She briefly glanced into the kitchen to see if she could spy Chris, but there was no sign.

The pianist finished a song and Jeff softly clapped for him. Ellie noticed that he and the other man made eye contact for a moment before he went into another song.

Then suddenly Chris popped up beside her and her mind went blank.

"Ellie!" he exclaimed. "I'm so glad to see you again so soon." He glanced at Jeff. 'And who is this with you?"

"Don't worry, buddy - we're not together," Jeff said without looking at him. Ellie tried to smile, but Chris seemed a little taken aback.

"He was on the flight with us," she said. "You just didn't see him. He's my colleague ... I mean friend... Jeff."

Chris seemed to think about offering his hand to shake, but reconsidered, as Jeff seemed off in his own world watching the piano player.

"So have you recovered from the flight?" Chris asked Ellie. "Are you on Crete's time zone, or San Francisco's?"

"I napped for most of the afternoon and feel a lot better now," Ellie admitted. She looked around. "So, nothing appears to have burned down anyway," she joked, recalling how he'd mentioned on the flight that he was worried the restaurant would burn down in his absence. "Unless all of this is new."

Chris laughed. "Yes, everything was fine. But I've been

thinking about what you said earlier. About how everyone comes running to me because they see me as the competent one. If my parents had someone else or were forced to make decisions on their own, things might run a little more smoothly around here."

Ellie smiled, happy that he'd been thinking about her, though she still felt guilty for the brief information she'd gleaned from him about the restaurant on the flight.

"So has anyone brought you a menu yet?" he asked then.

She shook her head.

"Good. Then I will be your waiter tonight." He bowed solicitously, before going off to pick up two menus. "I will give you a moment, and then offer some recommendations if you need any, but please take your time."

Ellie thanked him and was looking down at the menu when she noticed that Jeff had since got up and was talking to the piano player.

Great. Abandoned already.

CHAPTER NINE

SHE GLANCED at the menu and very quickly knew what she was going to get. She'd already familiarised herself with Thasos's offerings via her research, and there was one dish in particular she was anxious to try.

Her thoughts meandered back to Chris and how he'd been so kind and solicitous towards her, completely unaware that she was at his restaurant under false pretences.

If she hadn't gotten so lost in her thoughts she might have noticed Jeff walk away from the pianist and pull his phone out to show to Chris.

It was Chris's light laughter that broke her from her reverie.

Jeff draped a casual arm over the Greek man's shoulders as he swiped through pictures on his phone - the ones of Ellie draped all over him on the plane.

Her face burned with mortification. She could have jumped up and tackled Jeff to the ground right then.

They walked back to the table, chuckling like two schoolboys.

"Do you need more time?" Chris asked as Jeff sat back down.

"No, I think I'm ready to order," she said through gritted teeth.

Jeff said he was too. "Can I have the grilled Psari? That's enough for me for the moment. It looks like plenty."

Chris nodded. "Good choice and it is, believe me. My mother spared nothing when she created that dish. I think she had a growing teenage boy in mind when she did. I used to eat anything I could get my hands on when I was younger."

He took Jeff's menu and then turned to Ellie. There wasn't the slightest smirk on his face as he waited and she had to marvel at his manners, given the photographs of her at her worst he'd just seen. He really was a true gentleman.

As his delicious brown eyes bored into hers, she gulped, trying to remember what she had decided to get.

"Can we start with a side of spanakopita?" she asked. "And for my main dish may I have the moussaka? And for wine, can you choose something that you think would accompany everything for both of us?"

"Of course," Chris said, smiling and taking her menu.

When he was gone, Ellie rounded on Jeff. "I can't believe you …" But he simply, shushed her, once again absorbed in the pianist's music.

Her phone vibrated with a text message. She pulled it out thinking it would be her mom or Maria checking that she'd arrived OK, but it wasn't.

Send me pictures of the food or anything else you think is useful.

Swallowing hard, Ellie surreptitiously snapped a couple of pictures of the restaurant just to show her boss that she and Jeff were there as arranged and sent them to Zack along with a message: *"Awaiting appetiser. Will send more as food arrives."*

"Do."

Feeling like a heel, she quickly put her phone away when

Chris came back with a plate of spanakopita and a bottle of white wine.

"This is an Assyrtiko from the small island of Skiathos - a beautiful place to visit if you are ever able," he said.

Jeff nodded. "I visited for a few days with my father when I was still in college. It was ..." he paused and thought for words, "a very hard place to leave."

Chris uncorked the bottle and poured some for Ellie and Jeff to taste.

It was dry with bitter citrus notes. Ellie wasn't much of a wine enthusiast, but she liked it. Jeff seemed to also. Theatrically he swished the sample around in his glass and then in his mouth before drinking it.

"It's got a lot of surprises to it actually," he commented. "How much does a bottle of this typically cost?"

"In American dollars? About $300."

Ellie felt a sting of sticker shock but then remembered that it was Zack and not she who was paying for this.

"I like it," she said, breathing a sigh of relief. Chris filled both their glasses and then stood back and waited for Ellie to try the spanakopita.

Cut in hand-sized triangles, the spinach pie - a Greek speciality - felt like it was cooked perfectly. Not too soggy, not too crispy. It had a nice weight to it, too.

She took a bite and smiled. Feta cheese and butter made everything in life taste better— even spinach.

In college, she had a brief encounter with vegetarianism. For one year she fought the fight, and it was dishes like spanakopita that made it last as long as it did.

It was a small Greek restaurant a stone's throw away from her dorm that introduced her to spanakopita. She ate there at least once a week, and when she did she always got an extra spinach pie to take home. She had thought at the time that she would never find anywhere else as well able to make that particular dish.

She was wrong.

"Everything about this is perfect," she said to Chris. "The spinach isn't too dry or too wet, and the breading is simply wonderful."

"Yes, I know," he agreed with a smile. "It's my mother's recipe. I didn't know how good it was until I started eating out on my own as a teenager. It was then that I realised my parents were offering something important to the restaurant world."

"How long have they had this place?"

"My whole life," he told her. "But we just own the restaurant, not the building. This we rent. The owner was an architect my father knew. Somehow he got permission, the architect I mean, from the city to construct this building around the remains of a temple that was standing. These columns you see outside have been at this geological location for over a thousand years. The glass, the wood, and the lighting were all built around it. Everything but the stone is new. It's seamless."

"Did he know he wanted to put a restaurant here? The architect?" Ellie asked.

"Yes, and to tell you the truth, I'm quite positive he built everything with my parents in mind. I've seen pictures of him eating at our house before I was born. I think he already knew they could make something magical if he gave them the space to do it. Both my father and my mother were top-rated cooks long before this place was built."

"Sounds like he was a wise man," Jeff commented.

"*He* was," Chris said, emphasising for contrast. "His son though... " He shook his head.

There was a story there Ellie realised, but decided not to push.

At least, not unless she had to.

"Do you cook?" she asked instead.

"I do, a little - but my take on Greek food is a little different from my parents. They are more traditional whereas I'm a little more modern. One day, I hope to have my own restaurant as successful as this one. When I start it - perhaps when my parents are gone - I don't want anyone to know I was involved with Thasos. I want everyone to just like it for what it is and forget all about this place."

Interesting. Ellie realised, brightening a little. *He wants this place forgotten, too.*

Perhaps Zack had nothing to worry about after all, and Thasos would simply fade away in its own time?

She knew from her research that Chris's parents were in their late sixties, and wouldn't be able to keep this place going forever - especially if their son wasn't going to continue the family legacy.

"Your meals should almost be ready," he said. "I'll be back in a few moments."

When he was back in the kitchen, Jeff turned to her. "Some interesting information there," he said. "Did you catch it? Sounds like the place is already on a downward spiral if the guy isn't going to stick around. This might not even have to get dirty."

Ellie hoped not. For as little as she knew about Chris, she didn't want to hurt him.

The music stopped and Jeff rose again and went to talk to the piano player, who smiled this time when he saw him.

Clearly, he was making progress.

Ellie's phone buzzed once more in her pocket and she sighed.

She truly hated herself for doing so, but she sent a short message to Zack, detailing the dish she'd just eaten as well as the wine.

Family recipe. Incredible.

Zack shot back with: How do you know it's a family recipe?

Owner's son told me.

Great work! Keep talking to him!

On it :)

She wasn't one to use emoticons, but she wanted him off her back. A smiley suggested enthusiasm and energy for the task at hand.

Both things Ellie was sorely lacking just then.

She saw the top of Chris's head coming out of the kitchen and she quickly put away her phone.

"This looks even better than it normally does," he said to her and winked. "I'm not joking. I wish I could pull up a seat and share it with you."

Ellie chuckled, "You can if you want. You don't have to be formal with me."

She saw that he considered it, but he shook his head and said, "There are a few regulars in here. It would cause too much of a stir. It would get back to everyone in the kitchen and then my parents would find out. Then you'd be eating with my mother who, though smiling, would harass you to find out everything about your past, your parents' past, and what your grandparents did during World War 2."

Ellie laughed and said, "But really... it would be nice to talk with you some more. It's my first time in Crete and I'd appreciate some suggestions for places to see - from a local, especially."

Chris smiled then nodded then towards Jeff. "Well as your travelling companion seems already…. otherwise distracted, something tells me you'll be spending some of this trip on your own and we can't have that. Maybe the day after tomorrow, I can show you around a little before the restaurant opens in the evening?" he suggested.

"Sounds great." Ellie smiled and tried to convince herself that this was all in the name of more research on Zack's behalf, but she wasn't successful.

Chris was wonderful and she did want to spend more time with him.

"Where are you staying? I can pick you up," he asked.

She gave him the hotel name, deciding to not bring up the fact that she and Jeff had stupidly taken a taxi over and gotten swindled in the process.

"Perfect," Chris said. "I live close by. So did you have any particular plans? Would you like to do something early?"

"Not really. But something early is fine by me. Maybe ten?"

"I'll see you then. For now, I must leave you to your food."

Ellie looked at her moussaka: alternating layers of thinly sliced potatoes and eggplant topped off with ground beef and drowned in a creamy white bechamel-parmesan sauce.

One bite in and she nearly wept. The textures alone made her ravenous for more.

She took out her phone and snapped off another picture.

We've got our work cut out for us …

In more ways than one.

CHAPTER TEN

HAVING SPENT her first full day in Crete catching on her sleep and familiarising herself with her surroundings, Ellie woke up early, the morning Chris was due to pick her up, and decided to walk around the town a little before he arrived.

Jeff, who had spent the previous day with Patrick the pianist, was once again out and about with his new friend.

He and Ellie had decided to spend the next few days uncovering more about Chris's family situation and future plans before they told Zack anything else about Thasos, or formulated plans for a rival restaurant.

Ellie tried to tell herself that today would be part of that research, but there was no denying that she was looking forward to seeing Chris again. There was something about him, something besides his good looks, that had drawn her to him right from the very beginning.

She knew it would be a huge struggle to put her professional feelings before personal where he was concerned, but for the sake of her new job, she had no choice but to do so.

But that didn't mean she shouldn't enjoy spending time with him in the process.

On the way down in the hotel elevator, an elderly couple got in.

Speaking Russian, their voices were soft and tender to one another. Though the man stood erect and stared directly ahead (Ellie suspected because she was there), his wife couldn't stop looking at him.

She scooted close to him and reached for his hand, and he took it without hesitation. More gentle words were exchanged between them, and the wife put her head on his shoulder.

Love seemed an inadequate word for these two.

Ellie ached watching them. That gentle knowingness and stillness that came from being with someone for years; that complete faith and confidence from knowing your partner loves you and would do nothing ever to slight you; a feeling that doesn't fade, transition, or mutate, but instead escalates and deepens with each passing year.

She wanted that.

The doors opened, and the man insisted Ellie exit first.

Outside, Hersonissos was alive and bustling. People chatted as they walked along the shore. Children laughed and ran into the water. Bells on doors jingled as shops opened their doors.

Ellie noted that people made a point to look her in the eye and say good morning as she walked by.

Were they just being polite to the lonely tourist girl? Or did people here actually take notice of one another?

It was a few blocks before Ellie realised that she didn't actually know where she was going, and that she had just been walking aimlessly. Then she saw a familiar sign and recognised she was nearing Thasos from the other direction.

Fate, as it would turn out, was at work yet again.

An older woman spoke to a man just outside the entrance to the restaurant. The guy looked not much older than Chris and he was doing most of the talking.

He gestured to the woman and then back at the restaurant with quick jabs of his forefinger, spittle flying from his lips.

The woman— late sixties or even early seventies— wore a blue bandana and a long, ankle-length white dress in the traditional Greek style. Whatever she was hearing was clearly news to her.

She tried to stand tall and defiantly to mirror the confrontational man, but the weight of her heavy breasts (or maybe the gravity of the news) only allowed her to do so in short bursts— like a push toy where every push and release of the button either makes the toy stand or collapse to the ground.

As Ellie got closer, her college Greek allowed her to understand one thing the woman was saying. *Eíste o gios tou patéra sou.* "You are your father's son."

She didn't say it indignantly, though. Rather it came out as a question. *Your father's son huh? Are you and he related?*

There was no question in Ellie's mind now that this woman was Chris's mother and the man was their landlord— the son of the architect he'd spoken about the other night and toward whom he'd hinted at mixed feelings.

The conversation abruptly ended then, and the man turned from the older woman and walked the five feet back to his shiny black sports car.

When he was out of sight, the woman who Ellie guessed was Chris's mother allowed herself a sob and staggered back into the restaurant. The built-in bolt clicked home, the lights turned off, and the shades fell closed.

Ellie wanted to console her, but what would she say? What

could she possibly say to a woman whose very livelihood was being threatened— not just by that man but by her boss too?

And she realised then that Thasos wasn't just a restaurant, business rival or threat to Zack Rose's world domination.

Behind it were real people, with feelings and lives at stake like Chris and his poor mother.

Now that she'd seen the place first-hand and the people behind Thasos, could Ellie truly - in all good conscience - be the architect of this lovely family's downfall?

CHAPTER ELEVEN

SHE MADE sure to be back at the hotel in time for when Chris said he would arrive to pick her up. She walked into the lobby and sure enough, he was already there asking the hotel clerk to call her room.

"I'm telling you I know her. She came to my restaurant the other night." By his tone, Ellie could tell he wasn't making light conversation.

"We met on a flight," he continued. "Her name's Ellie Moore. Why would I know her full name? If she didn't want to see me, why would I know she's even here?"

"Pígaine stin paralía. Ypárchoun korítsia ekeí."

Go to the beach, there are lots of girls there. Ellie's four semesters of Greek were about eighty per cent confident that's what the guy said.

"Hey stranger," she sang out, thinking it best to intervene before things got ugly. The normally affable Chris looked just about ready to punch his compatriot.

"Ellie!" he greeted and hugged her. "This man thinks I am

trying to stalk you - at ten in the morning." He looked at the clerk who shrugged and went back to his business.

"Good to know he's trying to be protective," she joked, trying to make light of the situation.

Chris gave the man one last stare down, and then asked, "Ready?"

"Sure. So where are you taking me?"

"I thought we should go somewhere a little off the beaten track. You're here for a little while, yes? What you see here in Hersonissos is not the *real* Crete. While my home town is charming it is..." he struggled, "now much like you'd find in any other touristy area. So I thought I would take you to the west. It's a bit of a drive, but worth it." Then his eyes travelled to her clothes. "You wouldn't, by chance, have anything else you can wear would you?"

Ellie blushed hotly. "I do, but... You don't like what I'm wearing?"

He chuckled a little. "No, no, that's not what I meant. I was thinking we might go walking. Crete's known for a lot of things - mostly beaches and old ruins, but one thing tourists don't seem to know about us is that we have excellent hiking trails. The best in the world, I'm told, but I can't say for sure as it's all I know."

Ellie beamed. "Hiking?" Her father used to take her hiking in Yosemite when she was younger, but she hadn't done so in a very long time.

Chris nodded. "I thought also we could pick up some, what do you call it in America, 'brunch?' A combination breakfast and lunch. We can pick up something along the way. Like I said, though, we will be in the car for a while, but if you're visiting Crete, then one place you must go is Sfakia. I would be derelict in my duties as a native if I did not take you there. But your friend, Mr. Jeff, will he be OK without you today? He's more than welcome to come along."

"Jeff? No, he's fine. He's with the piano player from your bar. They hit it off the other night."

Chris smiled but seemed a little surprised, his face suggesting he hadn't known either man was gay.

Ellie went up to her room and changed out of her skirt into shorts and a light t-shirt before heading back down.

Chris smiled appreciatively at her long toned legs. "So, let's have an adventure."

"Let's," Ellie replied, smiling back.

CHAPTER TWELVE

WALKING AROUND TOWN EARLIER, most of the cars she had seen were small, energy-efficient Hondas, or cute little Fiats.

Growing up, Fiats reminded Ellie of clown cars at the circus and with her height she couldn't imagine fitting in one, let alone driving one. People had cars of all sizes back in the US, but tiny cars seemed in absolute abundance on Crete.

So when Chris walked her back to an old, rusty-looking farm truck, she was a little taken aback, but pleasantly so. Here was a vehicle that wouldn't ensure her knees ended up in her eye sockets in case of a collision.

Chris unlocked the door and held hers open for her. No one in America had ever held open a door for Ellie, and it seemed fitting that the first one to do so would be the proud Greek owner of a beat-up old Chevy.

With a roar and one big plume of black smoke upon starting, Chris eventually got them up to cruising speed before heading westbound on Crete's northern coast.

The truck's elongated bench seating was comfy enough, but the seams were undone in many spots and leaking yellow foam.

The steering wheel was a faded robin-egg's blue and was so large that Chris barely had to turn it to take them into a hard turn.

He used this ability on many occasions when cars drifted into his lane. No one in Crete seemed to check their mirrors before merging; it was an unspoken rule that Chris be forced to yield to any and all incoming traffic.

Unlike Ellie, if she had been at the wheel, Chris was calm and unperturbed by everyone's seemingly senseless driving.

They chatted and listened to the radio as they drove. It was an old, metallic one with manual tuning and volume dials. Ellie didn't know what they were listening to, but it sounded like music to a film. When she asked Chris if he knew, he said he thought it was the soundtrack to *The Thin Red Line*.

"Sounds like Hans Zimmer," he said. "I've never seen it, but I've heard the soundtrack a couple of times."

"Are you talking about that war movie from the nineties?" Ellie asked.

"Yes. We have a soundtrack station on the island. This is one thing that surprised me when I travelled to your country. You don't have movie soundtrack stations. So much energy and enthusiasm for your movies yet where's the radio station to support that?"

Ellie had never thought about it that way.

They drove along the coast for the remainder of the morning. The truck sputtered and shook violently along the dashboard whenever Chris had to speed up, but it was otherwise a smooth journey.

Rolling treeless rocky mountains became visible at one point, and Ellie asked if there had been a recent fire.

"No, we call them the Lefka Ori, the White Mountains. Others call them the Madares, which translates to the Bald

Mountains. Most of the year they are white with snow. The rest of the time, the sun shines so bright on the limestone, that they still appear white. We're going to drive between them in a little bit and head over to Sfakia soon— it's on the southwest coast of the island. Are you hungry?"

"Yes," Ellie replied, playfully scolding him. "It's a good thing I had a bagel before you arrived."

Chris cringed. "Sorry. I'm not good with time. I hope you're not starving. But there is a small restaurant on the way that if you can make it, I think you'll appreciate."

"Why is that?" she asked.

"You seemed to appreciate our food the other night. The dishes I want to get for you there is - how do Americans put it - in the same ballpark."

Ellie said that sounded good.

"I'm so sorry again. Of course, I should have fed you by now. I just… I don't know, I suppose wanted to make sure I gave you a good tourist experience."

"It's OK. Really. I'm having fun and to be honest, I haven't really thought about food since we hit the road."

It was true. It was easy to ignore hunger pains while bouncing along the countryside and seeing so many new sites. By and large, Hersonnissos had given her the impression that Crete was your standard Mediterranean tourist haunt, but that wasn't even remotely the case. While certainly touristy, away from the coast the island was also wild and largely unsettled.

The truck suddenly bucked and started to slow.

Chris cursed.

She looked at him and asked, "What's wrong? Are we breaking down?" Her earlier fear had come to pass after all.

"No, no. I just … forgot to fill it up before we headed out. We're out of fuel before I thought we would be. Don't worry, I have some tanks in the back." He eased the truck over to the side of the road and turned it off.

"How much do you have?" Ellie asked anxiously as he got out. "Will it be enough?"

Chris nodded back to her. "Oh, I have plenty. I use leftover grease from the restaurant to make biodiesel."

She didn't know this could be done and said as much.

"One of the perks of running a restaurant. You have most of the ingredients to make your own gas. And you can make some for your car, too," he joked.

She giggled. He had such a cheesy sense of humour which only added to his charm.

Chris poured in several large gas tanks' worth of fuel and got back in.

Ellie had her doubts that the truck would start back up, but it roared right to life and they were quickly cruising down the road again.

"You have lots of surprises in store, don't you?" she said looking sideways at him.

Chris winked at her. "You have no idea."

CHAPTER THIRTEEN

ABOUT AN HOUR DOWN THE ROAD, Ellie's stomach started rumbling. She didn't think she would be able to make it much further without eating, and admitted as much to Chris when she stopped seeing any signs of buildings or homes.

"Well this is good," he said, and turned left onto a straight and long highway that went between the White Mountains, "because we're just at where I wanted to bring you."

Though the mountains that rose high into the air were bare, the valley they were driving through was wild and abundant with life.

Sounds of chirping grasshoppers, frogs, and birds filled the truck's cab.

Chris turned off the radio so they could hear better. "We're a little more than halfway to the trail. We'll fuel ourselves up, ride a little further, and then have a nice little walk."

The front of the truck dropped down when the road ceased being paved. Behind them, waves of dust swirled into an opaque cloud.

"It's a lot different on this side of the island, isn't it?" he said to Ellie. "Almost feels like a different planet. Crete still surprises me, and I've lived here my whole life."

Chris slowed and pulled into a small gravelled parking area where a few Jeeps and Hondas sat. He turned the engine off and pointed to a trail that went into the forest.

"The restaurant is through there," he said.

"Is it also a monastery?" Ellie asked, taken aback.

"No," Chris replied. "But the people running it will make you question."

They got out and Chris held out his hand. She took it automatically, as if it was the most natural thing in the world, causing Ellie to remember the old Russian couple back at the hotel.

Chris caught her eye and when she smiled shyly, he squeezed her hand.

Oh God, I think I'm already falling for this guy...

Was he like this with all tourists though, Ellie warned herself. She knew that Mediterranean men had a reputation for being charming but feckless, so perhaps she should be on her guard, but she'd met her fair share of players back home too.

Chris seemed ... different.

"In English, the restaurant would be called *New Valley*— Néa Koiláda in Greek. You won't find it in any travel guide. Not because the owners don't want foreigners inside, but because they have no interest in advertising themselves. They are happy with the money it makes through simple word of mouth."

"Not trying to take over the world or build any franchises?" Ellie replied dubiously.

Chris nodded. "Exactly."

They crossed into the shadow of the mountain, where the air was cool and moist. Large, heavy stones bubbled up from the earth, making it necessary to watch their footsteps.

"I don't feel like we're walking to a restaurant," Ellie said. "I still feel like you're taking me to a church. I like you and all, but I don't think we're quite at that stage just yet ..." she chuckled.

"It's just up ahead," Chris assured her, smiling.

Ellie checked to see that her phone was in her pocket just in case Jeff - or worse Zack - thought to check on her. It was, but she doubted it mattered— no one got any service in places like this. Not now nor in fifty years.

Some places were just removed from the world.

And that was a good thing.

A young couple walked by and Ellie almost breathed a sigh of relief because it meant they were going somewhere. Both greeted them in Greek and passed on, moving nimbly across the rocky path as if they had walked it a hundred times.

To the right, the ground quickly rose, and trees disappeared only to be replaced by solid rock.

A babbling brook flowed to the left, and the rock closed in around them in a gorge so tight Ellie looked up to see that they weren't walking in a well-lit cave.

Just as she was about to feel claustrophobic, the tunnel widened and opened out into a clearing. A dozen or more tables (some wooden, some stone), stretched across dark green grass. It looked more like a barbecue gathering in a park than a restaurant.

Chris sat down at a polished stone table encircled by milk crates for seating.

Ellie sat across from him, looking around at the 'restaurant' in both amusement and awe.

A woman draped in black cloth placed a small candle between them, and rather than light it with a match, went inside a nearby stone hut (where Ellie assumed they cooked the food) and came out with a candle already lit.

Holding this, she bent and lit their candle, then exited without saying a word.

Chris grinned at Ellie. He looked like a schoolboy waiting anxiously for a prank to commence.

"Are we going to get menus?" she whispered, leaning forward.

Chris shook his head. "No, they serve you what they want to serve you."

Another woman, this one older than the first, came out holding a tray with four glasses on it— two large and two small — and placed them on their table one at a time.

"The big one's obviously water," Ellie said. "What's the other one?"

"What does it smell like to you?"

Ellie brought the smaller glass to her nose and sniffed it. It didn't have a strong smell. Slightly nutty, maybe a hint of something sweet like honey, but it was otherwise bland...

She took a sip, and her throat and mouth were instantly lit with fire. She coughed and put the drink down.

"What is this? Moonshine?" she asked, wiping her eyes.

Chris looked at her confused. "Moonshine?"

"Moonshine. You know, white lightning, bootleg, Mountain Dew." Chris's vacant stare stayed locked in place. "Let me put it another way, if I had a barrel of it, and I sat on it and lit it with a match, would it get me to the moon?"

Chris's eyes widened and he erupted into laughter. His whole body laughed hard. Then he calmed and nodded, wiping away tears from his eyes. "It's alcohol if that is what you're asking me."

"What is it called?"

"Tsikoudia. Another word is Raki. Translates roughly to firewater. Is this your first time drinking it?"

Ellie said it was and took another sip. This time she almost coughed herself hoarse.

"The proof ranges anywhere from forty per cent to sixty per cent, so take it slow. I'm surprised you haven't had it yet, though I suppose this is only your second day here. Everyone on this island drinks it like water. A lot of the old locals think it's a cure-all medicine— some even put it on skin rashes and warts. I don't know about its medicinal properties, but I do know it will get you drunk. It's very good at that."

"So you brought me here to get me drunk?" she teased.

Chris picked up her hand and kissed it. "No, I brought you here to spend time with you," he said, as inwardly Ellie melted. "The firewater is just an added bonus."

CHAPTER FOURTEEN

"So they're really not going to let us pick our food?" Ellie just couldn't wrap her brain around that.

"No," Chris said smiling. "A lot of fine dining doesn't allow you to either."

Then he leaned forward towards her on the table and whispered, "Let me tell you a secret. This whole place is mine actually but nobody knows it - not even my parents. Don't tell anyone."

Her eyes widened. "Really?"

"Yes. The land is in my family's name. It's not exactly legal what we're doing here— hence the lack of advertising, and it's not going to be in existence long. It's just an experiment for me to try out various foods and a new concept should I ever start my own place."

Ellie was amazed. "How long has it been around, and how much longer will you run it?"

"There are a few more dishes I want to try out, so maybe another month. This is the only season it's been open. My friend runs it for me. We opened it at the tail end of winter around March. My friend is a great cook, but every meal I design."

The older waitress came back and set them each down a bowl of steamed leafy greens, and a small communal dish full of baked pastries.

"What is all of this then?" Ellie asked, excited.

"The main dish is *horta vrasta*, and the pastries are meat and cheese pies called kreatopitas. The horta vrasta is a vitamin powerhouse. Normally it's made from collard greens, but we've made it out of wild greens that aren't farmed anywhere. Made with collard greens, horta vrasta is great for you to eat, but since we make it from foraged greens, the nutritional value of it has multiplied tenfold."

Ellie took a big bite. The greens were similar to spinach but had a peppery bitterness to them that she liked. Chris had mollified their taste with what tasted like beet juice. She asked if she was right.

"Yes and no. It's a cousin of beets that's not farmed anywhere. It too, is foraged." He took a bite and added with a mouthful of food, "You can eat the greens on their own, but I like to pair them with the meat pies."

"Are those foraged for, too?" she asked jokingly.

"Yes. How do you describe it? Roadkill."

Ellie spit out her first bite and Chris reached across and grabbed her wrist grinning widely. "I'm joking. The meat comes from locally raised goats."

The meat pies were juicy and thick, each containing pockets of cheese that came from grass-fed cows. As they ate, Chris also informed her that everything was cooked in locally churned butter.

"One thing civilisation has forgotten," he said, "and I include America in this, is just how nutritious and healthy animal fats are for us. People didn't get sick as often as they do now. Pollution's not helping, but it's not the main culprit. How we eat is. It's why I cook with the ingredients that I do. Many of the ingredients before us are not cheap for me to obtain, and some are downright expensive. But I believe very strongly in it. Whole milk would go perfectly with this meal, but I included the firewater with it so it would detox the system. With the fresh food that's now flooding your system, you should feel wonderful by the time we get to the trail."

"Could you afford to do this in a proper restaurant setting, though?" Ellie asked, chewing.

"Of course, the profit margins would be much smaller," Chris agreed. "But I'm OK with that."

She then remembered his mother crying outside Thasos earlier after talking with the landlord, who obviously wanted more money.

In the world of fine dining, Chris's family restaurant was as successful as any, but a dramatic spike in rent could do it under as easily as it would any other business.

Profit margins had to be high for any such business to survive, and as Thasos' manager, Chris surely knew this. He should know better than anyone that daily upkeep alone ate into most restaurant's profits.

And what kind of cold-hearted landlord would raise the rent right after peak tourist season?

But since it was none of her business, she decided not to talk to Chris about what she'd seen that morning.

"Everything goes so well together," she said, forking some greens onto her pie. "This is the best meal I've had in a long time if you don't count dinner last night. I almost feel like my blood is energised."

Chris smiled warmly at the compliment. "And it will feel that way for a good while yet."

The pile of pies before them dwindled until they were gone, long finished before they could even grow cold.

Now overly full, Ellie tried to remain ladylike and attractive while also stretching her stomach out and giving it more room.

She had a feeling she was failing miserably.

CHAPTER FIFTEEN

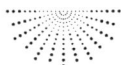

THE RIDE to Sfakia seemed to take far less than two hours. Chris's meal had indeed energised Ellie.

Legs wrapped under her, she asked him to change the radio channel as they bounced along the dirt road and give her something to sing to.

Loud and out of tune, she sang along even though she had no idea what anyone was saying, serenading Chris directly into his ear.

He wasn't a carefree singer like her but chuckled uncontrollably as she tried to not only hit notes she'd never hit but tried to sing in a language she didn't know.

Much like back in the restaurant when he'd kissed her hand, he surprised her again when he gently rested a strong hand on her knee between gear changes.

Forward, she thought but made sure he knew she didn't mind by scooting as close to him as she could, trying to convey to him that his touch certainly didn't offend her.

Soon he got bolder and left his hand upon her longer and longer— or at least as long as the truck would allow. It sputtered up a hill once, and Ellie wondered if it wasn't the steep climb that was causing the old truck to struggle but rather Chris's neglectful driving.

She hoped the latter, even though the truck sounded like a dying elephant.

The southern coast of Crete finally came into view at the top of one such hill. Far below, long, white beaches spread before the waters. Wispy palm trees dotted the sands and towered over the few post-summer stragglers.

"I liked the beach in Hersonnissos, but this one looks more unspoiled," she said.

"They're very different, but yes. It's roomier and there are not very many tourists out and about. Plenty of people still come, but it's a lot different from July and August."

Street parking was abundant there, also unlike Hersonnissos, but Chris had a specific place in mind and kept driving until he pulled into an area about fifty metres from a mostly intact ruin.

It didn't have that typical ancient Greek look to it, as the stone walls were still standing, and the thatched roof was still together save for a few spots, but it looked very old.

"Late eighteenth century," Chris told Ellie once they got out. "It's been cared for off and on over the years. It was used as a supply house during Nazi occupation. If the Germans had known about it, they would have surely destroyed it. As much as they respected our people, they never hesitated to lay waste to a lot of our monuments, despite what you may have read."

"I never would have suspected people were still recovering from World War Two here," Ellie said.

"Not so much my generation, but my parents'. They have a lot of stories they still tell. Their parents burned it into them, and they, in turn, feel a need to burn it into us."

It was hard to imagine Crete as a militarised zone. Probably even harder for its citizens.

The greenery that had been at Chris's experimental restaurant was still present here, only in Sfakia wildflowers grew on almost every square foot.

The forceful winds allowed trees to grow only sparingly, so grass and flowers ruled. The breeze that pulsed incessantly off the water shook and caressed the fields of green in great, unceasing, temperamental waves.

It was a warm day, but it didn't feel it out in the wind.

Chris pointed to a stone paved path that went uphill and back north from whence they came.

"This way," he said.

Ellie's heart sank a little bit. She would like to have stayed by the ocean. Everything was so still and quiet, yet loud and moving.

Sensing her hesitation, Chris turned back and said, "It's worth it. We'll be back. Have to if we want to drive home later."

The White Mountains rose like Titans just before the shore and Ellie gasped. Did Chris honestly think she was going to climb to the top of those?

From the looks of where they were headed, yes he did.

Firs, junipers, and spruces muted the ocean once they had walked for a few minutes.

With the trees blocking the coastal breeze, the air warmed up quickly. The trail was as unforgiving as any Ellie had hiked before. Mostly uphill, she lost her breath after just a few minutes.

As a San Francisco native, she had walked up her share of hills over the years, but this one was having its say over her. She leaned forward and pushed off her knees with her hands as she walked— a walk her father would call Neanderthal.

She could only envy Chris as he walked casually upwards ahead of her.

"You have some… interesting viewpoints on how a first date should go," she tried to say after they had walked well past the parking area, but what came out sounded like a series of heavy breaths.

Chris cocked his head. "Do you need a break?" he asked.

She waved him on and he resumed walking.

The ground eventually levelled off and they reached an area devoid of trees. Rough, bare rock rose like a tower still beside them, but they were high enough in the air that they could see rocky islands far on the horizon that they couldn't see at ground level.

"Is this where you wanted to bring me?" Ellie asked, admiringly. "It's beautiful."

"Not quite," Chris said. "Still higher." He pointed at the rock and walked up its steep embankment. It looked like he planned for them to just grab a ledge and climb.

"Chris, I'm honoured you think I can do that, but seriously… I'm no rock climber."

He turned back and looked forward a few times before realising the problem. Then he moved to the side and pointed.

Just a couple of steps past him was a break in the rock. Much like the monolith from *2001: A Space Odyssey*, it looked like an alien, foreign object on an otherwise predictable terrain— an open, straight black wound cracked into unblemished solid stone.

"It's a lot easier once you make it here," Chris said, emphasising the remaining five feet Ellie had to walk to get to him. "But it will be scarier in a few minutes if you don't like heights. You're not afraid of heights, are you?"

"I don't know..." she mumbled hesitantly. "What kind of heights are we talking about?"

"The kind you never forget," he replied, with a boyish grin.

Ellie's heart fluttered automatically. With that look in his eyes, how could she resist?

CHAPTER SIXTEEN

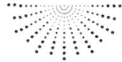

"OK," she said and pushed forward. "Lucky for you my father scared my fear of heights out of me a long time ago."

Chris offered her his hand and pulled her up the remaining slope.

Inside the tunnel, a stream of air gushed hard and then calmed once they were a few feet in. Moss and pockets of weeds tried to grow on what little soil had snuck inside the opening, but farther in and away from the sun the path became too rocky and dark for anything to survive.

The only light came from a lightning-bolt-shaped sliver of sky above them. Ellie could see and didn't feel in any danger, but she only felt comfortable walking forward because Chris was directly in front of her.

Without him there, she'd be scooting and sliding her feet just in case the ground dropped away.

Eventually, they came to a thick steel ladder bolted into the mountain. It went up high and far.

"Ready?" Chris asked. "You're sure you're not afraid of heights?"

"Lead on, cowboy," Ellie said. "I want to see where this goes."

Smiling, he started climbing up the steel ladder one rung at a time. Then he looked back down at her and said casually as the wind, "I like you very much, Ellie. You're a lot of fun," and resumed climbing.

She blushed as she followed him, unused to such direct flirtation. But with Chris, almost right from the very beginning, it had felt right.

The ladder was bolted into the mountain about every five feet or so, and its rungs were thick and perforated to prevent slipping. It was as safe and sturdy as it could be, but Ellie still felt crazy for climbing it.

Heart pounding, she followed after Chris, not bothering to talk or continue their light banter. Only the *ting-tang-ting* of their hands and feet slapping and pressing against metal filled the air between them.

Hand over hand, step after step, up, up, and farther up they climbed out of the shadow of the mountain and back into clear, white light, though they were still wrapped around the stone's cavernous wound.

They were so high now that Ellie wouldn't allow herself to look down. With sweaty hands and a nervous heart, add one more variable and it might all be over for her.

As her father used to say, looking down was a lot of people's last bad decision. "Wait until you're safe and sound at the top to do it if you feel like you have to," he said once while they were hiking up Half Dome. "At the very least, wait for a lull, because it's one thing to know, *but it's another thing to see.*"

They reached the top where some kind soul had continued steel handles and footholds on the ledge to make it easier to climb up and down. That was the hardest part about climbing— getting up and down from the top.

Ellie crawled to a stand, where she willed herself to look down, and was immediately glad she had followed her father's advice.

The bottom was only a small circle of darkness down below.

Yet they still had further to climb. The mountain still encircling them, Chris had walked over to the next ladder and was already a few rungs up waiting for her.

"Good?" he asked.

Ellie nodded. "How many more of these are there?"

"This is the last one. But it's taller than the others. If your hands are sweaty, I recommend getting them gritty on the ground before coming up. We're going to be on this one for a while."

Ellie rubbed her hands on the sooty ground and resumed following him.

Up, up, still further up. Both were still silent as they climbed.

What struck Ellie as wonderfully divine about where they were was the utter remoteness of it. The sounds of civilisation were long gone. No people sounds, no car sounds. The only thing she could hear apart from their climbing, was the steady rush of wind at the very top, and it was howling like a wolf.

"Are you ready to be on top of the world?" Chris asked, looking down.

"As I'll ever be," she answered, breathless.

"You're brave. There are many Cretans who have never done this. The first time I did this, I was with a group of five or six friends, and the only other person to do it with me was my friend Gregor— the one running the restaurant we went to this afternoon— and he complained the entire way."

"Well, this isn't my first rodeo," Ellie said, "and what's not to like? This is beautiful!"

Chris paused and looked down. "There are thousands of

places like this all over Crete, Ellie." He shrugged as if it weren't a big deal and added, "And if you'd let me, I wouldn't mind showing them to you."

Ellie met his gaze, realising that she wanted that too. She wanted to spend more time with this lovely Greek man who bit by bit was stealing her heart. They barely knew each other, but she and Chris had an intrinsic connection. It was undeniable. They both knew it.

Then Ellie suddenly remembered that whatever about Chris stealing her heart, she was here to essentially steal his livelihood, and the very thought made her stomach grow heavy.

CHAPTER SEVENTEEN

"YOU'RE JUST ABOUT THERE," Chris shouted down then. He grunted and pulled himself up.

Ellie looked up and saw he was out of sight.

She got to the top where Chris was waiting with his hand out. She took it and pulled herself free of the vacuum below her.

The light was almost blinding it was so bright. Her eyes adjusted, and suddenly all of Crete came into view. 360 degrees of it.

Ellie turned in slow circles, in utter awe at the beauty before her.

Chris chuckled knowingly and went and sat down to stare across the Aegean Sea. Blue waters were visible to the north, west and south, but to the east were green farmlands, brown chateaus, tiny white herds of sheep, and golden ribbons of road snaking in and out of view green, rolling hills.

Back to the sea, red, blue, and yellow sails pulled white dinghies across the cerulean waters.

It was overwhelmingly beautiful.

"My father's father ran away from home when he was a

teenager and spent a week camped out on top of this rock," Chris said. "He'd go down just long enough to fish, catch a few tuna, and climb back up. The whole town looked for him. My great-grandfather just happened to remember the look of awe on his face when he had brought him here as a young boy and decided to check it on a whim. My grandfather wasn't here when he arrived, but something told my great-grandfather to just wait. To just be still."

"Is this the grandfather who lived in the house we saw this afternoon?" Ellie asked, sitting down beside him. "The one you're using as your experimental restaurant?"

"Yes, the very same," Chris said. "My grandfather climbed up that ladder we just finished climbing, two fish slung over his back, and when he saw my great grandfather, he didn't run. He went and sat down beside him as we are now. The two cooked the fish together in silence. And when they had finished eating, they went back home."

"Did he do it just to see the views? Why'd he leave?"

"He wasn't that young. Germany had started assisting Italy in its assault on mainland Greece. Everyone knew Crete was next, including my grandfather. When it happened, he knew he was going to have to fight for his people. This was his calm before the storm."

"There's so much history everywhere here," Ellie whispered, still in awe.

Chris nodded. "And now I am on *my* calm before the storm, Ellie. My parents don't know it yet, but Thasos will go out of business soon. The landlord I told you about has been harassing us for months. He means to shut us down soon, which is why I've been experimenting with the other restaurant and doing so much research."

Her heart ached for him, and because it seemed this landlord was doing Zack Rose's - (and indeed her) job for him, she almost came clean.

Almost.

But still, Ellie couldn't bring herself to tell Chris the real reason she'd come to Crete.

Not yet.

Maybe never.

Instead, she sat with him and looked out at the waters, hugging her knees, her secret safe within.

"Thank you for using one of those days to be with me," she said, feeling sad for him. "Time must be precious to you right now."

"All the more since I met you," Chris said. He didn't say it looking at her. "You're something special."

He didn't say it after letting the air hang still between them. He said it matter of factly while looking out at the ocean.

And that made it even worse.

CHAPTER EIGHTEEN

AFTERWARDS, Chris took her to a restaurant in Sfakia that was right on the harbour. The little fishing village seemed sleepy compared to Hersonnissos, but not in a boring way.

Each town had its own heartbeat. Hersonnissos' beat was like that of someone walking excitedly to an adventure, whereas Sfakia's was like that of an old man sitting down for some meditation in his garden.

As an appetiser, Chris ordered them a simple portion of garlic bread. It was some of the tastiest bread Ellie had ever eaten. Crispy, but with pockets of warm butter that hadn't burned away, chewy but soft, and the garlic seasoning was mixed in with a sprinkling of parmesan cheese.

"This bread is made out of kamut grain, which is one that many gluten-intolerant people can tolerate."

"How so?" Ellie asked, through a mouthful of bread.

"It's an ancient grain, untouched by any modifications. The stomach can handle it because it's still how grains are supposed to be. The pasta we make at Thasos is made out of either einkorn or kamut. Gluten-sensitive people often ignore their diet while on holiday and eat whatever they want, regardless of whether or not they get hives or stomach aches. Many come to me the next day and ask me why nothing happened to them the night before."

"That could be a game changer for a lot of people, Chris. Do you advertise that? Have you bothered spreading that information around?"

He shook his head. "No. Many people in Greece know this. It's no secret to us, and wouldn't make me unique."

They ordered lamb gyros as their main dish, making sure to get two bowls of tzatziki to accompany it.

"As far as traditional food, gyros aren't high on my list. But here their tzatziki sauce is the best I've ever had, and tzatziki goes best with gyros. I've been trying to weasel the ingredients out of them for ages now, but they won't tell me. At four hours away, all I can do is insist I'm not competition, but they won't budge."

The gyros were massive (requiring two hands to lift), and the meat was cut to the perfect size. Dipped in the tzatziki yoghurt dip, Ellie abandoned all hopes of eating like a lady. She let her hands and face get covered with food, not bothering to use a napkin every time she got messy.

It hit the perfect spot after hiking all day.

They didn't get back to Hersonnissos until ten o'clock that night. Ellie fell asleep quickly after getting into his truck, but this time she purposefully found his shoulder to sleep on.

Her conscious and subconscious were now in full agreement that Chris was a wonderful guy.

If only there was a way to help him.

. . .

LATER, collapsed in bed at her hotel room, sure she was about to sleep the soundest sleep of her life, Ellie's phone chirped with a text message from Zack Rose: *"Update...?"* He'd even added an ellipsis, indicating his impatience.

She considered pretending she was asleep but decided to get it over with: "Spent the whole day with the manager. Honestly, all you need to do is wait. Landlord raised the rent so high it seems they have no hope of staying open. He expects to be out of business within a month or two."

"Shame. Any other insights into their success so far?"

Ellie's eyes widened at her boss's reply. No surprise or confusion? Just a simple *'shame'*?

"Truly, there's no secret that will help you, Zack. It's a terrific location, and the parent's love of cooking is palpable. You can feel it when you walk in. The food is delicious, but it's not the food that makes it great. It's the environment."

"You can 'feel it' when you walk in? Have you been sampling the local firewater? I need something concrete, Ellie."

"Sorry, it's all I have— but I'm positive there's no better answer. It's just a good place run by good people."

Especially Chris, she thought.

Zack must not have cared for what she said, because he replied, *"Where's Jeff? He seems MIA."*

And he will be for quite a while, Ellie thought. *He's fallen for a native, just like I have.*

But of course, she didn't admit this to her boss.

Then all of a sudden a thought came to Ellie and she decided to just jump straight into her suspicion: *"Are YOU behind the sudden rise in rent? Maybe the one pushing the landlord to get them out?"*

No hesitation from him this time. *"Guilty."*

Unbelievable....

Ellie gritted her teeth and shook her head.

*"This is why I hired you, Ellie. I knew you'd be able to see through things. Keep using those eyes of yours. And awesome job cosying up to the son by the way. Never knew you had **that** in you."*

Ellie almost responded back with a sharp retort but fought the urge. Zack was her boss after all.

But she was annoyed, not because of what he had just implied, but because of his additional subterfuge and admission about the landlord.

It dispersed a lot of confusion though. The likelihood Thasos was the target of two forces out to get it after operating in Crete peacefully for thirty years without any issues hadn't quite added up.

She was so angry she could spit. What Zack was doing behind the scenes was downright low.

If Ellie hadn't spent all day hiking, she might stay up all night boiling in her anger, but her body laughed at the thought of staying awake.

So she threw her phone on the nightstand, her boss's insulting text remaining as the last communication between them.

CHAPTER NINETEEN

SHE SLEPT WELL INTO MID-MORNING, and when she awoke she immediately wanted to talk to Chris. To tell him she had had a wonderful time hiking and talking with him, and that the entire day spent together had simply felt magical.

But she didn't want to call him because he was probably already busy at the restaurant getting supplies ready for the evening.

Instead, she sent him a text message:

Thank you for yesterday. You showed me another world.

Too cheesy? Too clingy? She didn't care. He needed to know that he was on her mind. Continuously.

He wrote straight back.

"No, thank you. Thanks for listening to my crazy ideas and maudlin rants. I was afraid I was too much of a downer last night after I talked about the restaurant...

So let me make it up to you tonight. I usually eat dinner before the crowds come in. Would you like to come to us for an early dinner today? 4:30?"

"Love to," was all she wrote back.

Ellie could only hope Chris was grinning as much as she was right then.

SHE MET Chris's parents on her arrival at Thasos that afternoon.

Their English wasn't great, but Ellie was able to communicate to them that they had a really great son and that they could cook amazing food.

The father was delighted to hear this, but the mother seemed unsure, continuing to stare at Ellie as if she'd said something insulting.

She kept asking her why she was in Crete, and nothing Ellie told her seemed to satisfy her.

Annoyed, the older woman eventually left and went back to the kitchen.

Chris's father stayed around though, and asked Ellie if she'd enjoyed the hike the day before.

"It was breathtaking," she said.

In very bad English, he then began to tell the same story Chris had told her about his grandfather.

She didn't have the heart to tell him she had already heard it but noticed that Chris stopped doing what he was doing to listen too. He listened and asked questions as if it were the first time he had heard it.

Ellie could see he loved and respected his dad.

When his father was finished, Chris asked, "Ellie, do you have your phone on you? Can you show my father that funny picture Jeff took of us on the plane? He would love it."

Blushing, Ellie did so, and he and his father burst out laughing, Chris laughing just as hard as the first time he'd seen it.

"Your mother and I don't even sleep that snugly together," Chris's father joked in broken English. "I'll arrange the wedding tomorrow. You two are meant to be together!" He slapped Ellie and Chris on the back and she blushed while Chris grinned.

"Mother should see it, too," he said to Ellie and took off to the kitchen with her phone. She didn't argue. The older woman didn't seem to like her much, so maybe the embarrassing picture would help endear her to her.

Just then Jeff and Patrick the piano player came in.

"Have you heard from Zack?" she asked her colleague in a low voice. "He says you haven't been answering his texts."

Before Jeff could reply, Chris's mother howled in the other room. She sounded as if a loved one had just died in front of her.

Alarmed, her husband ran to the kitchen door, but she pushed it open and pointed a finger at Ellie and Jeff.

"Zoýfia. Arouraíous sto spíti mou! Ádeia! Vges éxo tóra! Tha sas katára méchri to kókalo. Ádeia!"

Vermin. Rats in my house! Leave! Get out now! I will curse you down to the bone. Leave!

It was amazing how much college Greek flooded into Ellie's brain just then. She wanted to run to the old woman and ask her what was wrong, but Jeff gripped her arm and kept her from moving.

Chris came out of the kitchen next, his skin pale. He looked like he might either vomit or punch a hole through the wall.

"Ti symvaínei me ólous?" Chris's father asked. *What's wrong with everyone?*

"Chris, please tell me what's the matter," Ellie pleaded, astonished at the look on his face.

Chris staggered over to her and placed her phone back in her hand. "I shouldn't have read this. It's none of my business— you have, after all, been nothing but nice to me. But I accidentally clicked out of the picture sent by your friend. And I couldn't find his message again. But I found another. One where you and someone by the name of Zack Rose, who I can only assume is *the* Zack Rose, were discussing how my family's restaurant is being pushed out of business. He asked for insights, you sent him pictures of our food, he admitted to paying our landlord money to make us leave. I... you're an amazing actor, Ellie. I thought what we had was real. You've been lying to me since the very beginning? What is it you do, anyway?"

She swallowed hard. "I'm Zack Rose's employee," she admitted, shame filling her.

Then Chris turned to Jeff and whispered, "And you?"

He shifted and said, "Same."

Chris nodded, then went and sat down. "Please do as my mother said," he whispered, ashen. "Please leave, and don't ever come back."

CHAPTER TWENTY

ELLIE HAD NEVER CRIED HARDER in all her life.

The worst part about it all was that after what she'd learned the night before, she had already decided *not* to help Zack anymore.

She didn't know how she was going to work around it, but if she had to, she'd decided she was going to quit her job if he insisted on her being part of Thasos' downfall.

He wasn't playing fair and this wasn't right.

Jeff sat in the hotel room with her, looking out over the Aegean Sea as she tried to get control over herself.

Rain pelted against the balcony doors.

"What do we do, Jeff? I feel so terrible…"

Jeff turned to her and said, "Nothing in life is easy, Ellie. Especially the good stuff. Patrick is upset with me too. I don't know how I'm going to get him back, but I'm going to because I know this: he is worth fighting for. What we need to ask ourselves is would Chris or Patrick fight for us if the roles were reversed? Patrick would. We've only known each other for a few days, but I know he would fight for me. Ellie, do you think Chris would fight for you if he was in your shoes?"

She didn't have to think about it. Those beautiful brown eyes didn't look at her like she was just some girl. They looked at her with something far deeper— something that often took a lifetime to develop.

"So let's fight this, Ellie - let's fight *Zack*," Jeff continued passionately. "We'll make sure Thasos is around this time next year. And the year after that too. Instead of being its assassins, let's become its guardian angels."

"But where do we start? What do we do?"

"I don't know yet - all I *do* know it's the only way out of this. *But*," Jeff added determination in his eyes, "'we're marketeers, remember? We'll figure it out."

CHAPTER TWENTY-ONE

"ADDITIONAL FOOT TRAFFIC isn't going to help them," Ellie argued shaking her head.

It was the middle of the night, the rain had stopped, and she and Jeff had drunk two pots of coffee between them. "They're packed every day, so extra bodies aren't going to help."

"Maybe they could look at getting their overheads down to help recoup the rent increase?" Jeff suggested.

Ellie shook her head, overwhelmed with the task before them. "I don't think so. Food costs what it does, and staff need to be paid. We ask a restaurant of Thasos' calibre to get their chicken from a can and they'll die long before their landlord moves in."

"Couldn't they increase what they charge per cover then? Current menu prices are more than reasonable."

"Yes, but Jeff, these are all things Chris himself would surely know to do— not to mention his parents. He likely hasn't increased prices because he already knows what his patrons can and will pay. Every restaurant has a sweet spot and Thasos likely found theirs a long time ago."

"But you said yourself he's given up and is facing the inevitable. We've got to do something. Come on, Ellie. Both our love lives our on the line here. Think, dammit."

"There's nothing we can do," she said, exhausted. "From a marketing perspective, we can only look at generating excitement for a place, but Thasos already has that and more. They're booked out every single night. If we want to help them, we need to go bigger. We need to…" She stopped.

Finally, something was coalescing in the back of her brain.

"Ellie?"

Lightning flashed outside, and the wind picked up. Rain was coming again.

"Ellie, talk to me."

But this time thunder was coming with it.

She had often complained that brilliant ideas never came. Well, no, that wasn't right. What she'd thought was that people themselves generally don't come up with brilliant ideas all on their own. They're simply receivers of information. Or in the right place at the right time.

Truly big ideas— *Moby Dick*, the Eiffel Tower, real eureka ideas— came from somewhere else. Somewhere *out there*, far beyond the human condition.

This particular idea wasn't hers either. She wouldn't take ownership of it in a million years because sometimes you had to give credit where it was due.

Thank you, was all Ellie could think when Mind (with a capital M) gave her a plan of action.

"Why did Zack send us here in the first place?" she asked Jeff, her mind racing.

"He wants to rule the world of course," her colleague replied deadpan.

"Specifically, he wants to rule *Greece*, or at least be known better here," Ellie went on. "But more importantly Zack Rose wants people all over the world to know that his kinsmen not only know him but admire and respect him, too."

Jeff sighed. "And the way he plans to go about that is by opening up his own restaurant here in Crete, but he doesn't want Thasos as competition so people will just come to him and not them. I know why we're here, Ellie," he said, confused.

"But really think about it. Do you think Zack truly cares about a restaurant here? When I was researching for this job, I learned that most of his money comes from ad revenue for the TV shows. The restaurants and the books merely maintain and rejuvenate excitement for his TV show."

Jeff nodded. "True. Without ad revenue funding his celebrity, he's just another cook."

"So what we have to do is take this to the TV show," she went on.

"And how in the hell are we going to do that?"

"Through Zack's ego, of course," Ellie said smiling. "You of all people should know that."

CHAPTER TWENTY-TWO

ELLIE WASN'T ALLOWED into the restaurant the following day but insisted enough that Chris finally came out to talk to her.

"Just listen," she said when he appeared in front of her, stony-faced. "I have an idea. But first, yes, I'll admit was asked to come here to spy on your restaurant and figure out what made you so successful. Zack Rose has a bit of a Borg personality and just wants to assimilate, assimilate, assimilate. Once he's assimilated, he destroys." She had hoped this might make him smile but she was wrong.

Still, he refused to meet her gaze.

"Chris, of *course*, the time you and I spent together was real," she said gently. "I could never fake how I feel for you. The butterflies you give me, the way you make me blush and speed up my heart." When he still didn't react to her essentially baring her soul, Ellie swallowed hard. "Anyway, things have changed. I've met you and your family and I won't let Zack destroy Thasos. But I need your help."

Now he looked interested. "How so?"

"What I need you to do is this: go on to Thasos social media today and announce a menu change. Make it a copy of the menu you designed for your other 'secret' restaurant."

Chris looked at her suspiciously. "But the people love the food my parents crafted here for the last thirty years. They don't want a change," he argued.

"This isn't about them. It's about *Zack*. But if you don't go along with what I'm planning, they'll get a change when you're out of business in a few weeks."

At this, Chris seemed to acquiesce a little. He sighed. "Continue."

"OK. I'm sorry but next, you will have to lie a little. Take full ownership of the new menu, but add that it is heavily influenced by the work and craft of your Greek kinsman, Zack Rose. Post this on your social media, and tag Zack - I'll help you with the details. Ask him to check out the new menu for himself, and give you feedback and advice. Talk about how much you've always admired him."

Chris looked horrified. "Why on earth would I do that? I know nothing about Zack Rose except he's an idiot celebrity who's trying to ruin my family's legacy. I certainly don't admire him."

"Like I said, you'll have to lie. The thing is Chris, all of this - Zack moving into Crete and destroying Thasos - it's all about his ego. He wants - *needs* - to be respected here, by his fellow countrymen. It's the only reason he's set his sights on your restaurant."

"Then he truly is an idiot. No true Greek would do such a thing to another."

"Well, you and I know that, but Zack doesn't. Again, this is all about him and his obsession with what people think about him. So I want you to mention him on Thasos' social media because he has a hugely active online presence - millions of followers."

"But why do you think this would do anything?" Chris asked. "Social media is—"

"About 80% of online communication these days. Trust me, Chris, if you want people to know something, you share it online. I'm telling you, I sat in Zack's office and listened to him gripe about Greeks not respecting him. All he wants is for his own people to flatter him. That's it. It's not about money; your restaurant is simply a means to an end for him. He's got fame, but what he truly wants is for his kinsmen to acknowledge him and call him brother."

"I'm going to need to check with my parents—"

"No, Chris. You're the boss. You make the call. This is how we keep Thasos from falling into the sea. This is how we keep it above water. Zack already has you in checkmate. The clock is counting down to your demise as we speak. We need to convince him that he's stronger with you than without you, and we need to do it soon."

CHAPTER TWENTY-THREE

THE FOLLOWING DAY - using an ego-stroking spiel specifically crafted by Ellie - Thasos, one of the best-known traditional restaurants in Greece, paid tribute to Zack Rose, Crete's long lost son, asking him to visit them in person sometime, oversee the menu and ensure they got things right.

It was a masterstroke.

Ellie watched the interaction get retweeted and reposted around the foodie world in seconds, mostly due to Jeff's nimble administration of Zack's social media accounts.

While the hashtag of #ComeHomeZack, might have been a bit over the top - even for Jeff - she guessed that her boss would have no choice but to take notice.

Jeff and Ellie sat beside each other on her bed at the hotel that afternoon, watching Thasos' post go viral, waiting for their boss to react.

"GET BACK HERE - *NOW*," Zack demanded over the phone, barely an hour later.

"What's this about?" Ellie asked, feigning ignorance.

"You know well what this is about. I'm not an idiot, and neither are you. Get your ass back here pronto, and bring Jeff with you."

"Do you think he's going to fire us?" Ellie asked, hanging up.

Jeff looked up from his laptop. "Probably."

THE FOLLOWING DAY, Ellie texted Chris at the airport telling him that she had to leave and that she hoped to see him again one day.

Jeff had decided not to join her and had instead gone off in search of Patrick.

"I know you feel betrayed," she told Chris in the message. "I understand that. And I know it's a cliche thing to say, but I tried so many times to tell you. I really did. It was selfish but I just didn't want to ruin what I hoped we might be developing.

If I could turn back time, and find a time portal like in that Stephen King book, I would. I wouldn't hesitate for a moment. This is my number. If you ever want to talk, please call me - regardless of what time it is. But for what it's worth, I think our plan worked a treat."

She left it at that. It was hard, but she knew he had every right to be angry with her.

Ellie had ruined everything.

Including no doubt, her brand new job.

CHAPTER TWENTY-FOUR

THE FOLLOWING MORNING, she was back in San Francisco and in front of Zack's desk.

"What the hell happened, Ellie? Spare me the bullshit. I know you're behind this ruse."

She faced him down, no longer caring about her job. She guessed she was going to get fired anyway.

"I realised Thasos wasn't what you wanted. The fate of the restaurant was the least of your concerns. So I had a brainwave."

"Which was?"

"What better way to show the world that your people love your work than to have a beloved native Greek restaurant pay homage to you."

"Hence the idiotic *Come Home Zack* hashtag?"

"Well that was Jeff's idea but…"

"So you seriously expect me to go all the way to Crete, sample their new Zack Rose-inspired menu, and give them the thumbs up?"

"Preferably with the TV show."

"But how does that help *me*?" he demanded. "I only see how it would help them."

"To everyone around the world, it will seem like you are a king visiting his subjects, doing a good turn for your fellow countrymen by putting Thasos even more on the map. Give them a good plug and your homeland will love you even more."

Zack pursed his lips. "If you're trying to save the place, know that the landlord will likely still want to raise their rent even if I back out. If it's not me, it's someone else. There are a lot of other businesses that would jump on that location."

"Then why don't we—"

"You're in love with him, aren't you?" Zack asked. "The manager. This is all a ploy to save *him*, isn't it?"

Ellie finally teared up. There was no point in lying. "Not all of it. But yes, I'll admit that I liked Chris - a lot. He and especially his parents ... they don't deserve what you'd planned. This way, you get what you want and they can stay in business. They're no threat to you, Zack, honestly."

The chef ran his hands through his spiky blond hair. He appeared slightly mollified.

"OK," he conceded sighing. "If this works out the way you think it's going to ... maybe I'll think about it. In the meantime, go home. I honestly don't know whether to fire you or give you a raise. I'll decide in a few days. Oh, and not that he cares, but tell Jeff he's fired. I can't believe he ran off with a Greek piano player. Talk about cliche ..."

Ellie texted Chris as soon as she was home and told him what Zack had said.

But once again, her message remained unanswered.

CHAPTER TWENTY-FIVE

Soon after, Zack got the go-ahead from his producers and sponsors to film a visit to Thasos in person for the TV show.

In the meantime, Ellie checked the restaurant's social media religiously to make sure the place was still open.

Business seemed to be carrying on as usual so if their landlord had indeed raised the rent, Chris and his parents must have all tightened their belts and were braving the storm.

When the visit to Crete eventually aired, it became the Zack Rose show's highest-rated episode ever. And as Ellie anticipated, the chef's fellow countrymen had little choice but to embrace him with open arms.

She watched the segment at Thasos over and over - especially the parts in which Chris appeared.

Incredibly, Zack didn't fire her. When he'd informed Ellie he'd decided to keep her on, he said it was only because a little voice within him had told him not to.

"I rarely get intuitions, Ellie. My brain and every fibre of my being told me to fire you, but it wasn't my brain that got me to where I am today. It was my intuition. So, by the skin of your teeth, you're safe. Now get the hell out of here."

Ellie tried to move on, and in one idiotic moment of self-pity she printed out that stupid picture of her asleep and wrapped around Chris on the aeroplane, and put it on her desk.

If nothing else, having it there was a constant reminder that she needed more out of life, and that there was someone out there for her.

If not Chris, then perhaps someone like him.

THEN ONE DAY, a Google Alert for Thasos announced that they had revealed to customers that the restaurant was going out of business.

The headline simply read, "Beloved Cretan restaurant Thasos closes its doors after 30 years in business."

Zack was having his morning coffee when Ellie barged into his office.

He put up his hand and said, "It's for the best. Their lawyers couldn't find a way to get the landlord to back off, and the owners - the parents - were ready to let it go."

"What about Chris?" she asked, lips quivering.

"I talked to him briefly. He's got plans of his own. You were right; he's a great restauranteur. Anyone would be lucky to get him."

That day, Ellie went home early. She texted Chris for the first time since the aftermath of her departure, telling him how sorry she was about the closure, and offering to do anything she could.

She'd also made a decision. It was impetuous and likely fool-hardy but she was going to follow her heart.

"I know you don't want to see me, but I'm coming back to the island to talk to you. I need to see you - I'll do anything."

This time he texted back. "The best thing you can do for me is stay where you are."

Ellie's heart sank. It was the coldness of his response that did her in, morphing her sadness into a wave of heartbreak and disappointment that he truly didn't care about her.

Yes, he had every reason to be annoyed, but hadn't she done her best to make things right?

Clearly for Chris, Ellie's best wasn't good enough.

CHAPTER TWENTY-SIX

THE NEXT MORNING, she decided to go into the office early.

Her brief interaction with Chris had left her battered and sore, but Ellie knew she needed to move on with her life as soon as she could.

She parked in the garage and walked around to the street entrance so as not to disturb Zack while he was recording.

Today though, the door to that entrance was locked. Ellie peered inside, hoping to see someone who could let her in, but she was obviously the first to arrive.

Reluctantly, she walked back to the attached parking garage, and went through that door, recalling her first day.

The same rat-like bespectacled sentry stopped her in the hallway and made circle motions in the air to tell her they were recording.

I know, I know.... Ellie slipped off her shoes.

The small man smiled and turned to escort her to the offices. As she followed him, she heard Zack in-studio talking to another person.

A man with a thick accent and warm lyrical tones that Ellie

would recognise anywhere. She stopped short and looked into the studio.

Her boss was standing to the side and watching none other than *Chris* making bread.

"What's the grain called again?" Zack was asking.

"Kamut. K, A, M, U, T. If you are gluten intolerant, don't bother working with it, but if you are merely sensitive to gluten, give it a try. Here I see so many gluten-free products in your grocery stores. In Greece, we don't cook with American grains. We use the old grains, and very few of us have trouble with gluten. Go into one of our grocery stores and you won't find entire shelves and aisles devoted to gluten-free products. I give you no guarantee it will work, but try it. Take little bites. Listen to your body. You'll know if you can eat it pretty quickly."

Zack looked at the camera and raised his eyebrows. "Give it a shot, folks. Only don't sue the network if anything happens." At this, both men laughed. "If you're just tuning in, my friend Chris here is making us some Greek bread with a twist— he's using Kamut flour instead of traditional ..."

Not caring they were recording, Ellie burst through the studio doors.

"You're here!" she gasped to Chris. "What are you doing *here?*"

Out of the corner of her eye, she saw Zack motion to the production team.

Chris looked back at her, grinning wickedly as if he'd fully expected Ellie to walk onto the set in the middle of the show. "My parents and I eventually realised it was the best thing to happen for all of us. They've finally retired and I'm charging ahead with my restaurant — it's no longer just an experiment. We've added a modern building around my grandfather's old hut, and have most of the cooks from Thasos. We're not even open yet, and we're booked solid for our first three months."

"Who's *we*?" Ellie asked, overwhelmed but happy for him. "And what are you doing here?"

"Zack. He's my patron, the one funding all of it." She looked around for her boss but didn't see him. "So I came here to America to help return the favour - and something else of course."

She looked at him mystified. Chris and Zack teaming up? Why hadn't her boss said anything?

"Ellie," Chris continued, moving towards her, "I have everything I need to get started with my new business except one thing - a marketing guru. Know anyone who might be any good?" he asked, eyes twinkling. "And most importantly, someone who'd be willing to make a go of it with me - on an island in the sun?"

Without saying anything, Ellie melted into his arms, gripping the front of his shirt, afraid to let go in case all of this was a dream.

"I thought … I thought you hated me…" she whispered, drinking in his scent, unable to believe that he was really here, and not only that, but he wanted her to go back to Crete with him.

Ellie didn't even need to think about that - she'd do it in a heartbeat. He was the one for her; there was no question about that. What's more, her subconscious had known it even before she did - right from the very beginning on the flight.

"Kiss him!" Zack shouted from the shadows then. "So we can call this a wrap."

She did so, not needing to be asked twice.

But for Ellie and Chris, it wasn't a wrap.

It was just the beginning.

VILLA AZURE

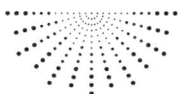

CHAPTER ONE

HEADING HOME FROM THE OFFICE, Joanna Nelson got her colleague's attention and tossed him a memory disk with the author interview he needed.

He caught it and promptly pantomimed worshipping her. *I'm not worthy, I'm not worthy.*

A stranger observing the exchange would assume Joanna was the boss and Liam was the understudy. Or at the very least, that they were equals at Herod Publishing in NYC.

But both of these assumptions would be wrong.

Liam was a senior editor of New York City's most prestigious publishing house and had been for the past twelve years, but his days were quickly getting numbered.

Not because of ineptitude but because he was losing touch.

When collaborating on a piece, he insisted on using Microsoft Word instead of Google Docs, Dropbox all but bamboozled him, and he couldn't be baby-stepped into loading attachments sent to him via email.

"Where does it go when I download it?" he'd complain to Joanna. "What's the point of all this magic if you can't find it?"

Her boss was a walking and talking anachronism. A caveman pretending to be a hipster.

They were both up for review the coming week, and it was widely assumed Joanna was going to get his job.

She wasn't worried about Liam though. He was likely just going to be moved into a horizontal position with fewer responsibilities, staying nearby to give advice whenever it was needed. By the time people stopped asking him questions he'd probably retire.

Joanna smiled and waved goodbye.

"Yeah, Donna, I know Harry's interested," she said to her close friend on the phone as she walked out. "He's practically stalking me on Facebook. But I've been with Peter for over a year now, you know that."

"You're like some elusive Mediterranean goddess," her friend replied. "None of the boys care about who you say you're with. Not when they get a glimpse of those legs and the bounce of your ebony locks."

"Well, I care. I'm with Peter."

Joanna maneuvered through the revolving door out onto Park Avenue and was immediately bombarded with sirens, honking horns, and the rattle of construction work.

It was early spring and New York was restless as always.

"Have I been egging him on? I didn't mean to. I just thought he was interesting. That's why I talked to him at that party."

"No, that's just who he is. And you have that effect on every guy you meet Jo. Anyway," Donna said segueing into a different subject, "any plans for the weekend? Want to go skinny dipping or rock climbing for old time's sake?"

Joanna laughed. "Nah, I don't do that stuff anymore, but there's something I am about to do that's out of my comfort zone. I'm pretty nervous about it, actually." She took a deep breath, guessing what her friend would say. "Peter's been asking me to move in with him since our six-month anniversary. And well...this Wednesday marks one year since our first date."

Joanna's dark curly hair whipped to the side as a Porsche drove by.

"No, don't tell me you're—"

"I'm going to tell him I want to give it a shot. I think I'm ready."

She hailed a cab as she waited for her friend to respond. A bright yellow taxi amongst a sea of shiny metallic movement pulled over and she got in. Inside the air was warm but smelled of menthol.

"West Twenty-third and Tenth, please," Joanna said to the driver. He nodded and turned back to the wheel, his eyes glancing down quickly to check her out.

"What brought this on?" Donna asked.

"I don't know. A lot of things. It's just— I think it's time to be a grownup. I think it's time to start doing all of the things I always said I would do. Marry a guy with a decent job. Settle down. Have a kid or two - "

"Wha—have a kid? Have you talked about getting married to Peter? You two have actually *had* this conversation?"

They stopped at a light and a homeless man stared at her and started shouting something inaudible over the taxi driver's radio.

"Joanna?" Donna prompted.

She pulled her mind back. "I'm sorry, yeah. A few times. Peter wants to marry me, I know that."

"He's proposed?"

"Well, no. He's just talked about it. About what kind of apartment he wants to buy. About where he thinks our kids should go to school. About the kind of life he wants and the life he can give me."

"Wow." Donna hesitated. "How ... romantic."

"No, no, it's not like that," Joanna explained smiling a little. "He's just very matter-of-fact about things, and I like that. There's no guessing with him. I know exactly the kind of man he is and what he wants. And we want the same things. That's important, don't you think?"

"So I assume he's finally mentioned the L word then?"

Joanna sighed inwardly and thought about lying, but this was Donna she was talking to. She'd known her since she was a freshman at NYU. This was the girl who went and bought her a pack of cigarettes and a 6-pack a couple of years back when her mother died so she could cry all week and properly curse the heavens.

She couldn't lie to her.

"No, but I know he does love me. He's just not good at that kind of—"

"Do me a favour, Jo. Get him to say it before you agree to move in with him. If after a *year*, the guy can't tell you he loves you, he doesn't deserve you."

Joanna was silent.

"How do you get a man to tell you he loves you?" she asked.

"You don't. A real man knows how to say it - and when."

Joanna glimpsed the Brooklyn Bridge for a brief moment before her cab turned right onto 23rd.

I guess it's time to cross that bridge, she thought, feeling more nervous than she expected.

"I TOLD HIM," Peter was saying amidst a mouthful of steak as he and Joanna sat in the trendy Brooklyn restaurant, "I told him he's got to come down ten, maybe even twenty per cent if he wants to sell, but I don't think he's listening. Guy has it in his mind he's going to make three or four million dollars off of it, but he's not going to come anywhere close. Not in this market. The poor have gotten poorer, and the rich are hoarding everything they have in Panama. They're not investing in overpriced apartments— even ones that overlook Central Park."

Joanna managed a smile to indicate to her boyfriend that she was listening, but she was still thinking about her conversation with Donna.

"So what is he hoping to sell it for?" she asked, pushing her hair over her shoulder and crossing her legs.

Peter shook his head and chuckled. "He thinks he's going to get twelve million, which is a joke. His only hope is finding a Chinese investor, but they're not known for overpaying. They like deals. I mean, who doesn't?"

Joanna sipped her wine and looked closely at her boyfriend.

At 29 his hair was already thinning. She had never really noticed until he started cropping it shorter, which he started doing recently. At least he wasn't being weird and trying to comb it over.

As her mother, Ruth used to say: "Embrace what you have. There isn't just one way to be sexy."

But Peter's looks weren't what attracted Joanna to him. Thin and wiry body, he had the build and look of a long-distance runner who spent his evenings looking down microscopes.

So why was she attracted to him?

Well, he was direct. He was confident. When they first met he was able to look Joanna directly in the eye and have a conversation with her without ogling over her breasts. It sent the message that he was disciplined and that if he was talking to her it was because he wanted to.

Sex wasn't the only thing on his mind, and to Joanna, this was a refreshing first.

Was the sex interstellar? No. And that was the other thing about Peter. Nothing about him went off the charts, but he was above average in every category that mattered. A steady, unwavering horizontal line.

If Joanna was asked to come up with something about him that really bothered her, she wouldn't be able to find a single thing.

He was pleasant.

He was safe.

He was...

Donna's words floated back into her brain. *If he can't tell you he loves you, he doesn't deserve you.*

"What's wrong?" Peter asked. "You seem distant this evening. Do you not like the food? I heard nothing but good things about this place. The chef has gotten two Michelins, and he's only like, twenty-two or something. A food prodigy."

"No, no, the food's great. I like what you ordered. Thank you."

Peter frowned. He was anxious.

Joanna took a big gulp of wine and asked straight out. "Peter, do you love me?"

His head shot back as if he'd been slapped, and Joanna waited. She didn't want to soften the question by filling the silence.

"Joanna, you know I care about you a lot," he responded matter-of-factly. "We've talked about marriage one day. Having kids. Surely you know how I feel."

"I've been thinking," she said. "I think I'm ready to take our relationship to the next level."

Peter relaxed and smiled, openly chewing his food when he said, "Really? You're ready to move in with me?"

"Yes, but I'm only going to move in with you if I know—"

"Joanna, you're exactly the kind of woman I've always wanted. You're beautiful. You're intelligent. Together we're a power couple. We're unstoppable. Of course I love you."

Joanna smiled.

Of course.

"I love you, too, Peter."

He put his fork and knife down and reached across the table for her hand. His palm felt dry and cold. He squeezed quickly and went back to his meal.

Joanna sipped her wine.

He had said it.

Hadn't he?

MUCH LATER, Joanna's phone vibrated on the nightstand at Peter's place.

She glanced at the number. 30-2427-555-6795

Well, that's a lot of numbers. With a foggy brain, she sent the caller to voicemail and went back to sleep.

Whoever it was didn't need to speak with her in the middle of the night.

Whatever it was could wait.

CHAPTER TWO

THE FOLLOWING MORNING, Peter dropped her back at her place a little before lunch. Saturdays were a busy day in New York real estate, as many clients weren't free to look at apartments until the weekend.

Joanna dropped her things onto the counter, kicked her heels off, and started up some coffee. Her place was small even by New York standards, but the one thing it had going for it was a balcony that overlooked the Hudson River.

She slid the door open and welcomed in the cool, constant breeze off the bay. She was about to sit down when Donna called.

"Spill," her friend demanded. "How'd it go? Did the bastard say it?"

"He said it," Joanna replied, smiling. "And he's not a bastard. Be nice."

"Whatever. How'd it come up? Tell me everything."

Joanna told her about their dinner date and what Peter had said.

"So you had to ask him? That's kind of forcing his hand, don't you think?"

"You don't know Peter. I *do*. He wouldn't lie to me to just placate me. How it happened is how it needed to happen. He's going to start saying it more and more now I'm sure."

"And will you say it back?"

"Of course I will. Will you stop it? I know what I like. This isn't about the past. It's about the future."

"Just keep your apartment, OK?"

"What? He works in real estate, remember."

"So what? Just keep it to be safe. You never know, he might turn into a controlling jerk when you move in."

"Bye, Donna," Joanna said and hung up.

Yes, she could be annoying sometimes but she also knew Donna was being a good friend by voicing all of the doubts and uncertainties she wouldn't allow herself to actively think about.

Once again her phone rang. It was the long number again from the early hours of this morning. She had completely forgotten about it. She thought about sending it to voicemail again so she could soak in fully the spring morning air but decided at the last moment to answer.

"Hello?"

"Yes, hello," a male voice said in a heavy European accent. Joanna couldn't place which one. "Am I speaking with …" he paused, "Miss Joanna Nelson?"

Frowning, she told him he was.

"Good, good. My name is Nick Artinos. I represent your father."

Joanna laughed. Her father? She had never met the guy - didn't even know his name or what he looked like. "My father?" she repeated.

"*Nai*, yes."

Joanna's heart pulsed in her throat for a moment and she sat down.

"Is this a joke? You're joking, right?"

"No, it's not a joke. No joke."

"I don't know anything about my father, and I doubt he knows anything about me. What is this about? Who are you?"

"I'm your father's lawyer. He did know about you, Miss Joanna, but I'm sad to say he passed away a couple of weeks ago. I represent him in his death. He's left his daughter, he's left *you* an inheritance. Here in Skiathos."

Joanna's brain whirled as she tried to process this.

"Skiathos?"

"*Ellada.* Greece, Miss Joanna. Skiathos is in Greece. It's where your father's from. It's where… well, it's where your family's from."

Her mouth dropped open in surprise. She knew from her mother that she was the result of an ill-advised vacation romance in Europe some thirty years before but …

"How soon can you get here, Miss Joanna?" the lawyer asked.

"I— is this for real? I can't possibly go there. I've got a job. An important one. I'm very busy." Then she added in a whisper. "What did he leave me?"

"That, I'm afraid I cannot tell you," the lawyer replied. "You must come to Skiathos to find out. That is one of the conditions."

CHAPTER THREE

"MY MOTHER NEVER TOLD ME MUCH," Joanna said later that afternoon. Peter had come over and they were sitting on her balcony.

She still hadn't managed to change out of the clothes she wore the night before. She had spent most of the day outside trying to wrap her brain around that call.

"The only thing I was able to get out of her was that she made a mistake one night while travelling in Europe, and she didn't even tell me *that* much until I was in college."

Her Greek father had left her something. An inheritance.

A man whom she had spent many nights pondering and making up stories about. But if he knew about his daughter - if he cared, why didn't he contact her before he died?

Peter had his arm around her shoulder and was attempting to console her.

"I mean, I guessed he must have been Mediterranean - Spanish or Italian even. She had red hair. I have black. I tan, she'd burn and burst into a million freckles. But we were a lot alike, so I never really focused too much on our differences.

God, I wish I had nagged her more. My friends always jokingly called me a Grecian goddess. I didn't know they were actually right. About the Greek part, I mean."

She had called Peter because he was supposed to be the person she'd call in these situations, but a hell of a lot of good it was doing her. She wanted to be angry at him for just sitting there and listening, but what else could he do?

There wasn't a damn thing anyone could do. Not now. Her father had been alive when her mother was dead, could have contacted her, could have formed a bond, but had chosen not to.

Instead, he had left it up to a lawyer.

How many nights had she spent wondering who he was?

And how the hell did this guy - George - know about her? Did her mom contact him when she got back to the States to tell him she was pregnant? She must have. There was no other way for him to know about her.

So all along Joanna had a father on the other side of the world who hadn't cared enough to come and see her. To meet her. To get to know her. This was why her mother didn't want Joanna to know anything about him and who could blame her?

"Are you going to go there?" Peter asked. "To Skiathos?"

"I don't know," she answered truthfully, thinking about what the lawyer had said, about the 'condition'. "What do you think it is? What do you think he left me?"

"If a lawyer's involved, and the guy's only question was when you could come over, then it's got to be a house of some kind. Why he didn't just tell you over the phone is strange though. But anyway, if it's indeed a house, you should sell it. No ifs, ands or buts. Sell the place, take the money and run."

"Why?"

"Skiathos is a big tourist destination. It's one of the most beautiful islands in Greece. Wherever that house is, it's going to be worth a fortune. Sell it, and you and I will buy a beautiful apartment and fund a lavish wedding without breaking a sweat. Probably have enough leftover for the honeymoon, too."

Joanna considered that. It would be the smart thing to do if they were going to get married soon.

But that word. It held so much power.

If.

Joanna thought she wouldn't be able to concentrate during the work week, what with her inheritance and potential promotion coming up.

But instead, she found throwing herself into work made things a bit easier.

At his insistence, Peter's guys got in touch with her father's lawyer, and suddenly Friday came with Joanna being promoted to a senior editor at Herod Publishing.

"Congratulations," Liam said to her, popping his head inside her new office before heading out for the weekend. "You deserve this."

"What about—"

"Senior Advisor. Now what the hell that means, I don't know." Her colleague stretched his arms and yawned. "Same office, slightly more pay. Just pushed to the shadows a little so a more vibrant plant such as yourself can start fruiting. I'm OK though. It hurts less that it was you they chose. See you Monday morning."

Joanna waved goodbye to him, then turned around and stared out at the city. She had a great view of both the Chrysler Building and the Empire State.

She was making it, going up in the world. Doing what she'd always wanted to do. What she'd always said she'd do.

Her phone vibrated in her purse, and she assumed it was Donna calling to see if she got the promotion, but it was that number again.

Greece. The Greek lawyer.

Joanna answered it without hesitating.

"Joanna Nelson," she said.

"Hi Miss Joanna, this is Nick, your father's lawyer again. I've been contacted by a lawyer from your husband about selling your father's property."

"Well, he's not my husband, but yes, that's right."

"Oh, I'm sorry. My apologies, Miss Nelson. I'm calling because I was hoping I could make you reconsider. As I said, your father forbade me to tell you what he left you. You see, he wanted you to come to Skiathos to see it for yourself. He doubted you would come otherwise. I'm not trying to be coy. It was his very last wish to me upon his deathbed."

"You knew him?" Joanna asked. "You knew my father well?"

"Oh yes. We all knew George. He was very much loved by everyone who knew him. He was somewhat of a local celebrity in fact."

Joanna got up and closed her office door then went back to her desk. "Can you please just tell me what he left me?" she pleaded.

"No, I'm sorry. I cannot."

"You mean you won't?"

"No Miss Joanna. I cannot tell you. You must come to Skiathos to claim your inheritance. That is the condition. It cannot be sold until then. Right now I am its caretaker. If you don't come, it will remain in my name. I am more than happy to keep it, but that is not your father's wish. I could have kept it from you and you would never have known. But I too, really think you should come."

"My father really did mean something to you then?"

"Yes, Miss Joanna. He really did. Even in death, I will do anything for George."

Joanna put her feet up on her desk, "I don't even know his surname."

"Georges Herod. Though we all just called him George."

She laughed. "I don't believe it! I work for a publishing company called Herod Publishing."

"I know. I thought that was strange, too, when I found you. My friend and I had a good laugh about it. It is one of God's little messages. Subtly hidden."

"Nick, why do *you* think I need to come to Skiathos?"

The lawyer hesitated, but when he answered his tone suggested the answer was obvious. "It is your homeland, Miss Joanna."

"No, I'm from New York. I'm a New Yorker, Nick. Always have been, always will be."

"But half of you is Skiathan. And all Skiathans must return home at least once. Come, for just a little while. That's all your father wanted. He didn't care about money or anything like that. He just wanted you to see where your people are from."

"But why didn't he contact me before he died? Why this grand gesture after death?"

Again the hesitation. "Miss Joanna, again to answer that, you must come to Skiathos."

Joanna exhaled and wanted to hang up. The most difficult part about all of this was that Nick was being sincere. It was clear in his voice.

To make it worse, he was actually the person who would benefit from her *not* going, and yet here he was doing everything in his power to persuade her.

If she were younger, she'd be head over heels for the

mystery. Would have put the entire trip on a credit card and gone in the blink of an eye.

But, as Donna frequently reminded her, that part of herself had been dormant for a couple of years now. Possibly since her mother's death.

"I just got promoted today— just a couple of hours ago in fact," she told the lawyer. "I'm now one of the senior editors at Herod Publishing. I can't just leave. The company's transitioning, and I'm a major part of that change. If I were to—"

"Miss Joanna," Nick interrupted her. "Please forgive me. But there will be a wedding at your father's property in a month. The weather is beginning to turn here already. In a month, every flower will be in full bloom. The birds will have returned, and the outdoor terrace of every restaurant will be pulsating with life and activity. Spring is the most beautiful time of year in Skiathos. If you would, I would like to take you as my guest. The marriage is between a young man and a woman whom your father knew since their birth. They both loved him dearly and considered him to be their godfather. Their wedding will be as much a celebration of your father as it will be of their marriage."

"It's in a month?" Joanna asked.

"*Nai*, yes, a month. It will be on a Saturday. Surely you can arrange for a few days by then? I will show you around the island myself and introduce you to everyone who knew your father. I do this because it's what he wanted and because I sense anger from you. I know that if you knew George, knew more about him, you couldn't possibly hate him."

"OK," Joanna agreed, impulsively. "Let me see, what I can do."

CHAPTER FOUR

"WILL this be your first time in Greece?" an older lady seated next to Joanna on the flight to Athens, asked.

A month had passed since her conversation with Nick. When she had told Peter she was going to Skiathos, and that she would like to wait until she got back to move in with him, he became annoyed and distant.

"I just need time to process all this," she said. "Don't be angry."

"We don't even know if this guy is legit! You're putting our life on hold for some faceless stranger from some godforsaken island in Europe?"

"That faceless stranger was my father," she argued. "I need to find out who he was."

He had mostly sulked that weekend but eventually warmed up.

The last couple of days before the trip, he kept asking her if she wanted him to go along too, but it was an empty gesture and they both knew it.

He couldn't leave. He was in the middle of closing three multi-million dollar deals in Brooklyn.

Now Joanna smiled and nodded to the old woman.

"Yes, it's my first time," she said. "I'm headed to Skiathos."

"Oh, my favourite island!" she enthused. "You lucky thing. Skiathos is heaven. Pure and simple. It's a secret that only a few blessed know about."

"What do you like about it so much?" Joanna asked, intrigued.

"Well," the woman exclaimed and slapped the handbag on her lap. "Too much to say. I adore the Greek Islands in general but the way I describe Skiathos to people is by asking if they have a special place they travel to in their dreams. Strange, I know, but it's the only way I can get it across. Do you have anything like that, dear? A place where you wake up while you're still sleeping and become aware you're in a dream. And when you realize where you are you become overjoyed? Like heaven on earth."

Joanna shook her head.

"Me neither. Not anymore. But I did when I was younger. It was a magical land that in my dreams, was on the other side of this forest behind my grandmother's house. Skiathos is the embodiment of that dream for me. The air, the light, the people. Some of the old gods are still alive there, believe me. Living and breathing heaven into the water and the earth. You'll see. Once you go there you're never the same again."

Joanna didn't know what to say. That was one hell of a sell.

"I'll leave you alone now," said her elder companion. "I'm a Gemini and we talk too much, or so we're told." She put on some headphones and began playing a word game on her phone.

Joanna looked out the window and watched New York float farther and farther away as they rose into the clouds.

Heaven on earth?

She'd soon find out.

CHAPTER FIVE

"MISS JOANNA! Over here! Miss Joanna Nelson!" Joanna turned and saw an arm holding a sign with her name over everyone's heads.

She turned towards the voice, knees still wobbly and shaking from the landing.

Land being a precious commodity on the tiny island, the airport on Skiathos was built on a small stretch of upraised ground flanked by water.

It was exactly what Joanna imagined landing on an aircraft carrier would be like. No room for errors. If you miss, well then you're out of luck.

She had almost slept through the transfer from Athens but had woken up to zipping backpacks and the jostling of people manoeuvring their carry-ons onto their laps. She looked out the window as the plane arched and turned into alignment with the runway.

"Is that what we're landing on?" Joanna asked the person seated beside her on the smaller plane.

The man laughed. "Yes, they call it the Saint Martin's of

Greece. If we live through this, you should watch it from below. It's quite the show."

Joanna closed her eyes and went through the rosary in her head.

Now, her heart was still beating as if she had narrowly avoided death.

"Miss Nelson? Are you Miss Joanna Nelson?" said the man holding the sign with her name on it.

Tanned with a swimmer's physique, he looked to be in his early-to-mid thirties. Mussed black curly hair, chiselled cheekbones and deep brown eyes you could get lost in.

Whoever the guy standing in front of her was, he was a dreamboat.

"Miss Joanna! I'm so glad you're finally here!"

"Nick?" she asked, reaching out her hand.

"Of course!" The lawyer pushed her hand away and kissed both sides of her cheeks.

She blushed.

"Have you been waiting long?" she asked. "I'm sorry I couldn't get here sooner. The only way here involved two layovers and one connection."

"Nai, yes, there are no direct flights from New York."

"What time is it here?"

Nick looked at his wristwatch. "It's almost four. How long are you staying?"

"A couple of days. Flight back isn't until Tuesday."

Nick chuckled and shook his head.

"You won't be leaving Tuesday. Not when you truly see where you are."

She chuckled. "Yes, I'm told this place is heaven on earth."

Nick took her luggage from her and grinned. "I should be

humble and say it's the only life I know, but I went to the university in London. I couldn't get back here fast enough."

He took the lead and manoeuvred them through the hordes of people. He wore a simple v-neck t-shirt tucked into fitted khaki pants, yet he seemed immaculately put together.

Joanna wished she had worn something other than jeans and an NYU hoodie. It had seemed like a good idea at the time before the long plane ride. Now she felt like the stereotypical American visiting Europe.

"Are you hungry, Miss Joanna?" Nick asked, turning around.

"I am, but I would love a hot shower and a change of clothes first," she said. "If it's not too much trouble. I know I look horrible."

Nick looked her up and down with his dark brown, almond-shaped eyes. "This is your home. And you look beautiful. Relax."

"No really, sitting and sleeping in the same clothes for so long, I just want to strip everything off of me and burn them."

Nick laughed. "OK, OK," he said. "Let's go to your father's place first and you can freshen up."

"My father's? No, I got a room at..." Joanna stopped. She couldn't remember the name of the hotel. The details were on her phone.

"You were going to go to the Elsa. I cancelled it. The owner is a good friend of mine. No, you'll be staying at your father's."

"But if there's a wedding there... won't I be in the way?"

Nick laughed. "No, Miss Joanna. It's big enough. And of course, there's always room for you. Come, come. Let's get you there so you can see. See what your father left for you."

. . .

THEY EXITED the airport and the first thing Joanna noticed about Skiathos was its air. It possessed an element of sweetness to it. Like a bale of flowers, but more herbal and purposeful.

The smell of the sea was present too but, it didn't smell like anything you'd find on the East Coast of the US.

She breathed it in again deeply through her nose. Gently aromatic, yet still cool and heavy from the Aegean sea, which was mere moments away.

Walking behind Nick she couldn't help but also check out his body.

His broad back and shoulders... *Wow*.

Nick sensed her staring and turned around, and she quickly diverted her eyes as if she just was taking in everything around her.

Parked in the shade of two tall cypress trees, Nick's car was a tiny, light blue vintage Volkswagen, with the back two seats taken out for extra storage. He popped the trunk threw her luggage in, and then opened the passenger door for her.

Peter never opened doors for her in New York— be it a taxi, convenience store, or restaurant. Never.

Nick did it without a second thought.

She thanked him and got in. The seats were leather and deliciously warm.

Nick got in the driver's seat, then turned to Joanna and seemed to consider something about her before nodding and pointing to her.

"Your father was right. You needed to come. Something about you has already changed since you've been here these few short moments."

Joanna furrowed her brow and asked, "What do you mean?"

"Your avra. It's clearer already."

"My avra? What's an avra?

Nick traced her body three feet away in the air. "Your avra. You know avra."

"Do you mean my aura? You can see my aura?" Joanna laughed, sceptical.

He didn't answer, but continued, "People would say you're just excited to finally be off the flight, but it's more than that, I think. You'll feel it, too, once you get a good night's sleep."

Joanna couldn't help but scoff at him but wasn't able to keep herself from blushing either.

This guy was a hell of a charmer.

CHAPTER SIX

THE DRIVE from the airport was surprisingly pleasant. After that plane landing she'd feared the romance movie cliche of crazy drivers in the Med might be true.

But it wasn't. Nick didn't speed or see any need to show off any nonexistent driving abilities. He drove like they had all the time in the world.

"This isn't the fastest way, Miss Joanna," he commented, with the window down. He grinned at her, wearing dark Rayban sunglasses and added, "Actually it's the farthest, but I thought you might like to see a bit of our homeland. The Skiathos National Airport is on the southeastern side of the island. We're driving north of it now, but your father's place is to the southwest. Most people who live on Skiathos live on the southern tip along the coast. North of the southern coast is mostly unbridled land. Where we're driving, there was a great fire some ten years ago."

Joanna sat up to see the green rolling hills and rising mountains and looked questioningly at him.

"It's so green, I know," Nick boasted. "The land here recovered, and within a year everything was back."

"How did it happen so quickly?" she asked.

"A geologist could answer that question better than me. I'm sure there's a technical reason with nothing magical to it. But to all of us who lived here, who lived through it and survived, it was nothing short of a miracle. There are a lot of churches on the island. Greek Orthodox. But every one of us, without talking to one another, felt it was old magic. Something, someone from the days of mankind's infancy."

"Zeus or Apollo maybe?" Joanna jokingly offered.

Nick looked at her and nodded seriously. "Yes, Miss Joanna. *Nai.* The old gods."

She couldn't tell if he was being serious, but he gave no sign that he wasn't.

The crystal blue expanse of the Aegean sea dominated the horizon, and it was an easy thing to see how such epics as *The Odyssey* had been written.

Looking past the undulating waves, there was mystery, a manifestation of the infinite.

And the water was so clean-looking. In New York, the water had a greyish-white hue.

Maybe it was the light, maybe it was the state of the Hudson River, but here, looking west, everything was nothing but blue.

Dark blue ocean, clean blue sky. No contrails dispersed into a foggy white haze.

This was the world as it was. As it should be.

Joanna chuckled to herself as the thought struck her.

Maybe the gods of old *were* protecting Skiathos.

THEY STOPPED after about an hour of driving.

Joanna's stomach was growling, but she was more than happy to wait. The island was intoxicatingly beautiful, and her senses were devouring it.

They pulled past a beach and started coming upon civilization again.

A teenage boy and girl on a mango-coloured moped zipped past, and boats with their sails drawn dotted the waters lazily.

"Joanna, do you mind if we visit someone quickly before I show you to your accommodation?" Nick asked.

"OK, sure," she agreed, somewhat hesitantly, wondering what he was up to.

"It's a woman I know will want to meet you. She loved your father more than anything in his last few years."

Joanna looked at him, interested. "Were they an item - together, I mean?"

"Who's to say?" he replied, shrugging. "I'm not even sure what *they'd* say."

They pulled onto a brick-paved roundabout that didn't seem to go anywhere except a flight of stone stairs.

Nick turned off the engine.

"Where are we?" Joanna asked, getting out with him. A park? Maybe a public garden?

She couldn't tell what was at the top, but tall, conical cypress trees intermixed with solid, white marble columns flanked both sides of the path all the way up the steep hill.

It was all so incredibly …. Greek.

"Come on," Nick said jogging up. "She's up here."

Joanna followed, glad to loosen up a bit and move her limbs.

"Oh, but before we get too far, just turn around and see this," he said, grabbing Joanna by her shoulders and gently turning her around. "Isn't this a spectacular view? I think it's the best in all of Skiathos."

Uninhabited, small green mountainous islands rose from the waters for as far as the eye could see. It was indeed breathtaking.

"Come on," Nick said, playfully. He reminded Joanna of Peter Pan trying to show Wendy all of the wonders of Neverland before nightfall.

Were mermaids next?

They climbed to the top of, not at a public garden, but instead … someone's estate? A large entryway in dire need of power-washing.

"*Eínai aftó tis? Eínai aftó i kóri Georges?*" a shapely older woman said, coming to the front door.

She was dressed in an all-white figure-hugging gown and had short, cropped black hair. She appeared to be in her late fifties but had the body of a toned, voluptuous younger woman.

"*Nai,*" Nick said. "*Aftí eínai i Joanna Nélson. Kóri tou Georges.*"

The woman startled Joanna and placed both of her hands on her face to gaze into her eyes.

Nai, you are his daughter," she said and smiled, displaying straight white teeth and healthy pink gums.

She kissed her on both cheeks and pulled her in for a hug.

Joanna kept her hands to the side, overwhelmed by this strange woman's onslaught of affection.

The Greek woman squeezed her hard one more time and let her go.

"You are a gem to us," she said. "*Efcharistó!* Thank you for coming!"

Joanna looked at Nick and asked, "What did I do?"

"You are George's daughter," Nick explained. "It is enough."

"What time did your plane land?" the woman asked, taking one of Joanna's hands and clasping it with both of her own.

"Around four," she replied.

The woman then looked sternly at Nick who promptly snickered and put his arms up to defend himself.

"That was hours ago and I'm sure she's tired and hungry," the woman scolded, raining down playful blows upon him. "Romance her after she's rested! I'm so sorry, Miss Nelson. If you weren't pretty he wouldn't have bothered you. You would have been here at four-twenty. Come, come. Come inside your new abode."

"This is…"

"*Nai, nai,*" the woman said, shaking her head. "*This* is your inheritance, all of it. Welcome to Villa Azure, the best hotel in Skiathos."

CHAPTER SEVEN

NICK BROUGHT her luggage in while Joanna walked around the lobby of Villa Azure, slightly dazed.

The walls were cracking and peeling paint, and the air smelled like a muggy enclosed swimming pool.

"I didn't properly introduce myself," the Greek woman said then. "I'm Crisanta Lekas, but you can call me Chris."

"How did you know my father?" Joanna asked, wandering around in circles, her mind spinning.

"I worked for him the last four years of his life. He was a great man."

Joanna stopped and leaned before a picture of an old man standing between the columns that lined the staircase.

"Is this him?" she asked, pointing.

"Your father? No, but that is your grandfather. Priam. He's the man who built this place. Would you like to see a picture of your father?"

Joanna nodded.

"Nick," she hollered and the younger Greek shrugged and set Joanna's luggage on the floor.

Chris seemed to think for a moment. "He wasn't a vain man, you see, Miss Joanna. I don't think he had anything like that in his room. We're still going through his things and belongings, and it's hard. None of us have the strength or time to do it. I don't think I've seen any pictures of him in there. Eímai ilíthios!" Chris suddenly slapped her head. "My phone. Let me find my phone. Just a minute, dear."

She walked behind the check-in desk, dug into her handbag, and came back with a white iPhone.

"I forget about how much these things do." Chris pulled up her photos and scrolled to one of her sitting next to a man with both hands resting atop a carved cane. "On the night of his last birthday, I got someone to take my picture with him. This is him. This is your father."

Joanna snatched Chris's phone from her hand and went and sat down on one of the old, leather couches. She zoomed in on his face. Unlike most older American men, her father was fit and thin before he died.

His teeth were slightly crooked, but they were still his own. No dentures for him. He had a pen behind his ear. Was he a writer? His shirt was pressed clean. His tie was tight and…

Suddenly overcome with emotion, Joanna broke down.

"Miss Joanna," Chris cried. "What's wrong? Is it just seeing your father? Nick, get her a glass of wine." She then ran to the check-in counter for a box of tissues and held the box for Joanna as she pulled some out.

"I'm sorry, it's just … I feeling a lot of emotions right now," Joanna sniffed, distraught at this unexpected show of feeling for a man she never knew. "I'm confused. If he was so wonderful why did I never have a chance to meet him? I don't understand. Why the distance? I think we would have liked each other perhaps."

Nick reappeared with a glass of wine and Chris took it from him, holding it out to Joanna. "Here, please. Take a sip. They don't call it spirits for no reason."

Joanna laughed sheepishly and drank it quickly.

"I wasn't going to tell you this but … you have me feeling bad for you now," Chris said and playfully slapped Joanna's knee. "Tomorrow, I will show you his room. I found a box of letters before that I couldn't bring myself to throw out. Now I know why. Your father must have been on the other side, encouraging me to keep them."

"Who were the letters from?"

"Your mother, Miss Joanna. So many of them."

"What?" she asked, wiping her eyes. "From when? What are they about?"

Chris patted her hand. "You'll just have to read them and find out for yourself."

CHAPTER EIGHT

THEY SHOWED Joanna to her room only after Chris had forced olives and cheese upon her. "You need to eat. You look pale."

It was the master suite - the only room on the fourth floor.

Its balcony and outdoor patio covered almost the entire area and the length of the third floor below. There was a large king bed in a separate bedroom, living room, and kitchen. It was three times larger than her apartment in New York.

"No, please, it's too much. Give it to some of the wedding guests. I don't need this much space. I promise."

"Óchi, óchi. Enjoy, Miss Joanna," Chris persuaded gently. "It's already done. Relax."

Nick placed Joanna's luggage on the bed for her and said, "After you take a shower and rest up, come down to the lobby. I'll take you to town for dinner and show you around some more."

"OK," Joanna said, her heart fluttering a little at the idea of going to dinner with the handsome Greek.

Chris smirked and shook her head at Nick.

"Keep your eye on him, Miss Joanna," she joked as if reading her mind. "Greek men aren't usually this polite to women. Even if they're the daughters of Georges Herod."

They left Joanna alone, and she walked out onto the patio to call Peter.

To the right, the sun was setting and casting the clouds in a wonderful peach-pink glow. The water rippled and shimmered in quiet ecstasy.

Were there any bad views in Skiathos? She loved how everything was mountainous and wild. Poseidon and Apollo were putting up a great show and if she had to prove her devotion to one of them, she'd be hard-pressed.

She calculated the time difference between Greece and New York. It was only eleven in the morning back there. She dug her phone out and dialled Peter. It went straight to voicemail.

"Hi, honey. I've arrived safely in Skiathos. You're never going to guess what he left me. It's beyond belief. Give me a call when you can. I'll probably be in bed before too long, so give me a call if you're not too busy."

She hung up. He was probably already at work showing some Wall Street investor a new high-rise apartment. She decided to take a hot shower and get ready for the evening.

Inside, the bathroom was direly in need of remodelling. The paint, the towel rack, and the shower rod all looked like they were probably dated even in the seventies.

She turned the hot water on, half expecting to see brown, muddy water seep out, but to her surprise, it was clear and immediately hot. So hot, in fact, she wouldn't be able to shower at full temperature.

"At least something's going right," she muttered.

She really wanted to talk to Peter about what her father had left her.

Was this place a goldmine like he assumed? The land maybe, but not the building. It needed so much work.

But the bones of it seemed strong. Perhaps it just needed to be spruced up a bit. Once upon a time, she could imagine it had been quite regal. Whenever that 'time' was, was open to debate, but it could be brought back.

But it really couldn't be on a better piece of land. The views were spectacular. She tried to keep her brain occupied with the logistics of owning an internationally visited hotel, but soon her brain went back to her parents, and to the letters they had written to one another.

Ruth had never really loved anyone, Joanna thought. Not from what she had seen. Hell, it was debatable if her mother even really loved *her*.

Over the years when she was a child, she had watched Ruth try to date men. Everyone she dated, no matter who it was, always ended badly.

She never went out with anyone for more than a couple of weeks. Joanna had just assumed at the time that her mother wasn't able to find anyone with whom she connected. That all of the men she dated were jerks of some kind.

Had she just been comparing them all to her father? Had they all failed to impress and had Ruth lived her whole life hoping to find another George Herod?

She'd never even mentioned him. The most Joanna ever got was that one comment: "It was a mistake."

Was *she* the mistake? And what were all of the letters about?

CHAPTER NINE

A WHILE LATER, Joanna got out of the shower and dried off. She opened up her suitcase and contemplated what to wear. She had brought a long, black flowing sundress but looking at it now, was it too sexy?

She wasn't concerned about that factor so much as she was about comfort.

A little voice in her head, one that sounded surprisingly a lot like Donna said, *Yeah, you tell yourself that's why you're wearing it. Nick isn't exactly hard on the eyes, is he?*

He's not, Joanna conceded. And I bet *he'd* answer the phone if I called him from another country...

A few minutes later she went back down to the lobby where she found Nick reading the paper, and Chris talking with a guest.

"Joanna," she waved. "Come, come! This is Mr. Balis. Mr. Balis, this is the new owner, George's daughter. You're going to bring this place back to its former glory, aren't you, Miss Joanna?"

She coloured. "Oh! I have no idea what I'm going to do yet…"

Mr Balis took Joanna's hand and kissed it. He had white hair shooting out the sides of his old golfer's hat and was maybe in his mid-eighties. His eyes looked a little confused, and Joanna couldn't tell if he knew what was going on. Then he surprised her by speaking English.

"Your father," he began and shook his head. "Your father was the best friend anyone could ever have, but he didn't give a shit about this place. He let Chris here worry about everything. But he always made sure we had whatever we needed. Before I married my wife, I wanted to buy her some flowers as a surprise. I wasn't the only guy interested in her, you see. He lent me the money when I jokingly said I was going to lose her to Janus down the street. Janus's father had money, just like George's father did, but George didn't walk around trying to look better than everyone else. I tried to pay him back, and he wouldn't let me. Told me to buy her another bouquet. He said the trick is not just buying a girl flowers, but buying her flowers more than once. I took that to heart. Been buying her flowers ever since."

"Your English is very good," Joanna commented, smiling.

Balis gave a curt nod. "Deal with tourists most of the year. We all speak some English here. Learn some Greek if you're going to stay, but it doesn't matter. We'll talk to you even if you don't. Skiathons are talkers."

Then he walked out the back to the outdoor pool and bar.

"Is he here for the bar?" Joanna asked.

"No," Chris replied. "He got in trouble with his wife. Shouldn't have given her so many flowers. Now when he makes her angry he's got nothing to give her."

Nick had been so involved in his paper that he hadn't

realised Joanna had come down. Right then he noticed her (as well as what she was wearing) and tossing the paper to the side he bounced over.

"Joanna," he exclaimed. "Ready for dinner?"

"I am. Where are you taking me?"

"What do you like?" he asked charmingly.

"Something fresh," she said.

This confused him a little. "Something fresh?" he repeated, cocking his head to the side.

"You know, a nice salad or something with vegetables. Nothing greasy or fried."

"I see," Nick said and laughed. "I think you mean Greek food."

She smiled. "Then lead the way."

"Are you going to take me the long way again?" she asked when seated in Nick's old Volkswagen.

"Do you want me to?"

"No, I just want to eat," Joanna sighed. "You've been promising me food all day."

He grinned. "We're going to a restaurant that only Skiathan natives know of. No tourist, to my knowledge, has ever gone there."

"They won't throw me out then, will they?"

"No, because you are part Skiathan too. One who can't speak any Greek perhaps, but you *are* Skiathan."

Nick looked at her and saw her face. "Miss Joanna, no, I'm teasing. If you knew me you'd know I only tease people I like."

Joanna thought they were going to drive straight along the coast and into town, but soon he turned left where the road suddenly became a dirt path and curved and wound its way up one of the many mountains on the island.

"What are you doing?" she urged, becoming a little irritated now. "Don't drive me all over this island because you've got nothing better to do. Feed me!"

Nick grinned. "We should have brought a donkey, but I think we're going to make it. How strong are your American legs? You might have to push. My car is old."

Joanna bit her lip and stifled a laugh. She hadn't bantered with a guy like this in a long time. Peter was serious and so literal. He didn't really know how to banter.

Nick stopped at the peak of the hill in front of a modern, glass-walled building. There were no signs that it was a public place other than the fact that there were parking spaces.

"This is a restaurant?" Joanna asked dubiously.

"It is. Not the typical tourist taverna you were expecting no?" he joked.

Inside, Nick spoke Greek to the waitress who smiled warmly at Joanna and then took them outside to a terrace.

"Look," Nick said, pointing. "Both coasts of Skiathos. That's the southern end, and behind me is the northern coast. Great view, still not as good as the one Villa Azure provides. But I like it here. I feel like I'm at the top of the world."

It was a stunning view but grey clouds had begun to form, and it was looking like it was going to rain any minute. The sky rumbled and the wind picked up.

"If it rains, we'll go inside," he told her. "I just wanted to show you the view."

Joanna tried to decode the menu but couldn't read a word.

"Just tell me what you want, and I'll tell her," Nick offered.

"But I don't know what I want. I can't read it. I don't know what they have."

"They have a little bit of everything."

"Anything you'd recommend?" she asked. "What's the best thing they have here?"

"I don't know. Just let me know what you prefer. They have lots of good stuff."

Nick was quickly becoming the antithesis of Peter, who would have jumped at the opportunity to tell Joanna what she wanted, whereas Nick made no move to assume such a thing.

He took out a cigarette and lit up.

"I just want a really big salad, I think. Nothing extravagant. Can you tell them to make me their best salad?"

He nodded. "Of course. No country makes better salads than Greece."

He took her menu from her leaned back into his chair and crossed his legs, enjoying his cigarette. He quickly got lost in his thoughts as he gazed at the storm clouds on the horizon. There was something so easygoing about him.

Joanna wished she could talk to him in his native tongue, and hear how his mind would naturally express itself.

"Tell me something about my father," she asked, trying to pull him back from wherever he was. "Tell me a funny story, or about why you liked him so much. Something to illustrate why you'd be so willing to arrange for his estranged daughter to come from the US and spend the day with her. How did you know him? Villa Azure seems a little far from the town. Did he make his way there often?"

"Your father was always involved in town affairs. He wasn't a hermit," Nick replied.

"But how did you come to know him? How did the two of you meet?"

He stretched and looked at Joanna. There was warmth in his deep brown eyes.

"My father manned and operated a fishing boat. Every week he'd go out to sea and come back with fresh, delicious fish to sell at the market. It was normal for him to be gone for a few days at a time. He never caught too much. Just enough to feed us and sell to the restaurants. One day he went out and got caught in a freak storm. We never saw him again. Your father supported my family until we were able to get our feet on the ground again, and it was your father who said I should go to school. I was going to become a fisherman like my father. I'll never forget what he said to me. It was on a Sunday. On Sundays, we would walk through the hills to go to church on the northern side of the island. It was a ritual that he got me into. There are numerous closer churches, but he liked the walk and invited me to go along with him. After church one day, it was about to rain as it is now, and we had stopped to catch our breath and observe the sea. He said to me, 'Nick. It is noble for the son to take up the trade of the father, and there is no such thing as a petty job. If it puts food on the table, then it is a noble job. But I have known no father who would have his son walk in his footsteps simply to repeat his story. All fathers want their children to have their own story. You are not meant to be a fisherman, Nick.'"

"How did you take that?" Joanna asked, rapt. "Was it what you wanted to hear?"

He looked away into the distance. "Yes and no. I was still upset over the loss of my father and was angry at the gods for having taken him away from me. I think that's why your father would take me on walks. I tended to sit inside and read all day. He knew the walks were good for my anger. On that same walk, he told me he would help me go to school, and said I could go anywhere I wanted. That he would pay for it. I can still remember how my mother wept with joy when I told her.

Naturally, I went to the University of Athens. I wanted the city life, but was too afraid to go too far. I studied international politics and philosophy. When I came back, full of book knowledge and anecdotes of eccentric professors, he listened to all of my stories and everything I had learned. When I was finished, he looked at me and asked, 'Where do you want to go next?' He had already changed my life and given me countless wonderful experiences. I was already set to get a good office job somewhere and climb the corporate ladder. 'Where do you want to go next?' he asked again. I was flabbergasted. I said I might want to study law. He looked at me and said, 'Nai, I think you should, but the best universities are in London. You're going to need an umbrella. It's a cold, grey place there.' And he sent me to London just like that to study law."

"Did he know you before all of that?" Joanna asked.

"He knew of me. He made a point to know me. He went out of his way to help me when my father died."

The waitress came out then and Nick ordered for them, as well as some wine, and she came back with a full bottle and two glasses.

"The wonderful thing about my story, Miss Joanna," Nick said once the waitress had gone back inside, "is that it's not unique. Your father did the same for many other children on this island."

"How many?" she asked, amazed.

"I don't know," Nick said. "Considering how large his funeral was, I'd say it was a lot."

He poured them some wine and put out his cigarette before continuing. "Now you know why Villa Azure is in the state it is. He spent all the profits on us as if we were his children. He knew his hotel needed work, but he cared more about people than he did about that."

"So you're saying he left me something that was just an afterthought to him?"

"I don't know. I don't know if I would say it like that."

"What do you think are in the letters?" Joanna asked, her thoughts segueing to all of the other things she didn't know about her elusive father.

"Something interesting for sure. There is a history there that none of us know about. I think you're going to find out what happened between Georges and your mother, Joanna. I think you're going to find out why you didn't grow up in Skiathos."

CHAPTER TEN

LATER, Nick dropped her off at the hotel and walked her inside.

"Where do you live?" she asked. "Do you have far to go?"

"A houseboat. I'm just a few minutes away from here."

"So some of your father is still in you then," she said and smiled.

"Yes, but I leave it to others to do the catching. Goodnight, Miss Joanna." He waved goodbye and left. Joanna had expected him to kiss her on the cheeks again, but he didn't. Had she done something?

Chris saw the exchange, though pretended she was watching TV on a small portable television.

She looked at Joanna's perplexed face and shook her head.

"Kissing on the cheeks is a sign of familiarity here. It's something that a brother and a sister, or a father and a daughter would do without a second thought. To kiss both cheeks is like saying 'I'm comfortable with you. You are a good friend.'"

"So you're saying that—"

"Nick doesn't want to be your friend, Miss Joanna. He wants something more."

Joanna didn't know what to say. Chris waved her on and said, "Go and get some sleep now. Think about it tomorrow."

PETER CALLED Joanna back after she had changed and brushed her teeth for the night. She considered not answering but did to tell him all about Villa Azure, the hotel of which it seemed she was now the proud owner.

"Ooh, never mind what it's like on the inside, if the views are as good as you say they are, sell the place. Whoever buys it is probably just going to bulldoze it and start over anyway. They'll pay you for the land, and you can use that as a bargaining chip. Land is a huge commodity in the Greek Islands. Your big chain hotels are always looking for mom-and-pop places to buy so they can swoop in and run it like it's supposed to. They'll make millions more because they'll put in what tourists want."

"Uh-huh," Joanna mumbled, thinking that a generic tourist hotel would be awful in a place like this.

"I can help you out. We've got a lot of international connections at the company. We'll get you the money you deserve. We'll dance with investors. You're probably going to become a millionaire overnight. We'll be able to have our wedding wherever you want."

"That sounds … good I think. But I'm going to need a little more time here first."

"Time?"

"There are some things I need to deal with, some letters belonging to my father. Probably other things as well. The letters are between him and my mom. Seems this whole thing was more than just a one-night stand."

"Oh, well, clean his room out and then sell. I don't get what that has to do with anything."

147

"I'm just… I'm just not so sure I want to tear it down just yet. This place was built by my grandfather, and he passed it down to my father, who passed it down to me."

"A father you never spoke to passed it down to you Joanna," Peter pointed out. "You're not obligated to preserve anything for him. He did nothing for you."

Joanna remembered the story Nick relayed about what her father had told him.

"I have known no father who would have his son walk in his footsteps simply to repeat his story. All fathers want their children to have their own story."

Still, her mind wasn't there. She wasn't ready. Not yet. Not after having been here for less than a day.

"There's a story, Peter. I have to know it. If I walk away now I may never know it."

Peter was quiet. She could tell he was measuring his words. Crafting a way to try and get her to commit to selling. He was a good salesman, but he wasn't good enough to sell her on this. He knew it, and she knew it.

He exhaled. "Do what you have to do, Joanna. Just don't get lost in some dream that never existed."

CHAPTER ELEVEN

"GOOD MORNING," Chris greeted warmly the next day, as Joanna came down the stairs. "Did you sleep well?"

"I did," she replied. "Actually don't think I've ever slept so deeply in my life."

"We get that a lot," Chris chuckled. "Not just from tourists. Skiathons who stay at Villa Azure say that too. I don't know why that is. Something in the stones this place was built upon, I guess."

Joanna went and poured herself some hot coffee from a pot across from the clerk's desk, and noticed Nick already outside reading the paper in the back alongside the dated, chipping swimming pool. She considered running back upstairs as she hadn't put any makeup on yet but decided to go out and tell him good morning. He didn't seem the type to care that she wasn't wearing eyeliner and blush.

He saw her and beamed.

"Kaliméra, Joanna," he said, folding up his paper.

She cocked her head in confusion.

"Good morning," he translated with a smile. "Your Greek language instruction starts today."

"Now? Why is that?"

"Because I have a good feeling that you are going to fall in love with this island, and be ready for the challenge of renovating this place. It's early yet. Not even seven, and yet you are up and drinking coffee. It's a good sign for us who would have you stay."

"Hey, slow down, buddy - I've always been a morning person."

He shrugged. "You see they are getting ready for the wedding reception over there. Just behind you?" he said, pointing to some people putting out tables and arranging chairs. A young couple, freshly married, will celebrate their marriage this evening overlooking the Aegean Sea on the most beautiful place on the island. It's going to be quite romantic. And the rain has passed so it's even better. You will accompany me to the church, yes?"

Joanna was a little taken aback. She recalled that Nick had mentioned during that first call about the wedding celebration, but she hadn't expected an invitation to the church.

"What time is the ceremony?"

"I think around five." Then he took a key from his pocket and handed it to her.

"What's this?"

"Your father's room key. He lived in an inconsequential room that no hotel guest would write home about. Room 111. I will come and get you for lunch at noon. Is this OK? Chris left the letters where we found them in a leather satchel hanging in his closet."

Joanna took the key from him and stared at it - wondering if would be the key to her past - or future.

. . .

ROOM 111 WAS DOWN A DARK, quiet hallway, across from a loud ice machine that constantly hummed and vibrated. How did her father put up with that noise? If Joanna had to live next to it she'd go crazy.

She put the key in the lock and opened the door, terrified she'd see George's ghost standing there and waiting for her. She didn't know what she had expected, but what she saw unnerved her even more than a ghost.

A bed.

A wardrobe.

A closet.

A desk.

A bathroom.

And that was it.

Positively, unilaterally underwhelming.

She hadn't expected to find the studio of a genius or think he was the twenty-first-century equivalent of Leonardo da Vinci or anything. But there were no personal touches anywhere. No sign of character or illumination into who George Herod was.

He lived in a dilapidated hotel, and his room was as lifeless and neutral as any other.

She sat down on the bed and saw that on the desk was a hotplate he had apparently used to cook on with a kettle behind it. Coffee or tea? She stood up and looked around but didn't see anything indicating either. Tea perhaps, since there was coffee freely available in the lobby?

There wasn't even a particular smell in the room, odd for an older bachelor's place. He had left behind no aftershave, no cologne, no manly soap preference.

The whole room was still. Flat. Like a monk's.

She walked to the closet and saw the leather satchel Nick had mentioned hanging on a hook. She unhooked it and emptied its contents onto the bed.

It was nothing but letters. She scattered them out briefly and saw for herself that every single one of them was from her mother.

"Oh Mom," Joanna sighed. "What happened? Why didn't you let yourself be happy?"

She found the first letter. Someone had taken the time to number and date them. Nick or Chris? They hadn't given her any sense that they had lingered over the letters - or read them even. Plus the writing looked like it was done by a shaky hand.

Joanna opened the first letter. It was dated 1982, almost four years before she was born.

CHAPTER TWELVE

George,

I don't know how else to say this. I'm going back and forth between smiling so much my cheeks hurt, to fighting tears that you're not next to me right now.

I've been home for two hours. I'm tired, and hungry and I should go to sleep, but I'm not going to. I'm going to write and tell you one more time how much you changed my life. I don't know how long it takes for mail to get to Greece from New York, but I guess we'll find out, won't we?

Before I left, you asked me to tell you what my favourite thing we did was. I couldn't tell you at the time I was so busy fighting my tears and trying to be a 'strong woman.'

Now, after daydreaming about you for eleven hours on an aeroplane, I have to say it was the walks you took me on through the foothills to get to Moni Evaggelistrias. Such a beautiful church. But it wasn't the church I enjoyed. It was just being with you. Hearing you tell stories of your family as we idly walked, pointing out to me what plants were medicinal and which were poisonous, and just... being in silence together. Is that strange? I've never been so comfortable with someone before that I didn't feel a need to fill the silence with chatter. I'm a New Yorker: silence is a strange concept to us. It's like a word we got from another culture but don't understand what it truly means.

I meant what I said: I will come back. Time is the only thing keeping me from you right now and I will weather it. But I feel a bit like Persephone banished back to hell, only my punishment is far worse. If only my time in New York were but a season....

Please know that I will come back.

Utterly, completely, passionately yours.

Ruth.

JOANNA FOLDED the letter delicately and put it back in its envelope. There were little bubbles on the ink where it looked like someone had cried over it. Were they her mother's tears upon writing it? Or her father's? At that point, Joanna was seconds away from adding her own.

She didn't know if she had another in her, but the envelope labelled number 2 was right in front of her.

Why had he numbered them? How often had he read them? Would he spend his evenings recanting the romance he had with her mother? Letter by letter? Were men even capable of being that romantic?

Maybe Grecian men, but certainly not any others that she had ever met.

Delicately, she pulled out the second letter.

It too was from 1982:

GEORGE,

I got your letter today. I was so nervous when I got your reply because I couldn't remember what I had said in my first letter. It takes so long for mail to get between us. It's too much. I was terrified that I said something to make you not want to talk to me anymore. But then I read what you said, and saw that you, too, felt the same way that I did— and still do!

I smiled, I laughed, I cried while reading it, but I mostly smiled. Beamed with joy. My heart feels so light and giddy, knowing that you feel the same way I do. I've never felt this way before. To the rest of the world, I'm an old 39-year-old woman... in my heart, I'm a schoolgirl again. I blame you. Bless you for doing this to me.

I'll be able to take another vacation in a few months. Just five months. Sounds absurd, but knowing there's a light at the end of the tunnel makes it easier.

You've already noticed, I'm sure and combed through them, but I've sent you pictures of all the places I go every day, and given you a map with my daily routes. Try to walk with me. Try to visualize where I am. Every day I do the same. Every day I'm in Skiathos. Breathing the air. Feeling the light. Smelling the sea. It's my happy space. A mansion within my mind. Create a mansion of my world, and let's build a bridge between the two.

Say a prayer for me. Call out the old gods as I know you silently do. You're a man of magic. You've managed to keep it from everyone else, but I know your secret. I saw you communing with them.

I'm going to write as often as I can, and I'm going to call you as often as I can afford. My brain will always be mentally calculating the time difference between us, wondering what you're doing. Wondering if you're awake. Wondering if you've returned from your long walks. I compared myself to Persephone in the last letter, I think, but now I wonder if Odysseus wouldn't be a better comparison. Can I be a female Odysseus? Will you destroy the shroud every night for me? Protect my palace from encircling real estate investors?

Keep it. I know you don't love Villa Azure as much as I do, but keep it for me, so that I can return to the place where I fell in love with you, and will know where to look for you when I return home.

Because Skiathos will soon be my home.

JOANNA PUT the letter back in the satchel as she had the others. She guessed where the story was heading and didn't have the heart to keep reading right then.

A lot of things were starting to make sense, though.

When Joanna was a teenager her mother suddenly started dating again, but she never dated anyone for longer than two weeks. She never seemed to find just the right guy. A lot of them were great men. Charming, handsome, funny. But they had one handicap that they couldn't overcome. Now she knew what that was.

They weren't George. They weren't her father.

But what had happened?

Joanna had cleaned out her mother's apartment when she died a couple of years back. She didn't find any kind of memento or keepsake from George. Unlike he who seemingly kept everything he could relating to their brief romance.

Joanna walked out of the room and locked it up. She needed a breather.

George had apparently intimated to her mom that he wanted to sell the hotel. If Villa Azure meant nothing to him, why didn't he sell it and move to New York to be with her mom?

What on earth had gone wrong between them?

CHAPTER THIRTEEN

NICK LOOKED up when he saw Joanna walk into the lobby. "Is everything OK?"

"Yeah… I just need to get out for a bit."

He showed her his pearly white teeth. "Are you hungry yet?"

She shook her head no.

"OK. I think I know just the perfect thing to brighten up your day."

He instructed Joanna to go back to her room and grab a bathing suit.

"Where are we going?" she asked, as they trotted down the stone steps to Nick's car.

"My boat."

"Nick, we just met," she said, taken aback expecting he'd planned to seduce her.

He yelped like a hyena, the most absurd laugh she had ever heard, and despite herself, she laughed too.

They practically flew the thirty seconds it took to drive to the pier where Nick's boat was docked.

He turned the engine off before the car was even finished

stopping, and helped Joanna climb into his houseboat. He untied the ropes tethering the boat to the peer, and pushed it out as hard as he could with his foot before jumping in.

"Will you tell me where are we going now? What are we going to do?"

"Just sit tight," Nick said as he powered up the boat. "Inside the cabin is a small fridge. Grab a beer if you want. There's also some wine in a crate if you prefer. You can go ahead and change, too. It will take us a little less than an hour to get there."

"But where are we going?"

"There's a small island immediately to the north. It's the best fishing area on the islands— a secret my father passed on to me. Have you ever used a speargun before?"

"A speargun? Why the hell would I know how to use a speargun? Every American girl isn't Annie Oakley, you know."

"It's easy. I show you. If it's too big, don't shoot it, though. My speargun isn't that good. You'll just anger what you shot."

Joanna considered this. "Where'd you say the beer was again?"

A LITTLE WHILE later they were about four hundred meters off the mountainous coast of Skiathos. Nick's father's secret fishing spot was nestled between two barren, rocky islands that jetted out of the water like cavernous teeth.

It was quiet and peaceful. The only sound was the lapping of seawater against the side of the boat.

Why would anyone ever leave this place? Joanna thought, captivated.

Having dropped anchor, Nick suddenly took off his white t-shirt and tossed it inside the cabin, and she almost spat out her beer again.

He was lean, tanned and muscular, way too fit for someone who seemed to sit in a lobby all day reading newspapers. He then took off his pants to reveal he was wearing only a pair of black speedos and she gulped afresh.

"Already wearing your swimming gear?" she asked, trying not to stare.

He winked. "Always prepared."

Joanna had changed when she went inside to get a drink and was wearing a white one-piece. Nothing revealing, but her boobs looked good and she knew it. She saw him glance a few times as they chatted and she didn't mind.

What about Peter? You're being emotionally unfaithful, a little voice nagged.

Perhaps. But nothing's happened.

Hence the word emotional.

But Joanna couldn't deny that she was attracted to Nick, and when the question 'what about Peter' returned to her active, little brain, she didn't have an answer.

All she knew was that being with him felt like the most natural thing in the world.

He went into the cabin and came back with a speargun that was about five feet long.

"OK," he said, holding it out to her. "First we should practice on something." He looked around, visibly at a loss and then abruptly grabbed a life vest off the rails and flicked it into the water.

"I guess we're not going to need that then?" Joanna said dryly.

He grinned. "I hope not."

He handed her the speargun and got behind her, his hard body firm against hers. "OK, pick it up and aim as you would a rifle. It does have a little bit of kick, so put the stock into your shoulder." He put his chest into her back and helped her position her elbows correctly.

"What if I miss?" Joanna asked, turning back to him. His face was getting stubbly. He hadn't shaved in a day or so and it was tickling her shoulder. Not unpleasantly.

"That's why there is a rope attached to the spear," he pointed out.

"Oh, right." Joanna blushed at her own stupidity.

Nick stepped to the side and said, "Match up your sights and pull the trigger. Now in the water, it's unnecessary to put the butt in your shoulder, but it does have a kick even when submerged, so it's up to you. We'll practice a few times."

He got closer to her again and repositioned her elbows once more before she took the shot. She could smell him. He wasn't wearing cologne or deodorant, but he didn't have to. His natural fragrance was sweet and manly. She liked how he smelled.

Joanna pulled the trigger and the speargun kicked a little bit, stinging the flesh in her armpit. Instantly the spear struck the life vest with a loud pop and jostled the water.

"Well done, Annie Oakley!" Nick exclaimed.

Joanna rolled her eyes at him but grinned.

A little while later he went into the cabin and came back with snorkeling equipment.

"Ever snorkelled?" he asked.

"Yes, that I *can* do."

Nick handed her two fins, a scuba mask, and a snorkel. As she was putting everything on and tightening straps, he casually geared up and sat on the side of the boat and waited.

"Ready?" he asked. She nodded and he took a deep breath and fell backwards into the water with the unloaded speargun in his hand.

Show off, she thought.

She climbed down the ladder and shrieked the deeper she got into the water.

Gah, it was cold!

She gasped and shivered while Nick pulled the spear out of the life vest and loaded it back up.

"There are two fish abundant in this area worth hunting," he said while wading towards her. "The tuna and the red snapper. Catch one tuna and we're all set for lunch."

Joanna's shivers abated and she nodded. Her nipples had become two rock-solid little buds that he was definitely going to notice underwater.

Nick kicked his feet up and plunged beneath the waves.

That was OK, she was going to steal a few glances at him, too.

She kicked and dived after him.

The sea floor was only about thirty feet below the surface. It wasn't flat and smooth. It was quite rocky and cavernous like the island nearby, only it was underwater. The water was so clear that if it weren't for the rugged landscape she'd be able to see quite far.

A little fish darted between her legs and she jerked.

Nick got her attention and pointed ahead.

There was a school of large tuna swimming between two large rock clusters that connected to the tiny islands above.

He then pointed upwards and they went for air.

"We'll get in position, and I'll give you the gun," Nick said.

"Wait, I thought we were going to practice some more."

"No, my Annie Oakley doesn't need more practice. You'll be fine."

Joanna was going to protest but he plunged back down.

Beneath the water, they kicked with their finned feet closer to the school of large tuna. Nick handed her the speargun and gave her a thumbs up. The tuna were each three if not four feet long, and there were a lot of them.

The gun was easier to manoeuvre beneath the water and so she decided to hold it like a pistol this time.

The spear zipped through the water with the line attached and struck the tuna straight into its side. Puffy clouds of red erupted around it, and it darted and pulled the line out.

Joanna gripped the gun in case it should jerk out of her hands, but after a moment the reel stopped spinning. The tuna had met its end.

Nick pointed up and they surfaced.

"Great job, Joanna!" She laughed as he made gun sounds with his mouth as he pretended his hands were pistols.

They swam back to the boat and he reeled it in. It was a four-footer.

"Wow, this baby weighs at least thirty pounds," he said muscling up. "Are you hungry now?"

Joanna bounced on her heels and nodded.

CHAPTER FOURTEEN

NICK FRIED the fish while they both drank another beer. He told her she could steer them back to the dock if she wanted, but she didn't have to.

"Do you have any brothers or sisters?" Joanna asked him conversationally, dangling her feet off the side of the boat. "Any family in Skiathos?"

"No, I am all that is left," Nick said. "I think our mothers died around the same time. Did your mother have any more children?"

Joanna snorted. "No, my mother would have rather died than have another kid. Parenthood didn't suit her."

"So have you discovered anything from the letters so far?"

Joanna hesitated, then said, "She loved him very much… in the beginning. I've only read the first two. They were difficult for me to read. She was a completely different person when they met. She was… more like me, as I am now. Or how I wish I could be. What they had together… in the beginning, was a magical thing for her. I just can't bear to find out how it ended."

"He kept every one of those letters," Nick said, absently, flipping the fish.

"I know. And I also know my mom was probably the one who screwed it up."

"Still," Nick added, "she kept you, didn't she? She could have given you up, but she kept you. Something was going on within her." He flipped the fish over one more time and said, "OK, let's eat."

He got them some paper plates and they sat cross-legged on his bed and ate as they continued their conversation.

"Do you know what happened and just aren't telling me?" Joanna asked, in between bites.

"I have an idea. I've heard mumblings here and there. Half the town thought he was gay, including me for the longest time. I know now that he wasn't. He was just in mourning."

"You know this because of the letters?" she asked.

"No, they were too personal for me to read. I know this because I talked with a villager who saw something one night. I'll tell you if and when you're ready. I don't think we have time for you to shoot another fish if you get in another funk."

Joanna gave him her best schoolgirl scowl. Then she yawned, stuffed after the food and nicely chilled from the beer. "Oh, I could take a nap. Your bed is comfy. I can see why you don't think you need a house. Do you have a house? Do you get a lot of visitors? I bet you do, don't you?"

"This is your way of verifying I'm not married and that this isn't just my bachelor apartment, isn't it?" he said smirking.

"Well? Is it? Are you married? Is this your one-night stand bandwagon?"

"Like George, I'm sure most of the island believes I'm gay. I do not live anywhere else. I don't have a girlfriend. But I believe you, on the other hand, do have a boyfriend."

Joanna deflated a bit at the thought of Peter. "You're right, I do have a boyfriend. But, things have gone a little south lately."

"Does he know this? Men sometimes don't know when things go south. But if you don't mind me saying, this man must be an idiot to let that happen and risk someone like you slipping through his fingers."

They both eyed each other intensely, the sexual tension between them growing with each passing word.

"Take a nap, Joanna," he said quietly. "I promise to not bother you, though I have never had such a beautiful woman as you in my bed."

"That's not weird for you?" she asked, feeling little butterflies in her stomach at his words, and thinking that perhaps she wouldn't mind in the least being 'bothered' by him, as he'd put it. "Having a complete stranger sleep in your bed?"

"You were never a stranger to me. Draw the shades. You'll be asleep in no time, dreaming of worlds within reach that have yet to be explored."

He closed the door, and Joanna did as he recommended and closed the blinds. The gentle sway, to and fro, the constant rumble of the engine was soothing. He was right. She did fall asleep.

But she didn't dream of worlds yet to be explored. She dreamed of Skiathos, and in this dream, she stayed on the island and had all the time in the world to get to know Nick.

It was the loveliest dream.

CHAPTER FIFTEEN

LATER, back in her room, getting ready for the wedding that evening, she got a phone call from Donna.

"Tell me about this Greek hottie I know you're falling in love with," her best friend demanded without even saying hello.

Joanna dropped down to the bed, gobsmacked. "What do you know? And how the hell do you know it?"

Donna cackled over the phone. "Nothing! I was just playing with you. But who is he? Tell me more."

Joanna grinned and got out her nail polish. "His name is Nick. He's charming. He's funny. He's smart. He's been taking me all over Skiathos. We just went spearfishing. It was so much fun."

"Wow, so you killed something. How romantic." Donna deadpanned.

"Yes. And then we ate it on his boat."

"Please tell me Peter is out of the picture then," her friend enthused. "He's not right for you. I know you don't like me saying that, but he's not. He's a downer. And, quite frankly, he's been turning you into one as well."

"Well, that hurts Donna, but I think I do see what you've been trying to get me to understand. I've been having so much fun and I've only been here twenty-four hours."

"Did you want me to break it to Peter?" Donna asked. "I'll do it. I'll do it in a heartbeat."

"I didn't say I was breaking up with Peter!" Joanna exclaimed. "I'm just... I don't know. I don't know what I want."

"You will. Hopefully sooner than later. What did your father leave you in the will anyway?"

"A hotel. A rundown, beat-up hotel, badly in need of a makeover."

"Oh my god! Let's renovate it together! That would be so much fun. Oh let me in on this, please! I could come to Greece, and we could work on the hotel by day and drink ouzo all night. We would kick some serious ass together, I know it."

"Whoa, calm down. I haven't even seen the numbers. I don't know what the place is making and I definitely don't know what it would cost to fix it up. Like I said, I don't know anything. I'm still wrapping my head around this secret relationship my mom had and never told me about."

"What?"

Joanna told her about the letters and what she knew.

"And you've only been there a day? You must be exhausted."

"No actually... well I did take a nap, so I feel great, but I'm probably just on a vacation high. I'd better get going, though. I've got to get ready for a wedding now."

"OK, I'm serious. I'll come to Greece and help you renovate. I don't care about numbers. Whatever they are, we'll increase them."

Laughing at her friend's enthusiasm, Joanna said goodbye to Donna and finished getting ready.

She had already given Nick a glimpse of her boobs, so now time to give him a taste of her legs.

Tonight, she was going to turn some heads.

CHAPTER SIXTEEN

THE LOOK on Nick's face when he met her in the lobby to take them to the church, was enough to tell Joanna that she could have him eating out of her hand if she wanted.

Hair pinned up, she had on a sleeveless, black A-lined dress that could be worn on a red carpet. With an open back, the top was fitted more so than the bottom, but with her pins on full-out display, it was her toned, tanned legs that would make men speechless— Nick included.

"You are stunning," he said in a whisper.

But she wasn't alone. He too was quite the looker.

Navy blue sports jacket, white dress shirt, leather brown shoes that only a true European artisan could have made, and a maroon bow tie expertly tied, he was quite dapper.

Instead of a belt, he wore grey suspenders with bronzed metal clips that shimmered in the light. If it weren't for his devil-may-care-mussed-up hair, he would look right in place in a Rat-Pack movie. You could put him on a runway and no one would think twice when they saw him. He would fit right in.

Nick held his arm out for her and she took it. She was accustomed to walking in heels, but if he was going to offer her his muscular arm she was going to make the most of it.

Chris yelled out, "Have fun you, two. See you back here later."

In the car, Joanna asked, "Where's the church?"

"A few minutes north of here. Through several thick pine forests and climbing, dirt roads and just before the land drops again and descends to a rocky beach. It's an old church, so old that a bunch of wild cats see no difference between it and nature and have declared it to be their sanctuary. Monks feeding them fish might also have something to do with them being there too."

The air had cooled since their fishing excursion but had now taken on a flowery, ambrosial quality. Maybe it was where they were driving and the flow of wind currents across the island, but the air grew steadily more perfumed the higher they drove.

It took them about ten minutes to get there. There was no parking, so everyone parked on the road and walked the hundred meters or so to the church.

Nick was right. The place did seem to have a cat problem. Several were sleeping lackadaisically along the stone walls and regarded them both with indifference as they walked by. One stretched and playfully attempted to hook a claw into Nick's hair, but for the most part, they acted like tamed wildlife at a park, and not, as most foreigners would assume, pets.

At the stone entrance people were lining up, waiting to be seated inside.

Joanna noticed several women looking at Nick, and almost subconsciously she squeezed his arm tighter.

A broad-chested man with short, black hair turned around and greeted Nick in Greek.

He in turn placed his hand on her bare back and replied, "Joanna Nelson. Aftí eínai i kóri tou, George."

The man looked at Joanna, and then back to Nick before saying something else.

Ever the gentleman, Nick shook his head. "Let's speak in English, so she knows what we're saying."

"Hello, Joanna," the man said in perfect English, much to her surprise. He took her hand. "I am Markos. Your father was a great man. I'm sorry for your loss. We all mourn with you. Do you know the couple about to get married?"

Joanna shook her head. "No, Nick invited me. It's partly how he persuaded me to come to Skiathos."

He smiled. "Nick always finds a way to get what he wants. He is like a magician who can conjure the elements as he needs them. In America, he would be called a cocky son of a bitch. Here, in Skiathos, we just give him the space to do what he wants. He doesn't disrupt the waters too much."

Joanna turned to Nick. "And here I thought you were a good boy," she teased. "Is Markos trying to tell me you're dangerous?"

"Unsupervised, maybe, yes," Nick chuckled, shuffling forward. "Less so since your father passed away."

Markos pointed to Nick jovially and said, "He and your father used to get in a lot of trouble. I had to go and bail them out of jail in Athens once."

Joanna looked at Nick in shock. "Why? What did you do?"

He shrugged. "We may have had a little too much to drink one night. There may have been a speargun involved on a public beach, and then a fight with the locals." He looked at Markos and held up his index finger sternly and said, "I didn't need you, you know. I was moments away from talking myself out of that one."

"Friend, you were already in jail. You can't talk yourself out of it if you're already locked up. You should know that better than anyone."

Nick didn't submit. "If you're good you can. And I am. I almost had them drop the charges." He pinched his index finger and thumb together and looked at Joanna. "Almost."

Markos dismissed this with a wave and said, "It was your father who called me, Joanna, once he sobered up. He didn't give me any details. He just said he'd pay me back. Of course, I couldn't take his money. Not after all that he did for me. But when I saw them, I was able to put the story together myself. Shirts caked in blood— bloody knuckles, puffy lips. They caught something in the ocean and went into the city for another drink while covered in fish blood. They scared some of the natives, probably got thrown out of a bar, and from there, things got out of hand."

"OK, OK," Nick said, stopping him. "Let me tell it." He turned back to Joanna. "So your father and I would drink on occasion. This time we travelled to Athens, needing to see something new for a change. We went to a restaurant and ordered some fish, and they apologized and told us they had none. This perplexed us, you see. We said, 'We're in Athens. You're telling us you are all out of fish?' They nodded and replied that that was correct. So we left— I think we paid for the drinks, but I'm not sure. We got back on my boat, got an underwater light, went snorkelling with my speargun, and then went back, fish in hand. We may have looked a little crazy— I think this is probably the case. From there, you can imagine what happened next."

"Nick," Joanna said, wide-eyed, "You're a Grecian redneck."

"I don't know what that means," he said, cocking his head and contemplating her words, "but I'm sure it's an insult."

"No, no," Markos said and winked at Joanna, "it is the

highest of compliments. She means you are a great hunter. Like Hercules!"

Joanna laughed, wrapped her arm around his waist and said, "I'm just glad my friend Donna is not here. The things she would say about me. She'd be bursting to tell you the things I've done."

"Like what?" Nick asked, genuinely interested.

She pantomimed zipping her lips up and tossing away the key.

"What side are you sitting on?" Markos asked Nick. "Groom or bride?"

"Depends on what side you're sitting on," he replied.

"I was thinking bride."

"Groom then," said Nick, and the two men burst out laughing.

Some greeters at the church door escorted the three inside to a row of benches in the middle of the church.

The sun was beating down outside, and the church was welcomely cooler and darker— though it was muggy and perhaps a little too perfumed with incense. They were one of the first people to be seated on the bride's side. Markos and Nick sat on either side of Joanna.

"Shouldn't the groom already be here?" she asked them both.

Markos shook his head. "No. In Greece, the groom awaits the bride outside. He waits there with his entire family, and then the bride comes, escorted by her family. Then the groom gives the bride a bouquet, and they walk together to the threshold. This is why, even though there are so many people outside, we are one of the first people to be seated. We are not with either family. We are guests. And after the couple comes in, then their families will follow and sit down amongst us."

"I like that they walk together," Joanna said. "It's nice."

"Yes, it is symbolic. The journey they make through life will be together, you see. And so before God, they walk together to the threshold to show that they are together in their bond and decision."

"Are you married?" Joanna asked.

Markos shook his head and laughed out loud. "No, no woman will not have me. There's a reason your father called me when he and Nick were locked up," he said. "I was the only one he wasn't embarrassed to call."

Nick and Markos snickered, obviously two great friends who couldn't be together without laughing.

"So I'm seated next to two troublemakers, is what you're telling me?" Joanna teased.

Nick and Markos nodded at the same time emphatically.

"But we're also the smartest ones here," Nick said. "So you get and you give," he added.

"He means it's a give-and-take," Markos chuckled.

Outside a few people clapped and cheered, and then silence quickly followed.

A few minutes later, the air seemed to settle, and a hush fell amongst the crowd. Joanna turned around to see a young man and woman, dressed in typical bridal attire, begin to walk down the aisle.

The man looked similar to Markos— broad-chested, muscular— but had less of a mischievous air about him. The woman— could easily be Joanna's younger sister. Dark curly black hair, average height, round face. She was beautiful. Her eyes sparked something within Joanna and her stomach twisted a little.

Maybe they knew each other in a past life? And were destined to cross paths again.

Joanna tried to relax in her seat, realizing that all of Nick's mystical talk about Greek gods and destiny was getting to her.

The ceremony started and she tried to follow as best as she could. The priest spoke slowly and purposefully, resting a large bible on his arms as if it were a platter. He turned the pages as he spoke, but seemed to have the entire ceremony memorized as he rarely looked at it.

The bride's mother, just like a mother would in any other country, became a sobbing mess, and the bride turned to her sympathetically, tears streaming from her eyes, too. It was during this brief exchange that she looked up and she and Joanna locked eyes.

She feels it, too, Joanna thought, unsettled.

The bride seemed reticent to look away but went back to the priest when he turned the page.

"You're positive we're not sisters or anything?" she whispered to Nick.

"Hush, Joanna. I am positive." She duly felt like a scolded little girl and remained quiet through the rest of the ceremony.

The priest took the rings out and placed them on the couple's fingers, and then two people (best man and maid of honour?) swapped the rings a few times between the couple. It was very formal until the best man accidentally almost dropped the bride's ring and the entire church chuckled at him. He managed to keep his cool, but his entire face flushed red.

The priest resumed talking, and then brought out two... Joanna cocked her head. She couldn't tell what they were.

Nick leaned into her and whispered, "Stefanas. Floral crowns."

The stefanas were linked together by a ribbon, and again, the best man and maid of honour exchanged the crowns back and forth between the groom and bride.

The priest said another prayer and suddenly the entire church rose and started clapping and whistling.

Nick handed her a pouch packed with rose petals. "Let them have it!"

Joanna tossed her petals and they landed gingerly upon the new husband and wife, while again she and the bride locked eyes as she walked past.

The church emptied out.

"Time to catch the bouquet!" Markos shouted enthusiastically. "Catch it Joanna, and tie Nick down," he added grinning. "Nothing would make me happier."

She tried to object, but Markos guided her along to other singletons outside where the bride was already waiting. She had her back to all of them when she tossed her bouquet high into the air.

Joanna had no intention of catching it and had only just gotten her bearings when the mass of flowers smacked her in the face and landed in her arms.

If any of the others had known her, they might have tried to snatch it away from her. As it was, they all just looked at her and seemed confused as to who she was.

The bride turned around and saw who had caught it. She beamed and gave her a knowing nod.

Joanna was suddenly lifted by Markos and spun around. "Well done!" he exclaimed. "Now, go tell Nick the good news."

Nick was talking to the priest inside the church and the two were in serious discussion. Shoulders bumping, Nick talked and held the priest's hand as he escorted the old, arthritic man outside. The priest listened to everything he had to say, then patted him on the back and brought him in close to whisper in his ear. Nick nodded as if in agreement.

When they'd finished, Joanna stood still and shyly lifted the flowers for him to see.

He slapped his knee and laughed. "You see? You cannot leave Skiathos. Now that you are destined to be married here."

CHAPTER SEVENTEEN

"OH, MISS JOANNA!" Chris exclaimed when they returned to Villa Azure with the rest of the wedding guests. "Skiathos has captured you! It wants you to stay. Here, I will put the flowers in water and leave them in your room."

Joanna handed them to her, blushing. She'd never caught a bouquet before and was still embarrassed by all the attention.

"Come," Nick said to her. "The party is outside."

Two women walking beside them spoke softly to one another in Greek. Though Joanna didn't know what they said, she sensed an element of nostalgia in their voices, but with a tinge of sadness.

Then suddenly the woman on her right shook her head and hissed and they walked away— sighing.

Joanna whispered to Nick. "What did they just say? What were they talking about?"

"Are you sure you want to know?"

She nodded that she did.

"They said this place is still so beautiful and that they can't recall the amount of good times they had at the hotel. But now they are sad because it is to be sold. They think it is a sin that the daughter of George Herod would want to sell."

"Oh…" Joanna gasped. She felt like she had been slapped in the face.

"Everyone has an opinion," Nick said. "Of course, I wouldn't have you sell either, but it is your decision."

"I know but I didn't want to upset anyone …"

"Cheer up. They didn't even know it was you."

"That doesn't make it any better," Joanna said, biting her lip.

THE BRIDE and groom were still taking photos when they left the church, but most of the wedding guests were already pouring in.

Wine bottles and glasses were everywhere and everyone was already helping themselves. The sounds of a jazz band softly filled the air, and a few couples were dancing in the back, close to the hill's drop-off.

The pool, a mere cement hole with water in it the day before, was now adorned with blue, purple, and pink floating glass torches.

Round tables with pink tablecloths stretched almost the entire length of the hotel's property, giving everyone unbridled views of the evening Aegean sea. Upon each table was candelabra waiting to be lit when the sun set.

"Would you like some wine?" Nick asked.

"That'd be lovely."

He walked away and several small girls came up to Joanna and spoke to her in Greek. They were about five or six years old.

She leaned over and said, "I'm so sorry, I can't understand

you. I don't speak Greek. Are you maybe upset with me for catching the bouquet? I'm really sorry."

They looked at her confused and said something to one another. Then saw Nick coming and spoke to him in Greek.

He shook his head and then pointed his thumb to the side, telling them to scram. They gave Joanna a dirty look and skipped away.

"I'm an enemy here, aren't I?" she said as he handed her a glass.

"Some have figured out who you are, but not everyone."

"They were asking me not to sell, weren't they?"

He nodded.

Joanna turned back and looked at the hotel. Yes, it needed a lot of work, but she admitted to herself, it was beautiful tonight. With its red tiled roof, stone walls and walkways— it was the epitome of an upscale Mediterranean hideaway. Besides the views, she especially loved the climbing vines and ancient lanterns that hung sporadically around the property. It had a secret garden vibe to it.

"You must understand that your father was a town icon," Nick said. "In addition to helping out numerous local children in need of direction, he held a lot of parties and festivals here to keep us all united and together. It was never anything lavish, but he was kind of like Gatsby I suppose. He gave everyone a spot to unwind during tourist season and always made sure we knew how to laugh together. A lot of people have family on the mainland, and if any of them needed a place to stay while visiting they came here. This place has always been the heart and soul of the island."

"I just don't know how I could realistically keep it without abandoning everything I've worked for in New York."

He nodded, understanding. "Anyway…" He pointed at boats

on the horizon. "See those boats out there? My wedding gift for the couple is on them."

"You going to make them swim out and get it themselves?" she joked.

"Fireworks," Nick said. "Big ones. I'm not good at shopping for other people, so I found a way to get them something that was really a gift for myself." He tapped his brain and grinned. "Markos helped me. We had a great time picking them out. They're from a professional fireworks company in China. We got the salesman to come out this way and got him so drunk he acquiesced and let us preview them. Markos was afraid the coast guard was going to come and get us, but we were too far out in the water."

She giggled. "Did you take him spearfishing afterwards?"

"No, he confessed to us he was a horrible swimmer and had nightmares about drowning. But he was a lot of fun. Was fluent in Greek, and told the filthiest jokes I'd ever heard. Your father would have loved him."

Nick really did have a Peter Pan, fox in the henhouse mischievous quality to him. In many ways he reminded her of an overly intelligent, twelve year old— partly because he seemed mostly unaware of his own sexual magnetism. Well, if not unaware, then at least pleasantly preoccupied with other things.

She would never tell him this, but if he had been any way aggressive with pursuing her, she would likely have acquiesced. She was emotionally vulnerable, and very much attracted to him— a dangerous combination. He was also just so much fun to be with. And she could talk to him and tell that he was listening.

He wasn't just being polite and performing a role (as she

sensed Peter often did when they talked). He actually listened to her.

All of this had added up and scared Joanna to her core on the drive back from the church, while the bouquet rested in her lap.

Skiathos was magnificent and Villa Azure was so tempting, an alluring change of pace from New York.

It seemed the universe was being quite blunt in its attempt to tempt her with another path.

Or was her brain just frantically looking for a way to keep the vacation dream/illusion alive? She had only a couple of days left here, and yet it felt a bit like she only had a few more left to live.

She glanced at Nick beside her as the light turned an orangish pink to the west. He was simply majestically, beautiful. She could already see him as a dear friend and confidante certainly, but she also guessed he could be a wonderful partner — a passionate, soul finding, lover.

One with whom she could already see herself enjoying a very happy life with.

That was crazy, wasn't it? But it felt right.

This must have been what her mother had felt in the beginning with George, when she had first left Skiathos and gone back to New York.

Her heart was aching the same as her mother's had when she had written those first letters.

If only she hadn't asked Peter to tell her he loved her and agreed to move in with him. He didn't love her. He only loved the idea of her.

And yet she was guilty of the same. She loved the idea of establishing a 'grown up' life with him, and doing what people her age were supposed to do.

Her job? Of course she cared about her job. She had worked

hard for it. How many nights had she forfeited sleep so she could meet a deadline? Too many. But it had paid off. People had noticed and liked her work.

Now she was the youngest senior editor at Herod Publishing. She had broken through the glass ceiling, and she was still on the rise. Tectonic shifts were taking place in the world, and she was part of that.

But from this vantage point, here on the island, New York was beginning to feel like an empty existence. Surely God did not intend for people to live that way; constantly seeking, and constantly fighting, all in the vain hope of obtaining a title? A label. A label to be stuck on her by strangers she could care less about.

They were all ships passing in the ocean. Every one of them. Never to truly see one another again.

CHAPTER EIGHTEEN

NICK LOOKED at her and seemed to sense the turmoil taking place within her. He put his glass down, gently tapped her forehead and said, "Shh. Wherever your thoughts have taken you, come back to here. To right now."

Then he placed his hand around her neck and pulled her into a slow, heartfelt kiss. Their tongues never met, but it was passionate and heart-pounding. She never wanted it to end, and yet it did all too soon.

He whispered, "Whatever has filled you with fear, let it go."

Feeling a little bit breathless, Joanna nodded.

"Come," he said and led her to the dance floor before the jazz musicians. They were in between songs, and Nick went up to the singer and said something in her ear. The woman winked at him and nodded. She whispered the next song back to the band.

The drummer threw a few beats into the air and the woman began to sing in English a song that Joanna recognised.

"Is this 'My Blue Heaven' by Frank Sinatra?" she asked, delighted.

"Yes. And I'm going to give you a gift now I've not given anyone before. The gift of my horrible dancing..."

Nick began moving and jiving with the music in complete discord and disharmony to the beats established by the bass player and drummer. He locked his hands together and started doing a weird waving motion that he somehow, only god knew how mirrored with his knees. He then followed this with a pecking motion on his chin that made him resemble a chicken strutting to and fro.

"Nick!" she exclaimed laughing. "What are you doing?"

"I told you," he said. "I'm dancing. Join me!"

She didn't know how to compliment his particular ... style, so instead tried to match the beat of the song.

"No, Joanna. I meant it - join me. Come on!" He kicked his legs out like they were made of rubber, dancing like some sort of cartoon character.

Joanna got a case of the giggles and started mimicking him as silly as she could, jerking her legs and waving her arms.

"Good. She can shoot, and she can dance. I've found a winner!" he hollered.

"Only a good dancer could dance as poorly as you," she replied, over the crowd's laughter.

He winked at her, then turned around to shake his butt, to which all of the older women hackled and screamed in delight.

Not to be outdone by his friend, Markos appeared beside them, and the two Greek men started having the worst dance-off Joanna had ever seen.

She laughed so hard that tears streamed down her face and she had to walk away to the side, her cheeks aching from laughing and smiling.

Everyone clapped when the musicians struck the last notes,

but Joanna couldn't tell if they were clapping for the band or Nick and Markos.

She highly suspected the latter.

CHAPTER NINETEEN

THE WEDDING COUPLE arrived shortly afterwards, and then dinner began.

Nick had his arm resting on the back of Joanna's chair and the two were listening to the jazz band drift the evening away. Joanna didn't recognize any more of the tunes and Nick informed her that what they were hearing was the band's music.

It was slow but had an ethereal quality to it that was quite alien to Joanna's ears. At times fast, at others ambling, it was like water drifting down the countryside.

"I talked the groom into hiring them," Nick told her. "I heard them rehearsing one night a little way inland from my boat. I followed the music until I found their studio, and stayed outside until they came out just to meet them and get their names. They had no idea if what they were doing was going to be liked by the public. I told them, 'To hell what people think! Keep doing what you're doing.' But I also convinced them to learn a few crowd favourites so they could start getting bookings at bars and weddings."

"Are you their patron?" Joanna asked. It was a bit far-fetched, but she'd believe anything about Nick at this point.

"I was for a time," he admitted. "But they don't need me anymore. They're travelling to Athens in a week and will be there playing gigs for a few months."

Someone tapped his or her wine glass and the crowd hushed across the lawn.

The best man stood up with a wine glass in his hand, and Nick whispered in Joanna's ear, "We call him the koumbaro. The woman we call the koumbara."

The man started to speak, and Joanna paid attention as she had at the church, but she had no idea what he was saying.

"Let me translate this one for you," Nick said: "'Timeo and I, as you all know, have known each other since we were little boys. When he told me he was marrying Maia, I was not surprised. When we were teenagers, trying to make a few bucks doing odd chores for Mr. Herod, he always used the money Mr. Herod gave him to go take Maia out. I remember what Mr. Herod used to pay us for. Refilling the napkin holders in the lobby. Sweeping the already clean paths. And, my favourite, diving into his pool to pick up random leaves that had drifted to the bottom on hot summer days. Everything he paid us for he could have done in thirty seconds on his own. We knew it, and he knew it. Now, as a semi-adult— I don't think I'll ever feel grown up— I think I know what he was doing. He wasn't just giving two miscreant boys something to do. He knew why we wanted the money. Timeo needed the money to take the love of his life out, and build the lifelong connection that we are celebrating today... whereas I needed the money to buy twenty-year-old American Playboy magazines from Darius across the street— is Darius here? Hi Darius. That's not your wife is it?"

The crowd laughed, and as the best man continued, Joanna felt a tear in her eye, touched by these unexpected, kind words about her father.

"George saw what we were too young to see, as he did with a lot of people in this community. He wasn't just giving us money; it wasn't about the money to him. As many of you know, he didn't care one bit about that. What he was giving us was the life we needed— what he believed we were capable of and what we deserved. Timeo and Maia, I hope you don't mind, but I believe the toast I'm about to offer goes as much to George tonight as it does to you. You see everyone, his last grand gesture to them was the use of Villa Azure for this reception. His last grand gift to me was... well, I don't think I could speak to you about that without breaking down.

"'Before I finish, I need to talk about all of the celebrations we had here on nights much like this. When I think of my child-hood, the first thing I remember is those nights. In church, they talk about the holy communion. I know this is a horrible thing to say and that my parents are going to feel ashamed, but I've never felt religious ecstasy in church. But what I have felt is overwhelming peace and happiness right here, at this very hotel, eating, drinking, and laughing with every single one of you. That's no accident. George knew we needed each other, and gave us the space for it.'" Everyone smiled and nodded to one another. "I also know that this is probably the last time we'll have this. It saddens me to no end to think about it, but I am thankful for all of the times we did have, and know that what-ever the new owners build here will not, in any way compare to what we have right now together at this very moment... and that, in a strange way, makes me happy.'"

The man held up his glass, attempting to swallow his tears, but failing. "'To Timeo and Maia, may you capture and sustain the love that we Skiathons as a community have grown here and feel for you… and to Mr George Herod …'" He looked up at the sky, "'May the heaven you've travelled to be as beautiful as the life you gave the rest of us here.'"

Everyone raised their glasses and drank to the young koumbaro's toast, while Joanna wiped a tear from her eye, completely overcome by his words.

Nick waited for the applause to die down then took out his phone and texted someone.

Seconds later, a lone firework rose in the sky and exploded over the nighttime waters. All the children rose up from their parents' laps and ran to the edge for a better view.

"That couldn't have been timed any better," Joanna whispered to Nick, eyes glistening. "Are you going to tell them you did it?"

He shook his head.

"Won't they think you didn't get them anything though?"

"I got them some sort of glass bowl set they had on their wedding list. A little mystery in people's lives is a good thing, Joanna. They'll probably think your father did it for them. And that's OK because it's exactly like something George would have done."

"It seems like all the credit should go to you though," Joanna said, as more fireworks rained down from the sky.

For everything, she added silently.

CHAPTER TWENTY

"COME," Nick said then. "Let's meet the bride."

He guided her through the throngs of people to the happy couple who were standing to the side watching the fireworks.

"Maia," Nick said. "This is Joanna Nelson."

"Joanna? You are Joanna?" She dislodged herself from her husband and stared intently at Joanna. Then suddenly she embraced her and peppered her cheeks with kisses. "Joanna! My cousin! My American cousin!"

Once again Nick had surprised her.

"What? I still have family here?" Joanna asked, open-mouthed.

"Yes. She is your father's sister's daughter. Her mother, Alissa, who is just over there is your aunt."

Joanna grinned, amazed. "Why didn't you tell me this before?"

"They were busy with wedding preparations," he shrugged. "And... I wanted you all to myself."

I have family ... This time, it was Joanna who kissed a

stranger on both sides of the cheeks, fulling understanding the impulse to do so now.

Maia cried out in jubilation with her. "We are going to be like sisters, you and I!" her cousin said.

At that moment, Joanna felt like she truly was in the most beautiful place on the planet, and couldn't imagine being anywhere else ever again.

MUCH LATER, Nick kissed Joanna goodnight— not on the cheeks but on the lips. It was on the tip of her tongue to invite him in but they both seemed to know it was a bad idea.

"Tomorrow will you go out to lunch with me?" Nick asked. "I'll take you for some real lunch. Treat you to a full day in Skiathos before you fly back on Tuesday. Everything will be my treat."

Joanna's heart sank again at the mere thought of leaving Skiathos.

Her newly discovered family.

"That would be lovely," she managed to say.

And Nick...

Peter called her as she was sitting on the balcony, gazing at the moon's reflection on the waters, but she let the call go straight to messages.

She didn't want to talk and she didn't want to sleep either. Sleeping meant this wonderful day was over, and that she only had a few more left on the island.

"Joanna," Peter boomed in the message. "Oh, have I got some good news for you. I spoke to the northeast vice president of the Hilton Group about your hotel, had to pull a lot of strings, but I managed it. He made a few calls, and Hilton, I repeat *Hilton* are interested in buying your property. I can't— I can't even put into words how good this is for us. Hilton, Joanna! We are going to be so loaded."

CHAPTER TWENTY-ONE

"So," Nick said to her the following day with his hands in his pockets. "I've kept another secret from you."

"Why am I not surprised?" she replied.

They were in the town of Skiathos. Numerous business owners were outside sprucing up signs and removing 2X4s from their windows. Tourist season was now upon them and they had to get ready. Now that the wedding had come and gone, it was time for everyone to get to work.

"You asked me how your father and mother got together. I'm not sure about that, but I do know what drove them apart."

Joanna nodded. She had begun to expect as much, hearing about all of the adventures he and her father had had, and how close he and Nick were.

"At your mother's request, George never sold Villa Azure. She always promised him that she was going to leave her job and move to Skiathos and marry him. She wanted him to have the hotel so they wouldn't have to work. They could live their lives every day as if it were a holiday. He, on the other hand, wanted to sell. He wanted to move to New York so he could be with her. But she kept getting promoted, making more and more money, and delaying, month after month after month. She couldn't walk away from her job, and George felt like he was in a constant loop of hope, desperation, and disappointment."

"He cheated on her?" Joanna asked, believing she knew where the story was going.

"No," he said. "He never cheated on her. He loved her completely. But," Nick held his finger up in the air, "She thought he did."

They walked to the end of a street and turned left so they could be beside the main road that travelled parallel to the water. It was a tiny street barely big enough for one car to squeeze through, and yet there were numerous cars parked along the path close to the houses.

"Why would she think he did if he didn't?" Joanna asked, confused.

"There was a woman," Nick replied, "who was desperately in love with him. She was actually at the wedding last night, but she sat alone. I watched her. Charissa is her name. She ate nothing and said nothing. As they say, eternal life to those who are bitter and angry. But anyway. A native Skiathan, she hated that he was in love with a xénos, a foreigner. As much as she loved and adored George, she equally hated the idea of him leaving Greece. She found out when your mother was returning to the island, and made a point to follow them that evening. While they were walking down the street we are now, Charissa called out to George in an angry voice. Spoke to him as if he were her lover. Acted infuriated that he was with Ruth and not her. Told him he needed to help with their child or else she was going to sue him. It was all a lie, and your poor mother, believed every word of it. She ran away from him crying and hopped into a taxi. He thought she went back to the hotel, and so he made his way back there, hoping to find her in her room. But she didn't go back. He scoured the whole island, calling out for her. But he couldn't find her anywhere. No one had seen her. She had disappeared, though, and left all of her things back in the hotel. She never returned for any of them. If you look, I believe you'll find all of her things still in his closet."

They walked to the end of a long pier that went far out into the water. Waves lapped and rolled beneath them to the coast in an ever-constant rhythm.

"She said she made a mistake one night," Joanna said, repeating her mother's line. "I thought she meant that my conception was a mistake."

Nick shook his head. "No, running away was the mistake. She left him when she shouldn't have, and by then she was pregnant with you but perhaps did not know it."

"And George never got to tell her that the woman was lying?"

"He tried. There are letters in a shoebox in his closet from him to her that she wrote return to sender on. She never read them."

"When did she tell him about me then?"

"Not until very recently and only after she accepted that he was telling the truth— he never stopped writing to her, you see. One day - I think when she got sick - she decided to read what he had to say and then started replying again - only a few years ago. I remember the day he got the letter. He wept like a man spared the death sentence. He was going to go to New York, but she wouldn't let him. She didn't want him to see how weak she had become. But to his great sadness, he didn't receive the letter telling him about you until after she'd died. And then when he found out about you, Joanna, he immediately had me start looking for you."

At this, Nick looked pained. "But I failed him. It took me too long. It is and will always be one of my greatest failures in life not finding you fast enough. He never said one word in anger towards me about it though, but it was on his deathbed that he made me promise that you would come to Skiathos. He just wanted you to see, wanted you to know where he lived, who he was, what he did. He really didn't care much about the hotel. We do, those of us who knew him and loved him, but he didn't."

"So he *did* want to know me?" she asked, relieved.

"Yes, Joanna. The very prospect of seeing you, I believe, is what kept him alive for so long after he was diagnosed."

Joanna hugged her knees and leaned into him.

"Thank you, Nick. Even if what you say is not all true, thank you."

"Every word of it is. This I swear upon my life."

CHAPTER TWENTY-TWO

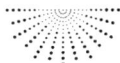

ON THE DAY of her return flight, Nick walked with her for as far as airport customs would allow.

"Will we see you again?" he asked. "When you sell, will you at least come back to see us?"

Joanna didn't know what to say. She hadn't told him she was going to sell, but she hadn't told him she wasn't either. He had interpreted that to mean she was going to go through with it when the truth was she didn't know yet.

All she knew right then was that couldn't bring herself to look in his eyes. Not out of shame, but because if did she knew she would start crying. She embraced him with every ounce of strength she had, breathing in his scent one more time before she left.

Nick patted her hair and said, "Come back when you can. You are Skiathan, Joanna, one of us. You always will be." He pulled her face to his, their foreheads touching, then turned and walked briskly away.

Joanna watched him for as long as she could before the crowds filled in around her.

. . .

ON THE FLIGHT back to New York, Joanna dug out the carry-on bag that she had stored at her feet and took out one of her mother's letters to her father.

The further across the Atlantic she travelled, the further the dream that was Skiathos was slowly fading away from her memory, and she needed some way to reconnect with it.

The letter was random but appeared to be one of the last her mother had written to him before she died.

GEORGE,

I pray every day that there is such a thing as reincarnation, one more chance with you. Even if it's only for one day, I would cherish it with my entire soul.

I worked my whole life to become something that few other women before me have ever been: Powerful.

Now, as I sit on my bed, drinking an orange juice that has never known refrigeration, eating a slice of stale cornbread and listening to gossipy nurses outside my room talk of some man named Dr Phil, I know that no one knows who I am nor cares what I did.

Where is the reset button on life? It's so fleeting! Surely it wouldn't be hard to just rewind a little bit?

If I could just go back to that one night. No, all those ensuing years... you sent me so many letters, so many opportunities, and I sent them all back like a maddened bull.

I expect nothing of you, George. I don't expect your forgiveness, I don't expect your condolences. Just know that I still dream of you every night, and wake up without you every morning...

I won't lie, I wish I didn't dream of you. Waking up from those beautiful, heavenly dreams is harder than I expect dying is going to be.

This I know with all of my soul.

Look for me in a white-washed hotel on a hill overlooking crystal clear waters. I'll be in room 111.

Waiting for you.

CHAPTER TWENTY-THREE

FOR ONE WEEK JOANNA TRIED. She really did.

She performed her duties as a senior editor at Herod Publishing. She assigned junior editors work, and went to meetings, fulfilled deadlines, answered emails.

She wanted to be thankful for the life she had earned, for the life she had fought for, but each moment she looked out her window and saw New York's famous steel titans looming on the horizon, she didn't feel like a modern woman in a sophisticated city anymore. Instead, she felt trapped and claustrophobic in a steel cage.

The city wasn't liberating. It wasn't inspiring.

It was imposing. It was finite. It was… wrong.

She put herself in autopilot mode and went day by day hoping she was just suffering a case of post-vacation blues, but of course, she knew better.

Her heart simply wasn't in New York anymore, it was in Skiathos.

She wished she had a picture of Nick. She needed to see his dark, brown eyes. His simple smile. His tall, lean frame.

She missed spending time with him. She missed... it was weird, she knew, but she missed how he smelled. She missed smelling him. Like a bundle of herbs taken from the forest.

Nothing of real substance had happened between them, but now Joanna wished it had. If her life was going to consist of petty fantasies of him, then at least she could have had that one real memory. Where she allowed herself to forego rules and normalities and indulged, even for just one night, in real passion.

She'd arrived back in New York early Wednesday morning but didn't bother calling Peter until Friday.

They never really communicated that much during the week, so it wasn't unusual, but he could tell something was up when they got together for drinks.

"Want me to help you pack this weekend?" he asked, talking about them moving in together. "We could get you over fully to my place probably by Sunday afternoon."

Joanna winced at the mere suggestion.

"You're probably still a bit tired from the jet lag though," he said in a rare moment of consideration. "Rest up. We'll do it next weekend, or whenever you're ready. Want to start moving forward with selling the hotel, though?" he added, a big smile on his face. "Ready to become a millionaire overnight?"

He then wagged his eyebrows and drummed the table excitedly. There was something carnivorous about him that Joanna truly hadn't seen until then, and something broke in her as she looked at him.

"No, Peter. That's not going to happen."

"Joanna," he sighed. "Do the smart thing. It's just a place. Think of it as a stepping stone to something bigger and better - for us."

"Peter, I'm not going to sell Villa Azure, and … I'm not going to move in with you either."

His face got still and flushed.

"The hotel has a lot of history for Skiathos," Joanna explained. "It's a lifeline for a lot of people. Selling it would guarantee its destruction. I couldn't in good conscience do that."

Peter clenched his teeth and turned his beer bottle on the table. "Don't be taken in by all that nostalgic nonsense. It's just business and that isn't a bad thing," he said.

"No. 'Just business' is what people say when they know what they're doing is wrong but don't want to feel bad about it. Did you hear what I also said? I said I'm not moving in with you."

"Yeah, I heard you," he replied, still turning his beer bottle. He finally looked at her, gritting his teeth. "So what was his name? Whatever slimy Greek Lothario you cheated on me with over there. What was his name?"

She didn't answer. "Before I left, I had to ask you if you loved me. Why is that, Peter? And I know you only said yes out of some sort of misguided loyalty. And what's worse is before I asked, it hadn't even occurred to me to care. We're in two different worlds, Peter. I stayed with you because I thought I was in a phase in my life where I should settle down. You were the mature, smart choice. And you were with me because I matched what you were looking for - on the way up the career ladder, lots of prospects. But you don't marry someone for power. You marry them for love."

Peter pursed his lips and she could tell he was biting back so many responses.

"But I wish you well. I really do. You've been nothing but good to me. Take care. I'm sorry it happened the way that it did."

With that, she stood up and left the bar, pulling out her phone and calling Donna as she hailed a taxi.

"Were you serious?" she asked her friend, without saying hello.

"About what?" Donna asked.

"About helping me fix up the hotel?"

"Hell yeah!"

"OK, let's do it then," she said, suddenly feeling like a great weight had been lifted from her shoulders.

CHAPTER TWENTY-FOUR

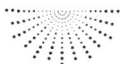

FLYING BACK SO QUICKLY HAD PUT Greek Customs on high alert. They seemed to think she was trafficking drugs or something.

"Nope, just a woman on a mission. I'm in love," she told them and they nodded agreeably, as if understanding.

At Villa Azure, Chris almost leapt out of her skin when she saw Joanna walk into the lobby.

"Where's Nick?" she asked.

The other woman frowned and shook her head. "He's not doing well, Joanna. He's been out fishing since you left. No one knows where."

"It's OK," she replied. "I know."

She turned around to leave, and Chris shouted, "Wait, Miss Joanna! Does this mean you're keeping Villa Azure?"

"That is exactly what it means!" Joanna turned around and shouted back. "But it also means something else. I have to find Nick."

She left and ran back down to her taxi driver, whom she had asked to wait.

They went to Nick's dock next. She had learned from him

that Markos, too, had a houseboat there and she was going to need Nick's best friend if she was going to get to him.

Lying down, listening to a Greek version of *Wheel of Fortune* and reading a book— Markos clearly needed something to do with his evening.

"Joanna! Are you back?" he said, startled. "Are you keeping the hotel?"

"Perhaps, but first I need your help."

CHAPTER TWENTY-FIVE

"STOP HERE," Joanna ordered.

She and Markos were stopped about a hundred meters or so from Nick's boat, nestled between the two small islands that were his father's secret fishing ground. "I want to surprise him. Can you tell if he's onboard, or if he's fishing below?"

"He's on board," Markos said, spying on his friend with binoculars. "And he looks rough."

"Good," Joanna said as she quickly undressed. "That he's there, I mean. If he moves off and I haven't made it to him yet, for the love of god don't leave me behind."

Markos' eyes widened as he saw Joanna's voluptuous figure spill out of her dress. And then he almost fainted when he saw she was wearing only a tiny black bikini beneath.

"OK," he said. "You want me to watch you as you swim? Make sure you're all right. I can do that."

Joanna laughed and dived in, not caring how cold the water was.

She was a decent swimmer, but she surprised even herself by how fast she made it to the ladder of Nick's houseboat.

Large tuna were swimming beneath the boat's underbelly and her first thought was to get his speargun, but then she figured that she - they - had more important things to do first.

She surfaced near his ladder and was ascending it when Nick yelled out something in Greek.

He was shocked and had probably just threatened her.

"Will you take me fishing tomorrow?" she asked him, water dripping off her.

"Joanna …" he gasped. "Joanna, is that really you?"

She climbed onto the deck but was almost knocked back into the water by the force of his embrace.

"You came back! Here to stay, yes?" Nick clutched her tightly.

She nodded and hugged him back, overcome at being in his arms once again.

This time it would be for good.

"Yes, I'm keeping Villa Azure. You told me my father would have wanted me to have my own story, that I didn't need to keep the hotel. But *you* are part of my story, Nick, and unlike my parents, we should have a life together. One free from pining and desperation, hoping and waiting. Together we're going to start living our lives now. And we're going to change things— the hotel included."

With that Joanna and Nick kissed and held on tight to one another, knowing they had all the time in the world, yet unwilling to waste another second.

SANTORINI SUMMER

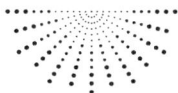

CHAPTER ONE

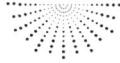

AT THE GRAND old age of thirty-two, Olivia Clarke was beginning to wonder if the best years of her life had already passed her by.

She shut the door of her flat behind her with a sigh after a long day at work. Heading into the kitchen, she tossed her keys on the countertop along with her handbag.

It was Friday night in London, one of the liveliest cities on earth, and she had nowhere to go and nothing to do.

Her fiancé had left and taken Olivia's so-called best friend along with him. She had become so downbeat and disillusioned over the past three months since the two people she'd loved most in the world had run off together, and staying in at weekends had become something of a habit.

She went to the cupboard and pulled out a bottle of white wine. Pouring a generous glass she slumped on the couch, unbuttoning the top two buttons on her grey blouse and piled her long dark hair in a heap on the top of her head, fastening it with a hair bobble.

Was this it? Her life couldn't be over already, could it?

"Ah you have to snap out of this," she chastened herself out loud.

She wasn't entirely sure how to do that though. Her heart ached and her pride stung every time she thought about the horrible end to her wedding plans.

She was in a rut and although no one would blame her after everything that had happened, it still didn't make it right.

Shaking her head, she got up and went to get her phone. Tonight was a takeaway night to be sure.

She ordered some Chinese food and went off to the shower. She knew they would not have the delivery to her until well after she was out of the shower and on her second glass of wine. She had ordered from Hu Hans Restaurant many times before.

Sipping her wine, she went into the bathroom and started the water running. Undressing, she adjusted the temperature then got in and stood there, enjoying the hot water as it ran over her body.

The shower was about the only place she could go to get away from things these days. It was so easy for her to meditate in the mist and shampoo and think of nothing at all.

Once she felt clean and refreshed, Olivia got out and dressed in her red silk pajamas. They were a gift from her aunt Carole, and she loved the feel of them on her skin. It was a little early in the evening for bedtime wear, but what the hell, she wasn't going anywhere.

She finished her first glass of wine and poured the second one. After only a few sips the doorbell rang.

The food was fast tonight, she thought, getting up and going to the door. She tipped the delivery guy and took her food inside, deciding to just eat it out of the box because she was suddenly feeling very hungry.

Sitting on her couch Olivia ate her Mongolian Chicken and

spring rolls with gusto, enjoying the flavors. Just spicy enough to get her attention, especially with the plum sauce. The spring rolls were also a special treat she had come to enjoy on her Friday nights in.

When she finished, she sighed with contentment and leaned back on her couch, enjoying the feeling for a time.

Staying home and enjoying a night to herself was not a bad thing, she reasoned, except she did it every weekend now.

Her friends from work in the accountancy practice had been pushing her to get out more, as had a few family members - Aunt Carole in particular.

Yet Olivia had not been able to find the energy or time.

Now this week, a work thing had gone sideways (another blow to her ego) and she felt more despondent than ever.

Sighing, she filled her glass a third time and her phone rang. Glancing down she saw it was her aunt. She smiled. Talking to Aunt Carole was always nice - the sixty-six-year-old was fun and full of chat and energy. Unlike her miserable niece.

"Hey Carole, how are things?" Olivia said by way of greeting, trying to sound upbeat.

"Great, love. How are you doing? I hope you're out and about enjoying yourself this fine Friday night - what are you up to?"

"Ah you know, same old thing," Olivia answered and took another sip of her wine.

"Chinese or pizza?" her aunt asked, deadpan.

"Uh, Chinese …. how did you know?"

"Friday nights you either have Chinese food or pizza. Saturday is usually Indian, or maybe Korean if you're feeling adventurous," was the response.

Olivia sighed. "You're right, Carole. I have fallen into a rut. I was actually considering going out tonight, but work was awful this week and I thought to hell with it," she responded.

She did not like moaning about her problems to people, but Aunt Carole was an exception. She was never judgmental.

"Ah no. You didn't get the promotion? I thought you were a shoo-in."

"I did too, but they gave it to that twenty-two-year-old newcomer, blond skinny and perky, you know the type," Olivia took a longer drink of her wine in disgust.

"That is ridiculous. You may not be skinny but you are perkier than most. What is their problem?"

Olivia had to laugh at that. It was true that she was more on the voluptuous side. Still, no matter how much they joked, being overlooked had made her feel even more old and past it. She sighed, despite herself.

"Talk to me, honey. I know your life has been hard the last few months but is it something else?" Carole asked.

Maybe it was the wine, but Olivia opened up further. "I suppose I just feel like I'm over the hill, Carole. My fiancé left me for my best friend and my job prospects disappeared in the flash of blond hair and blue eyes. To be honest, I don't have the drive to do much of anything these days. It's depressing and that just makes me want to stay home even more.

I don't know what to do. Will these feelings ever go away? Or am I destined to be a layabout for the rest of my life? I mean the food is good, as well as the wine but…" She trailed off and sighed again.

"First off, stop that line of thinking. You are nowhere near past it and I am going to prove it to you. Would you take my advice, love? Just a couple of small suggestions but I think they will help you in ways you cannot imagine," her aunt told her.

"OK. It is not like I have any great ideas at the moment,"

Olivia said with another heavy sigh. She realized she was doing way too much sighing lately.

"Good. Now start by getting that miserable ex's number and messages off your phone," was her aunt's first piece of advice. "You don't need to see Derek the Dick's name every time you scroll through your contacts. You don't need to listen to his voice, or read his texts either."

Olivia set her phone down and put Carole on speaker so she could scroll through her contacts and highlight her errant ex. She pressed edit and then delete. The message *"Are you sure?"* came up on the screen and she hesitated.

"Olivia, are you there?" her aunt asked and she realized she had been silent for too long.

"Still here, just doing it now," she told her, but still Olivia could not bring herself to press the yes command on the phone. Her eyes misted over briefly and she wiped them as her heart ached afresh.

"Okay then. Next, you need to call work and tell them you are going to re-evaluate your position and use up the rest of your current holiday leave. They won't like it, but they need you there and will go along with it, you know they will," Carole said in a cheerful voice.

This distracted Olivia a little from her heartbreak.

"And what am I supposed to do with the time off? I really do need that job you know," she said hesitantly.

"With your qualifications, you could get another in no time at all and they know it. They were probably hoping you would just go along with things. This will let them know they are at risk of losing you. It will also enable you to be on a plane to Greece first thing next week. You know my little timeshare in Santorini?" Carole asked and Olivia nodded, confused. "It's free at the moment and will suit you perfectly. The island is one of the most beautiful places on earth, and at this time of year will be full of people just having fun and enjoying themselves. You deserve to do the same. Use up your holiday time to relax, love. You can have the place for two weeks - my treat," Carole continued, and Olivia felt a lump in her throat at her aunt's generosity.

"Are you sure? I mean, this is too much..." she stammered.

"It's not enough as far as I'm concerned. You know, when your parents passed away the only thing that might be considered good about it was that I got to see you grow from a promising young girl to the proud and capable woman you are today. I am, and have always been, proud of you. I am sure they would be too. So take a break and enjoy yourself, Olivia, you need some fun," she finished.

Feeling a sudden surge of her old determination at her aunt's words, Olivia reached out to tap the "yes" button on her smartphone screen.

In an instant, Derek's name and his texts all disappeared into thin air.

Carole was right. Santorini sounded like heaven. She'd never been there, but over the years had heard Carole rave about her beautiful Greek Island retreat.

Yes, Olivia needed this.

And she was going to try her damnedest to make the most of it.

CHAPTER TWO

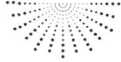

FIRST THING MONDAY MORNING, Olivia checked the time of her flight on the Departures board at Heathrow Airport.

She had called her boss's mobile the day after speaking with her aunt to let her know that she was taking two weeks holiday leave.

Julia had not been happy, but as Aunt Carole had predicted, she had still okayed the request.

Perhaps the company did want her to stay after all?

Olivia decided for the next two weeks it did not matter; all she needed to do was concentrate on enjoying herself.

She was going on holiday for the first time in years! She took out her iPhone and brought up the Santorini tourist website again.

The pictures were incredible, and looking at them was already melting her cares away. Her honeymoon with Derek was to be in France, but this looked far better.

The little Greek town her aunt's cottage was based in was lit up by lights from cafes and tavernas along the coastline in a dusky sunset shot, and whitewashed buildings with cerulean blue rooftops were bathed in golden light.

The entire area seemed to glow with warmth and in another daytime image, the Aegean Sea looked a heavenly blue. There were sailboats dotted about on the water that immediately made Olivia want to lie back on the deck of one and fall asleep beneath the warm sunshine.

Soon, she reminded herself, *soon you can do that and more.*

While going to such a destination was exciting, it was also a little daunting. She had never taken a trip abroad on her own before.

A flight announcer called her flight number then, and Olivia grabbed her things and stood.

"Here we go…" she whispered.

UNFORTUNATELY FOR OLIVIA, the flight was long and drawn out due to adverse weather over France and then there was a stopover in Athens that lasted for two hours, so the journey from London to Athens ended up taking far more than the anticipated four hours.

When she finally disembarked the plane at Athens airport to pick up her connection to Santorini, she was already exhausted.

Olivia got a strong cappuccino to keep her going before she went and retrieved her bags for the next leg of her trip.

She had packed as lightly as she could, but a two-week stay still required a couple of small suitcases. She retrieved her luggage and stacked it on a little hand cart. Her frustration level was rising with her fatigue and she managed to nab a passing sky car to help her make the connecting flight to Santorini. She had always been self-sufficient but decided enough was enough.

Fortunately, the Greek female airport attendant spoke English and Olivia could explain what she needed.

She almost melted in relief as her bags were loaded on and she was offered a seat. She thanked the woman twice as she sat down.

"You are amazing, thank you so much. I did not expect the flight to take so long. There were storms..." She trailed off and the woman kept smiling and Olivia could read the sympathy in her eyes. "I just hope I don't miss my connection."

"My pleasure Madam, it is my job and my desire to help you get where you need to go. Just sit back and relax now," the Greek woman said and got in to drive the cart.

In moments Olivia was on her way.

"I am Olivia, by the way. May have your name?" She had completely missed the lovely woman's name tag and was feeling flustered. She felt terrible.

"I am Alkippe, Madam. Thank you for asking. Are you going to be in Santorini for very long?" the attendant asked as she weaved them through the crowded terminal.

"Two weeks. Although it feels like it's already taken two weeks just getting this far," she joked and sipped her coffee. Fortunately, it was still warm but also very strong. They knew how to do coffee here, that was for sure.

Alkippe laughed softly. "I know travelling can sometimes feel that way. I am sure that once you get to the island all your cares will wash away. I have an old uncle who lives in Fira and I have spent much time there. It will be enjoyable for you, I am sure," she said encouraging.

Olivia smiled a little at the woman's sincerity, appreciating her effort.

"I am sure you are right. My aunt recommended Santorini as

the perfect place to sort myself out, and she is never wrong about these things."

Alkippe laughed again. "Aunts and Uncles Madam, they are always right. If they someday are not, we will just not mention it," she joked.

Olivia laughed and before she knew it she was at her departure gate. Between her coffee and Alkippe, she was feeling much better, and able to face the last leg of her trip.

"Thank you again for all your help," she told her, once her luggage was unloaded. She gave her a generous tip and Alkippe continued to smile.

"I am glad to have helped, Madam. Enjoy your time and I hope you have a wonderful trip!" she told her. Then the Greek woman climbed back onto the cart and was off to save someone else.

The friendly chat had been nice and helped Olivia feel not so mussed and dirty after her long and tiring first leg. She finished her coffee just in time to board the little plane to Santorini with the other passengers.

The plane was packed to capacity and Olivia realised she was hitting the Greek Islands in peak summer tourist season.

The thought bothered her at first, but then watching the excitement of her fellow travellers she began to relax and be happy that she would not be alone, and that there would be others striving for some kind of peace and fun, the same as she was. At least that was what she told herself as they soared over mainland Greece.

Even if they hadn't been through what she had, everyone had something they needed to escape from, didn't they?

CHAPTER THREE

THE FIRST THING Olivia did at Santorini airport was get something to eat and another coffee. The falafel was spectacular and the second coffee was even better than the one at Athens.

Then she roused herself to push her luggage cart out front and got a cab. The driver seemed nice, if a little uncommunicative, once Olivia had given him the piece of paper with her aunt's timeshare address on it.

But at this point, she was grateful for the silence.

Olivia sat in the back as they drove away and her jaw just about dropped to the floor as they travelled along a road next to the clear blue Aegean Sea.

The contrast of the crystal clear water, whitewashed buildings and dark volcanic rock was a treat to the eyes. She unrolled the windows a little and the smell of the salty sea was immediately intoxicating.

She had two weeks to spend in this incredible atmosphere and now that she was here, experiencing it, Olivia smiled to herself and chuckled softly.

Take that, Derek, she thought. He would be amazed to see her now.

She knew her ex had fully expected her to collapse in a heap after losing the likes of him - which she had for a while. But no more. She already had a feeling this place was finally going to help heal her broken heart.

The pain in her gut when she thought of him already seemed lessened.

THE LAST PART of the drive wound through thin streets of what looked like a pretty little fishing village, and Olivia looked up at the buildings they passed. All looked similar and very familiar: whitewashed paint and redbrick trim, with distinctive painted blue domed rooftops and awash with tumbling pink bougainvillaea.

Quintessentially Greek, she thought, admiring the look and feel of her surroundings.

Eventually, the cab driver pulled up to the little whitewashed cottage that was to be Olivia's home for the next two weeks, and helped her take her bags to the blue-painted front door.

She thanked him and tipped, waving as he left. Then she went up the small stone path, dragging her suitcases behind her.

Carole had told her that this was a cosy two-bed cottage, and it would be more than enough.

As soon as Olivia turned the key and entered the main room, she dropped her suitcases and walked to the picture window along the back of the house, her mouth open in awe.

The little town seemed to slope downward to the Aegean in a blanket of blue domed roofs and flowers, and from the veranda, the cottage had an unobscured view of a giant central lagoon surrounded by three hundred metre high cliffs with a dormant volcano silhouetted in the distance.

It was quite simply, breathtaking.

Olivia slid open the glass doors and stepped out onto her balcony with a big smile and a laugh from deep inside. The smell of the air and the sight of white sails on amazingly blue water was intoxicating, and she just stood there for a moment, taking it all in.

She walked up to the railing of her little veranda and saw a stone pathway leading down to the coastline, where little cafes and tavernas were dotted along a beachside walkway.

"Thank you, Carole," she whispered softly.

This was perfect.

After everything that had happened, the fact that she was here in this incredible place with stunning coastal views that were already good for the soul, would have seemed like a joke a week earlier.

Now Olivia was laughing with joy.

Something told her it was all going to be all right, that here in Santorini, she would be OK.

CHAPTER FOUR

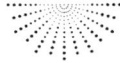

LATER THAT EVENING, Olivia waded out of the Aegean Sea feeling exhilarated and relaxed.

Swimming in the warm waters was a treat that she could get used to.

She pushed her hair back from her face and walked through the dark volcanic sand up to where she had left her stuff.

Just up from the beach, there was a patch of yellowish-white grass and a small group of palm trees with hammocks. She had already claimed one of them, and they even had little tables alongside each one for drinks and snacks.

Olivia took a long swallow of the pina colada she had waiting and sighed.

It was a very different sigh to the ones she'd been releasing since her wedding was cancelled. This was a sigh of pure contentment.

The angle of the hammock afforded her a hypnotic view of the water and coastline so she made herself comfortable.

It was a while yet before she would want dinner, so lying back and watching the world go by seemed like a fantastic idea.

The hammock swung gently, and the breeze off the water was heavenly as it ran over her bare arms and legs.

She was wearing a blue one-piece that was modest yet complimentary to her curves. She had brought a bikini too but was not quite confident enough to try that one out yet. It wasn't that she was overweight or that her belly wasn't flat it was just... she hadn't quite got her confidence back, that was all.

She reached over for the cocktail and drained the glass, before setting the empty container back on the little wood table, then put her sunglasses on.

It was so nice to just relax.

She had absolutely nothing to do, or any place to be, and for one of the first times in her life, Olivia did not mind. She didn't *need* to have something to do every second of every day, not anymore anyway, and definitely not for the next two weeks.

She closed her eyes and could hear the sound of children's voices laughing down by the water, and she smiled lazily. The sound of the surf, distant voices and the slight breeze took her to sleep in no time.

When Olivia awoke, she was startled and sat up. The movement of the hammock reminded her where she was, and she avoided flipping out of it at the last minute.

She realised she had slept the early evening away and the sunset was now in full bloom on the horizon, so she remained in the hammock watching the array of colours slowly change into dusk in front of her.

The Santorini sunset was breathtaking and a reminder that natural beauty trumped all else every time.

She waited until the sun had finally disappeared, and then she got up and stretched, gathered her things and headed back to the cottage to change for the evening.

She wasn't sure what she was going to do exactly, but felt

excited about her first night on holiday, and vowed to enjoy every minute.

AN HOUR OR SO LATER, Olivia was strolling down the beach to the string of beachside tavernas and cafes she'd seen from the balcony.

She entered the first one she came to, trusting chance. While waiting to be seated she gave herself a quick once over in the mirror behind the bar.

She had dressed in a red halter top and a white mid-length skirt. Her hair was in a ponytail and a few strands had come loose in the ocean breeze and hung around her heart-shaped face.

She was smiling and enjoying the natural lack of effort it took to do so. She used to always smile, but Derek had taken that away from her and she was glad to feel she could still do it.

She followed the Greek waiter who beckoned her to a little round table facing the water. It was one of the last unoccupied tables in the taverna, probably she thought, because it was so small and most people were in groups, enjoying the nightlife.

Olivia was quite happy this first night though, to be an observer.

A black-haired woman in a white blouse and skirt came over to take her order. Olivia was hungry and quickly ordered moussaka and some bread she had seen on another table as an appetiser.

The bread was delivered with hummus; the best she had ever tasted and seemed to compliment the wine the waiter had recommended.

Olivia sat back, watching couples walking past on the beach and felt a stirring in her chest.

That could have been her if her ex had not been such an ass.

She pushed that thought away. No more thinking of Derek the Dick as her aunt had so amusingly monikered him. He had no place in her relaxation time here, she told herself firmly.

It was still difficult though, surrounded as she was by romance and laughter. When her salad arrived, she dug in and found it to be as good as everything else so far. As she ate she continued to observe those around her and decided there were different kinds of romance.

Certainly, there was the romance of couples in love, but there was also the romance of a new place, exotic and exciting. A beautiful night in an idyllic location by the beach surrounded by happy people was also a romantic setting in and of itself, and Olivia did not need to be with anyone to make it so.

She felt her smile return with that realisation, and finishing her salad she leaned back in her chair, sipping her wine. As she did, she felt someone bump into her chair from behind and she turned her head, looking back.

"Oh, I am so sorry. It is getting a little crowded. I didn't mean to bump into you. No harm done I hope?" asked the tremendously handsome man Olivia was looking back at.

The attractive Greek had black swept-back hair and was wearing an open linen shirt. His bare chest was muscular and toned and his face was the chiselled sort beloved by romance writers.

Olivia smiled. "Not at all. It is getting busy, so no worries," she assured him.

"Glad to hear it. I need to catch up with my friends now, but maybe I will see you around?" he said with a hopeful note in his tone.

Olivia was not in any way looking to hook up with anyone,

but she appreciated his subtle offer, not to mention appreciative glances. It was a welcome boost to her confidence.

"Sure. Enjoy your evening," she told him.

"You too," he said and went out onto the beach with a last glance over his shoulder at her.

Olivia chuckled to herself, delighted by this unexpected interaction. Maybe she wasn't so past it after all …

"Excuse me, ma'am," said the waitress who had just then showed up to remove her dishes. "Would you like dessert?"

Olivia nodded in a sudden decision. "You know, I would. I was thinking of the Sfakianopita, do you have that here?" she asked.

"Ah yes, ma'am. It is a favourite of our patrons as well as the staff. I will bring you a serving immediately," she said and was off with a smile.

Olivia had heard of the famed Greek dessert and wanted to try it. Sfakianopita was a type of cheese pie with nuts and honey. Just thinking about it made her mouth water despite the big salad she had just eaten.

When it came she was not disappointed. It was decadent, delightful and just what she needed to end her busy day. She sipped the strong coffee that had come with the dessert and decided that, for her first day, she'd done enough.

It had been a long day, she was stuffed, had a little buzz on from her wine, and was ready for sleep.

Olivia paid her bill, including a hefty tip for the lovely staff and walked back along the coastline.

She was waved to by several people she had seen throughout the afternoon near the hammocks, as well as the handsome Greek who had bumped into her table. He was with a group of young people drinking down by the water. Everyone was having a great time and did not appear to have a care in the world.

She left the blinds open on her bedroom window and climbed into the bed, stretching out. It felt heavenly and she could see flashes of light from the village below, along with little glimpses of stars out the window.

What a wonderful, magical place.

Olivia went to sleep with that relaxing thought in her mind and had her first deep, uninterrupted sleep in a very long time.

CHAPTER FIVE

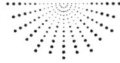

Ben Norton growled an obscenity when he saw the text from his agent. It simply said '*Call me*' and he knew straight away what *that* was about.

He had barely three months to get his next book to his publishers and he had not written a word. He was well and truly blocked and not a happy man.

Ben did believe in facing things head-on though, so he called Kimberly straight back.

"Might as well get it over with," he muttered to himself as the phone rang.

"Well, there you are, Ben. How is it coming?" his agent asked, and he knew she was not asking about his well-being. That was not her style.

Kimberly was all business. So he decided to be the same.

"Crappy, I have nothing yet, sorry - I am trying," he told her.

"I know, I know. I had a feeling that you might be blocked …" Ben winced at her words. No writer liked to hear that. "…so I went ahead and did you a great big favour - you can repay me later," she added and he was immediately suspicious.

"What kind of favour?"

"I reserved my family's time-share in Santorini, Greece for the next two weeks. It will be the perfect place for you to recharge and maybe get some inspiration. You know the guys at Herod are asking me all the time when the new script is coming, so I figured this might help us both," she said, referring to his publishers.

Ben had a brief notion of turning her down. Just because he was blocked did not mean he wanted to hear it or receive sympathy about it. The moment passed however when he realised this may be exactly what he needed.

The only thing he hated more than being reminded he was blocked, was actually being blocked.

Nice scenery, good weather, and solitude might be just what the doctor ordered. Besides New York could be hell in the summertime.

"I must admit, it sounds pretty good, Kim, and you are right, I will owe you," he told her.

There was a long pause.

"Really? I thought I was going to have to bully you into it! No one likes it when I have to do that, but you know I can," she said and Ben laughed, suddenly feeling some tension release.

"Oh I know; it is why I gave in so fast. When do I leave?"

"Is Thursday good for you? I will e-mail you the details and flight info etc. Two weeks of uninterrupted Greek sunshine, food, wine and hopefully for both our sakes ... inspiration."

Ben hoped for the same himself.

LATER THAT SAME WEEK, Ben sipped champagne on the first-class flight the agency had booked for him.

He was an hour out from Athens and he had had a good nap

231

along the way. The food had been passable but the drink was excellent, he thought, as he took another sip.

He had been recognised by a flight attendant an hour into the flight. She apparently had read everything he had written and loved every word.

Ben had a hard time believing those things when he was told.

Looking back, some of his earlier stuff was definitely subpar and he had been lucky to get it published. That did not mean that he did not accept the compliment or sign the copy she was reading of *Surrogate Damage,* his previous novel.

He had written a personalised thank you for her care on the flight. She had been ecstatic and suddenly he was getting even better service than before.

She did ask if he was working on anything new, obviously trying to get a scoop on his upcoming book. Ben did not feel like telling her the truth about his progress so he had hedged.

"I am kicking around a few things, outlining a few ideas. Mostly I am on vacation," he had told her smiling.

Half-truths at best. Ben felt a little guilty, but not too much.

As a heavy reader himself, he never felt it necessary to get all bent out of shape when his favourite authors did not produce as fast as he would prefer.

Then again, as a writer too, he knew the difficulties and dangers of rushing things. That thought reminded him he was pretty much in a position to rush things himself and that brought his mind back to the problem at hand.

It was just that nothing seemed interesting to him lately, not enough to write about anyway. He had fallen into a rut creatively and had to find a way to climb out.

Maybe this little jaunt to Santorini would be a good start.

CHAPTER SIX

WHEN HE LANDED IN ATHENS, he said goodbye to the flight attendant and went to get his bags.

It was the middle of the night in Europe and he wanted nothing more at that point than to fly on to Santorini and get some sleep.

He ran into a problem, however.

They could not find his luggage. It was logged into the system as having made it onto the flight, but they just could not find it in Athens.

Ben spent the next three hours waiting and pacing. He drank some coffee and paced some more before they found it. There were many apologies and promises of upgrades and free-flying miles but Ben just waved them off.

All he wanted was to get to his lodgings and hit the hay.

When he got to the departure gate for the little plane that would take him from Athens to Santorini he found he had another hour wait for the next one. He had missed the last flight by ten minutes.

More coffee and surfing the net on his phone ate up the time it took to get on board the connecting flight and be on his way.

By the time they reached the island, the sun was rising and Ben was famished. His frustration level had peaked with how his trip was going so far.

If this was any way like the way the rest of it was going to go, he was beginning to think he should have stayed at home.

Ben went to a café at the airport for breakfast and was greatly relieved by how good the food was at least. Eggs, sausage with a special goat cheese that was wonderful, and the freshest orange juice he had ever tasted.

Once he had eaten his fill, his frustration level had gone back down a little and he reminded himself that was always the way. When he got hungry he got annoyed.

So, he thought cheerfully, I just need to keep myself well-fed.

According to his information, there were lots of bars and eateries near the house he was staying at, so that would not be a problem.

Outside the terminal, he hailed a cab and loaded his baggage with the knowledge it should be smooth sailing from here on in.

THE TRIP to his lodging was a beautiful tour given by a silent cab driver which was nice. Coming from New York, Ben was used to chatty drivers.

He appreciated the quiet to admire the views and the beautiful village he was being driven through. The ocean was a crystal clear blue that was enticing and the white-washed architecture was quaint and distinctly Greek.

By the time the cab stopped in front of a cute little cottage, Ben had a smile on his face, fully looking forward to his time here.

The island had already charmed him.

He got out tipped the driver handsomely for the ride and put the key in the little blue door to what was to be his home for the next two weeks.

Inside, he saw it was tiny, with one main living-cum-kitchen area and a couple of doors on either side of that.

And then, much to Ben's surprise, out of one walked a pretty woman in a white bikini and an open red silk robe.

CHAPTER SEVEN

What the hell....?

The strange woman gave a startled cry and dropped her coffee, and Ben dropped his luggage as she jumped back.

She wrapped the robe tightly around herself and rushed over behind the counter in the kitchen.

"Who are you? What are you doing here?" she cried.

"I could you ask the same. I am staying here for the next two weeks," he pointed out.

"*I* have this place for the next two weeks!" she declared, eyeing him dangerously, and he noticed she had moved quite close to the knife block.

Ben could understand that, as any woman finding a strange man in her lodgings would want some sort of defence. But still...

He raised his hands in deference. "Hey, I will double-check the information I was given, but I suggest we both call our people and figure out what the hell is going on, okay?" he suggested.

His earlier frustration was back and he wasn't even hungry,

he thought as he found Kimberly's number.

The woman facing him was digging through her purse keeping an eye on him as she pulled out her own phone.

While the call went through he went out the front door.

"Ben, do you have any idea what time it is here?" Kimberly grumbled. "Shouldn't you be on the beach or something?"

She sounded like he had woken her up. Good, he nodded to himself.

"I just thought I should fill you in on how my trip is going, Kim. The flight was wonderful; First Class was a nice touch by the way. The airline did lose my bags but they found them again, and just now I walked into your place and scared the hell out of a woman who is already staying here - supposedly also for the next two weeks. What do you think so far?" His frustration and sarcasm were on full blast.

"Jesus Ben, are you kidding me? I don't believe this. I made the reservation myself. Okay, hold tight and I will make some calls to the management company and get back to you. We will be able to figure things out," she told him.

His news had immediately transformed his agent from asleep to alert and on the ball. That made him feel a little better.

"All right. Just hurry, please. The woman jumped and almost dumped her coffee all over me. She is not happy," Ben told her.

"I will do my best and if I have to I will get cranky with someone," Kimberly finished before hanging up.

Ben paced outside to give the other tenant a chance to make her calls before heading back in. He felt strange just loitering outside the front door like that.

"Okay Carole, just make sure they call me soon, will you?" he heard her say from the other room.

Then she came out to him, shutting her phone down. She had changed into a long flowing red and blue patterned skirt and white T-shirt. He had to admit she was very attractive - under that silk robe especially.

Ben held up his phone. "I am waiting for my agent to call me back. She offered me this place; said it's a family timeshare," he explained.

"My aunt booked me, she is part of the share too," she told him in return. They stood there for a moment in awkward silence.

"There's some coffee just made if you want some," the woman offered hesitantly.

"That would be great." Ben smiled gratefully and went back inside the cottage to pour a cup. "I've been travelling for hours and it already feels like it's been a very long day."

She glanced at his luggage. "You've just come from the airport?"

"Yes, and it was one helluva trip."

After taking a long drink of coffee, Ben sighed in satisfaction. "Thank you. That tastes wonderful. I really am sorry about this. Hopefully, we can get things worked out quickly," he said, and she nodded.

"Me too. Aunt Carole claims the calendar was free, that was why she booked it," she said by way of explanation.

"I think that is why my agent reserved it for me," he said.

"Your travel agent?"

"No my literary agent. My name is Ben Norton, I am a writer. I came here to try and find something ..." he told her cryptically, pointing to his head.

She grinned shyly. "I'm Olivia Clarke, an accountant and I am trying to lose something," she said pointing to her own head.

They both got a chuckle out of that, which immediately broke the ice.

"So, have you seen the view?" Olivia asked going to the

sliding glass doors. Ben had not noticed, but now that he could see the ocean he followed her out.

The coastal view across the caldera and out to the volcano was truly spectacular, and a little way down he could see direct access to a walkway along the beach.

Damn, he thought, this was nice. Kimberly had pulled out all the stops.

"I am positive I have never had a view quite like this," he admitted.

"I know. If it comes down to it, I may well arm wrestle you for it," the woman called Olivia said, although Ben was not certain if she was joking or not.

They stood in silence after that, sipping coffee and enjoying the warm breeze and the magnificent view. Then a phone rang.

Ben looked at his iPhone and knew it wasn't his. She did the same and then looked at him in surprise. The ringing continued and they quickly realised it was coming from inside.

He followed Olivia and saw a phone on the end table. A landline. She looked at him and he shrugged, so she picked it up.

"Hello, this is Olivia Clarke," he heard her say.

After a beat, she glanced at him. "Okay, thank you … yes he is here too. All right, just a moment," she said and put her hand over the receiver.

"It is Greek TimeShare Management from Athens. They want me to put this on speaker so they can talk to both of us," she told him.

Ben shrugged. "Sure, let's see what they have to say," he told her.

He had a feeling it wasn't good though. Otherwise, Kimberly would be calling to brag about what a great job she had done securing the place for him alone and getting Olivia kicked out.

"Hello Mr. Norton, as I was just telling Miss Clarke, there

has been a terrible mix-up. It seems the cottage was indeed booked by both Kimberly McNaughton and Carole Clarke. Somehow the system did not record either one, and as of a moment ago, the calendar is still showing the house as still available. We here at TimeShare Management are truly sorry for the confusion and would like to make it up to you. Our people have made many calls to try to find another available lodging in Santorini for either of you, but I'm afraid we have run into a snag ..." the man added hesitantly.

"Go on," Olivia told him, looking dubious.

"Well it's summer in Santorini - the middle of the tourist season and there is not a vacant bed available on all of the island. We were wondering ... if we managed to arrange some complimentary facilities - such as meals in some of our partner restaurants and entertainment for you both - if you would mind perhaps, sharing the bungalow for the ten-day crossover period of your stay?" he outlined with trepidation.

Ben looked at Olivia and she back at him. She had a calculating look in her eyes and he wondered if he would soon be arm-wrestling with her over it.

He sighed.

Yep. Helluva first day.

CHAPTER EIGHT

MUCH LATER THAT EVENING, Ben woke in the smallest bedroom in the bungalow.

As it seemed their individual reservations coincided by about ten days, and with no other accommodation available on the island, he and Olivia had little choice but to tell the management company they would try sharing the place for a day or two to see how things went.

The translation of that, he thought was, 'see if they were in each other's way'.

Olivia had told him she would be out and about most days in any case, which was good for him.

Ben liked to work from early morning to mid-afternoon, sometimes later. This first day was a waste as far as work was concerned however, because between his lost luggage, jet lag as well as the problems with the bungalow, all he'd wanted to do was sleep.

He checked his phone and saw it was now about six pm Greek time.

Just in time for dinner, he thought, pleased. He got up and

went into the main living area. He called out, but it appeared that his new roommate was as good as her word and was indeed out and about.

Ben grabbed some clean clothes and went into the single bathroom alongside the other bedroom - Olivia's 'side'.

He took a quick shower, enjoying the feeling of getting clean after the long trip. He finished shaving at the sink and got dressed before leaving the bathroom and was glad he had.

Olivia was sitting on the couch reading a magazine. She looked up at him, her face looking a little impatient.

"Hi. I just came back to change for dinner. Enjoy the shower?" she asked, immediately standing up and picking up a change of clothes on the couch next to her.

She had obviously been waiting for him to finish and was now *very* obviously annoyed by his hogging the bathroom.

Ben restrained from releasing a heavy sigh: clearly, they would have to work on their timing.

"Great water pressure," he answered lightly. "It felt amazing after the day I've had so far. Can you recommend a good place to eat around here?" he added conversationally.

Olivia nodded, moving towards the bathroom.

"Hali's is my favourite. It's just down the beach to the right when you get to the bottom of the trail off the veranda. It's about a half-mile walk down the steps to the coastline, and there is a whole string of cafés and tavernas along the beach," she informed him. "I tried out the management company's promise to compensate us at the partner restaurants they mentioned, and at the one I went to earlier they were falling all over themselves. So I don't think it will be a problem." She chuckled, looking a little more relaxed. "Hali's is on the list too. As far as I can tell almost every taverna down there is - have fun," she finished and headed into the bathroom.

Ben went into his room and put away his old clothes, then grabbed his wallet and phone before heading out to the veranda.

As the first time, stepping up to the railing was breathtaking.

The crystal clear water below against the darker colour of the volcanic rock was spectacular. He saw a few white sails silhouetted against the volcano in the distance and wondered what it would be like to spend a day on the water.

He then headed out the side gate off the veranda and down the path as Olivia described.

Just below, the path became steps and he followed about a hundred of them down to the walkway by the shore and out onto the beach.

As he walked along the coastline everything seemed like a treat for his senses. The water lapping up onto the shore. The feel of soft sand underfoot as he walked.

The scent of the evening sea air was invigorating, and despite the shaky start to the trip, now he felt an automatic bounce in his step.

He waved a greeting to a couple walking the other way, holding hands and taking turns throwing a frisbee for a little dog. They waved back with big smiles and he found himself smiling too.

His troubles did not feel so troubling walking down this beautiful Greek beach.

As he came up to the line of eateries he spied Hali's, the place Olivia had mentioned. It was a pretty whitewashed taverna with blue and white striped awnings fringed with bright pink bougainvillea, and open on the beach side with some tables beneath the awning or further inside.

Ben grabbed the only free outside table left so he could see the beach and passersby. The place was filling up fast and he was glad for Olivia's suggestion.

The restaurant felt comfortable and easygoing, yet he was excited at the same time. He rarely left the States and when he had in the past it had been for book tours with no chance at all for any sightseeing or downtime.

Maybe exploring Santorini a little, and perhaps even some boating would spark his creativity and be good for his imagination? he thought, as he ordered some red wine and looked over the menu.

"I wanted to ask first ..." he said to the Greek waiter who took the order. "I am staying at the bungalow further up the hill. There was a mix-up with my reservation and the management company said ..." The man grinned and immediately nodded in agreement.

"Ah yes of course. We were told. It is terrible about your lodgings. But at least you have a lovely roommate and all you can eat, yes?" he joked.

"You know Olivia?" Ben asked, surprised.

"Yes, she has been here a few times over the last couple of days. She was here for coffee earlier and we discussed the issue. She has fallen in love with our Sfakianopita. You may wish to try it for dessert sir, after your dinner of course," the man added, then seemed to realise he might be talking too much.

But Ben did not mind. As a writer, he was an observer, but also a converser. "I was pretty annoyed when I found they had double booked the cottage, but it definitely could be worse. Olivia is pleasant enough," he admitted to the man and looked back down at the menu.

"Do you mind if I take a minute to choose?" he asked. There was so much on the menu that looked good he could not decide.

"Of course not. Please, take your time and I will return shortly," said the waiter with a slight bow.

It took a few minutes and a full glass of wine for Ben to make his decision. He finally decided on Giouvetsi: a lamb dish baked in a clay pot that came with fresh vegetables and bread. The waiter duly took his order and said he was wise for such an excellent choice.

Ben was sure the Greek man told everyone the same thing but ordered another glass of wine regardless.

Watching the many people wandering along the path by the beach, he suddenly spied Olivia and could not help but wave. She had recommended this place to him after all.

Spotting him, she made her way over to his table.

"Hello there. I see you found it. Sorry about waiting outside the bathroom like that. I realised later that it must have seemed very rude," she apologised. "I should have just waited in my room and not come across as so impatient."

Ben had already forgotten all about the incident and shook his head.

"No problem. If anything I should be apologising to you for hogging the bathroom. And I should thank you for your recommendation. I am enjoying Hali's tremendously so far. Enjoyed your day?" he added, smiling.

"Yes, I swam in the sea a lot earlier and it always feels good to get cleaned up."

Ben's waiter reappeared at the table. "Ah Olivia, how good to see you again. Are you joining your friend this evening?" he asked and she looked startled and a little flustered.

"I was just saying hello, Ramone," she told the waiter but Ben had noticed the traffic on the beach, and how quickly the restaurants had filled up in advance of the sunset.

She would be lucky to find anywhere at this point.

"You are more than welcome to join me if you want. It is looking like finding a table here or elsewhere may be a bit of a wait. Not to mention you would have gotten out sooner if I hadn't held you up earlier," he added with a wink.

He was surprised by his own forthrightness but went with his instincts.

As soon as he said it, Ben realised he would actually like some company.

Someone to compare notes with about the locals and tourists would be enjoyable on this balmy summer Greek evening.

CHAPTER NINE

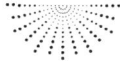

Olivia looked hesitant, glancing down the beach and around the crowded restaurant.

"The place does look busy tonight. Are you sure you don't mind, Ben? We did promise to stay out of each other's way …"

He could see she was just trying to be courteous too and he reflected that there was nothing worse than two people trying to be nice to each other in situations like this - people trying to be kind but ending up cancelling out each other's efforts.

He put a hand over his heart.

"I swear - on my next book - I really would enjoy the company," he promised with sincerity in his tone.

She seemed to believe him and relaxed, nodding. Ben immediately got up and pulled out her chair and from behind her, Ramone the waiter winked at him.

Olivia ordered a glass of red wine and already seemed to know what she wanted. She asked the waiter for something called a Kokkininsto and Ben recalled from the menu that it was a sort of stew.

Ramone quickly came back with her glass of wine and she

thanked him. Typically courteous, he bowed to her before moving on to his other customers.

"It did not seem as busy before, but of course, it is the weekend now. Thank you for the offer Ben, at least I know the food is always good here," she said and paused then laughed. "Listen to me, I act like I have been in Santorini forever instead of just a couple of days." She giggled a little, then took a sip of wine.

Despite the setback with the accommodation she was obviously enjoying her stay immensely. The mix-up with the cottage aside, Ben had already started to think he was going to enjoy this place too.

Particularly if he could get cracking on a decent story.

"You have been here longer than I have, so you are a veteran compared to me. May I ask what you have seen so far?" he asked curious as to what sort of adventures she had gotten up to since her arrival.

It turned out that in the three days previous Olivia had already explored a lot of the little town they were in, more so than he would want to in so little time, Ben thought.

She was completely taken with the place though.

Their food came at the same time and they each ordered another glass of wine and dug in. For Ben, the food was even better than it had been on his arrival in Greece in the early hours of that morning. He and Olivia relished their food with equal satisfaction as he finished his description of his travel adventures before reaching the island.

"I suppose the bright side is they still had your luggage," Olivia chuckled. "Could you imagine if your bags were on their way to Nome, Alaska or somewhere equally unreachable?"

He had to admit she was right. Things could have gone a lot worse.

"You have a point. And I have been to Nome actually. It was beautiful, but a bit out of reach of most things, though the inhabitants seem to like it that way. I would probably never get my luggage back though, and some Alaskan would get to live out his days in my beloved Gucci loafers" he joked.

After the main course, they both ordered the Sfakianopita - on Olivia's recommendation - and a coffee. It was the perfect finish to a delicious meal. The honey in the desert complimented the coffee nicely.

"Wonderful Olivia - great choice. You are turning out to be a fantastic tour guide," Ben told her and she laughed.

It was a sweet sound, particularly in this setting, he thought.

"Well, thank you. Though I'm afraid I have told you everything I know about the island so far. I will repeat however the naps in hammocks on the beach are fast becoming a daily thing. Lazy cocktails too… heaven," she added with gusto.

He laughed with her and thought he may well have to try that too.

He hadn't been kidding when he'd said she'd make a great tour guide. He was enjoying talking to her and would quite happily sit there for another glass or two except for the yawn that suddenly came out of him.

"Sorry, I couldn't help it. I think I am going to head back," he told her apologetically.

"Thanks for letting me share your table," Olivia said as he stood up. "I think I am going to stay on here for a bit. But I will be leaving the cottage in the morning early for a yoga class and then breakfast and I may not be back until later in the day so you will have the place to yourself," she added reassuringly.

"No worries, and somehow I think our roommate thing will work out just fine. Enjoy your evening and I will see you sometime tomorrow."

. . .

BEN STROLLED LEISURELY BACK along the beach enjoying the cooler breeze and the sounds of laughter and fun from the people he passed.

He saw the same couple with the frisbee from before and waved to them again and they returned it with grins. He was hard-pressed to remember ever meeting such happy-go-lucky friendly folks.

Everyone here seemed so cheery and cordial. It was a pleasant change from the hustle and bustle of NYC.

When Ben got back to the bungalow he looked in the refrigerator and saw glass bottles of water, frosty cold.

He grabbed one and went into his bedroom, then sat on the bed to read for a bit and let his brain switch off a little before sleep. It was an engrossing read about an exploration of the Ozark Mountains. The tale had seemed farfetched when it was referred to him, but now he was entirely caught up in it.

He hardly heard when Olivia came back a little while later. Merely the rustling of her steps and the sound of the veranda doors alerted him to her presence.

Soon it was pitch dark and he was reading by the light of the bedside lamp. He did not turn off the light until almost midnight and felt it had been a long but satisfying day, despite everything.

Or maybe because of everything?

As he felt himself drift off, he wondered what a man going out on the waters around these parts in a fishing boat would find.

What sort of mysteries could be discovered?

Ben did not know it, but he went to sleep with a peaceful smile on his face.

CHAPTER TEN

THE FOLLOWING MORNING, Olivia thanked the yoga instructor when her class finished.

For the last few days, doing yoga as the sun was coming up over the cliffs and bathing the island in its soft morning glow had been relaxing and exhilarating at the same time.

She said goodbye to her classmates and strolled off down the beach. This time she went in the other direction to find breakfast and explore a little more.

She was enjoying all the walking since arriving here, and keeping herself so occupied had helped her move away from moping over her ex.

About a half mile down the beach and up a side road of cobblestones further into the village, she found a café that looked good called Herodias Harmonies. She had an egg meal with potatoes and some of the wonderful toasted Greek bread.

Afterwards, she sipped coffee and watched the people strolling the whitewashed bougainvillea-lined streets in the morning sunshine.

She had gone back to the bungalow about an hour after Ben

last night and had been surprised to find he was still up. His door was open and he was reading and had not seemed to notice her moving through the living room.

So she got some iced tea and sat on the veranda, watching the stars over the caldera and just enjoying the nighttime air.

He was an interesting guy, she thought now, sipping her coffee. He was very polite and quite reasonable considering the predicament they had found themselves in.

They seemed to get along OK so far, and she agreed with him in that she did not think there would be any problem with them sharing the cottage for the duration of their respective trips.

Granted, at first the idea of having a strange man in the house had horrified her and made her immediately worried for her safety, but yet there was something about the confident and no-nonsense way Ben had handled things that was reassuring.

And once she found out he was a famous writer - and a celebrity of sorts - she suspected he would hardly do anything to risk his reputation.

She wasn't sure why, but her instincts told her to trust him.

Perhaps because he was so very different from Derek?

Both men were handsome but had completely different personalities. Derek was very forceful and commanding and completely believed in his own righteousness.

That was why Olivia had come to believe it had never occurred to him that sleeping with her best friend was something he shouldn't do.

He had never considered that there was anything he couldn't do if he wanted to.

Ben seemed so much more easy-going and open to enjoyment for the pure fun of it. There did not have to be a purpose behind it.

She wondered if that was his artist self showing. She imagined that being a writer would necessitate the ability to be open-minded.

Olivia realised then that she was indulging in whimsy; it was not like she knew Ben well or anything.

She just did not see any resemblance to Derek in him, and that was a good thing. Not only did she not need the reminder as a roommate, Derek really was a dick and she didn't need that either.

She was beginning to think like Carole, and wondering what the hell had she been doing with the guy in the first place. Olivia's heart gave a little tremble then, reminding her that she had loved Derek after all.

That was what she had been doing with him.

There had been a time when Derek had been nice, complimentary and even generous. She wondered now if all of that had been for show. Bait for the prize he wanted maybe. In any case, she would never know, or did she need to know?

Sod it, she decided. That was enough heavy thinking for today.

She had beaches to stroll and hammocks to nap in. Olivia felt herself smile at the thought and she got up to pay and continue on with another day in paradise.

DESPITE THE NUMEROUS signs and kiosks advertising same, she'd decided against parasailing or boat trips around the volcano.

At least for the moment.

She was hoping to get up the gumption to maybe try something more adventurous at some point though.

As she strolled down the beach she took off the linen cover-up she had on so she was only wearing her shorts and her bikini top. It was a bargain she had made to herself. Get used to one half of the bikini and then maybe she could risk the other half.

From the looks she was getting from the male locals and tourists as she walked along though, she had a feeling no one had a problem with it.

She also knew her reticence was a hangover of sorts from Derek. He had preferred that she keep mostly covered up and she now believed that far from modesty concerns, it was more of a possessive thing.

He thought she was his and no one could see her the way he got to.

Idiot, she snorted to herself as she reached the hammock stations. After four days in a row, the owner of the stand smiled when he saw her coming.

"I have been telling people, I have found the perfect customer. Miss Olivia - *she* understands what I have to offer. They do not believe I could find such a great customer!" Little Iason was a black-haired, stocky Greek with a permanent smile on his face and a cheerful nature that was infectious.

"Don't you think you are going overboard just a bit, Iason?" she asked laughing.

"No, not at all Miss Olivia. You understand the need for the peace and solitude my hammocks provide. It is an inspiration to me that I have chosen the right profession. Would you like your usual hammock and cocktail?" he asked solicitously.

"Of course. I'll want to live up to your kind words," she told him.

She took her icy drink to her preferred hammock frontline to the beach and got comfortable.

Taking a sip of her pina colada she smiled. She had always been a creature of habit and being here in Santorini had not changed that.

Derek used to complain she was boring and predictable and it had bothered her. She was beginning to think he was wrong on that front as well.

Just because she did like some structure, it did not mean everything she did was predictable and hell, even if it was, it was her life.

Olivia took another drink of the creamy refreshing pineapple drink, set it on the table and lay back, watching the water lap softly onto the shore.

All too soon she floated away into a dream of splashing water on a white-sailed boat in the Santorini waters, laughing.

CHAPTER ELEVEN

When she awoke she was refreshed and ready for the rest of her day.

After a light Dakos salad for lunch, she strolled further down the beach and scoped out a cave that was once investigated by Jacques Cousteau, the great underwater explorer.

Apparently, he had gone looking for traces of the lost city of Atlantis. Santorini was situated on what was possibly the only live volcano to host a city and he thought the history of ancient eruptions could have been a clue to the lost city.

He had found nothing conclusive, and the last eruption on the island had been over three thousand years ago. The cave was magnificent though; all lava rock that led to an underground lake.

When she got back to the bungalow it was almost four o'clock and she found Ben sitting on the veranda with a beer, smiling and looking relaxed.

She returned the smile as he got up and opened the gate for her before she got there.

Unlike Derek, he was attentive and thoughtful too, she realised.

"Hi, I hope your writing day went well," she said as she came up onto the veranda, a little sweaty and out of breath.

Embarrassed, she only then realised she was carrying her blouse and was still in her bikini top.

Ben did not, like many men, let his eyes immediately stray to her chest and Olivia appreciated that. She was also aware that her hair was mussed and had come out of her ponytail and hung around her face, but he did not seem in the least bit affected by her unkempt appearance.

He seemed so easygoing and nice to be around that she had a feeling that rather than a thorn in her side, her new roommate might become a welcome companion.

"It was fantastic actually. Last night I had this brilliant idea for a story and just went wild with it. I may have to experience some more of this wonderful place to keep the creative juices flowing. How were your adventures today?" he asked her politely, offering her a beer.

Olivia accepted and took a drink, letting the icy liquid cool her a little.

"Great, did some sunrise yoga, had some great food as well as a little sightseeing - and most importantly, my hammock nap and cocktail," she added with a smile.

He laughed. "Sounds idyllic. Well, the bathroom is all yours if you want it. I am done writing for the day and am gonna hunt down some food in a while. Have you tried the Café Eluent - about a mile down the beach? It's on the list and looks good. But more importantly, is the food any good?" he asked her taking another sip of beer.

"I haven't tried it but I saw it the other day. If you are still around later, I might pop in and join you for a drink?" she found herself saying.

He cracked open another bottle of beer. "Better yet, why don't I wait for you? I am in no hurry, this view can keep me occupied for some time," he said gesturing out at the Aegean Sea. "That's if you don't mind company again this evening."

"Actually I'd love that. Being on my own all day is nice, but can get quite quite boring."

"Ditto." He took another sip of beer and raised it in a toast to her.

"I won't be long," she said and Ben turned back to the sea as she went inside.

Olivia showered quickly and realised how easy it had been for her to agree to go with him to dinner. She guessed they were at the beginning of a companionable friendship and she was surprised at how simple, yet pleasant an idea it was.

Then again, she thought as she lathered up, they were both tourists and in the same situation of having no choice but to share accommodation.

It gave them a commonality that would make getting along a more natural thing. Kind of an us against them sort of thing.

Oh well, either way, it's nice to have someone to talk to at dinner, she told herself as she rinsed out her hair and tried to decide what to wear for dinner with a handsome American she barely knew.

CHAPTER TWELVE

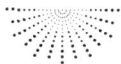

OLIVIA PICKED out a red summer dress, and flowing skirt with a thin waist sash and dried her hair, letting it down for a change.

Just a touch of makeup, she never liked piling it on, and she was ready to go.

When she came out Ben was waiting on the veranda but had also since changed into blue cotton pants and a white, short-sleeved, linen shirt. She gulped a little at the sight of him. He was very handsome.

They walked down the beach together smiling and waving at various locals and other tourists that Olivia had gotten used to seeing. Ben pointed out one couple with a dog, holding hands and smiling.

"I saw them here yesterday too," he commented as they exchanged waves.

"They've been around since I got here. I think they are locals just revelling in the fact they live in such an amazing place," she said looking at him.

"I think you're right and it reminds me we should all appreciate where we come from. I am from New York City and few cities can compare to it, yet I hardly think that way. You are from London, right?" he asked.

She nodded, realising they had never actually talked about where they were from."Oy, how can ya tell guv'na?" she joked in her best Cockney accent.

Ben laughed.

"Just a guess. You do have a lovely accent though. I visited London on a book tour once and always wished I had taken the time to look around. It is a pretty spectacular place too," he complimented.

"It is and you are right. It is easy to forget the things we have and always look for something else. Humans are weird," she said.

"True enough and thank goodness for that - it gives me plenty of material to write about," he quipped and she laughed.

When they got to the taverna Ben mentioned, it was one of the few enclosed restaurants on the seafront, but they were early enough to get a good window seat facing the beach. That and the management company had pulled out all the stops because here too, they got the red carpet treatment.

Olivia had to admit this was a nice touch by the company and was going a long way to making up for the problem with the cottage.

She and Ben ordered a nice wine and then went with the house special of broiled fish and herbs, with a rice and veggie dish.

As they settled into their wine, a man approached their table. His hesitant tone and the fact that he was carrying a book, suggested to Olivia that he was possibly a fan of Ben's.

Hi, you're Ben Norton, yes?" The thin man asked hesitantly in a Scottish accent.

Ben smiled and looked up at him. "That is what my mom named me," he responded cheerfully.

"I am such a huge fan. I was wondering if you could sign my copy of *Surrogate Damage.* I love how you wind it up at the end. I can't believe I was sitting over there re-reading it then looked up and the same guy on the cover was actually sitting in this restaurant," he said excitedly. "I'm such a fan."

Ben reached out and took the book and the pen from him. He opened the cover while Olivia just watched quietly, sipping her wine. The thin man did not appear to have noticed her and she thought that was funny.

"What is your name, I could put "to fan" but that would be weird even for me," Ben joked.

The man laughed nervously. "Oh yeah, sorry. I'm Jack and I am from Glasgow, Scotland," he said.

"Good to meet you Jack from Glasgow. I hope you are enjoying Santorini," Ben said as he wrote something in the book before signing it with a flourish.

"I am; it is my first holiday in Greece. There is so much to do and see, I feel like I don't want to leave," Jack said.

"I know what you mean. It is a beautiful place. Here you go. I hope your vacation continues to be great for you," he told him.

"Thanks, mate, I appreciate you taking the time. I see the new book is coming out at Christmas - I am looking forward to that," Jack added with an eager look in his eyes.

Olivia was taken aback. From what little Ben had said he had only just started writing it. She glanced at him but he showed no sign of nervousness or hesitation.

"That is the plan. I hope you like it as much as you did *Surrogate.* Have a great evening," he said with a smile.

Jack left then and Ben shrugged.

"Sorry about that. I don't usually get recognised by readers, but when I do they can be … determined," he said as dinner was brought over.

"No worries. I found it an interesting experience to behold, to be honest. I have never been near a real-life celebrity. I need to read one of your books to keep up," she laughed.

Ben smiled, not at all put out that she had not known who he was. She had a vague memory of hearing his name upon meeting him yesterday, but that was it.

They started in on the fish and it too was excellent. Though being inside the restaurant was stifling and she missed the breeze off the water.

"I thought you handled his last question well. Didn't you just start writing your new book?" she asked.

He nodded and looked a little disgruntled. "Yep. Just today actually. I would have appreciated my publisher letting me know they'd set a release date. Probably figured I wouldn't hear about it in Greece," he said. There was annoyance in his eyes for a brief moment, but it was quickly followed by amusement.

"It is that whole Stephen King thing," he told her, as she swallowed her bite of fish.

"Stephen King thing?" Olivia asked. She'd heard of that writer of course.

Ben nodded and dipped his bread in the sauce.

"Yeah, King went and said in his book, *On Writing* - an excellent book by the way, kind of his life story - that writing a book should take no longer than three months. But people - editors in particular - tend to overlook the fact he was discussing how *he* writes. Most of us have different time frames. Anyway, something like that enabled publishers to whine if you don't get it done in quick time," he said with another shrug and took a bite of his sauce-soaked bread.

"It does seem wrong for people to use such a prolific writer as a benchmark. Let's face it, even I know he's written practically hundreds of books at this stage," Olivia said in agreement. She then dipped her bread in the sauce and they were both silent as they finished up their meal.

Afterwards, they both leaned back in contentment.

"If it is okay, I was going to ask what your new book is about, but I am not sure about the protocol surrounding such questions," she said. She knew she never would have asked such a thing before, but Ben was such good company and the wine was so good she figured, why not?

He chuckled. "I don't mind at all. I just have a rough plot outlined, but basically, I'm fascinated by those white sailboats you see out on the water all the time. So far my story is about a man who takes a boat and goes out searching for something," he told her, and she noticed his voice softened a little as he said it.

Olivia realised with a start that he was really trusting her by telling her that much and she resolved to not abuse that trust. She of all people knew how that felt.

"Searching for what?" she asked and he shrugged.

"I have no idea. I want to be just as surprised writing it as hopefully readers will be reading it."

"That makes sense. But you could always rent a boat yourself and see what's out there in reality. I took a cave tour today and there's been stories around here about the Lost City of Atlantis."

He laughed surprised. "Here? I'll be damned. I will admit I had been thinking of taking one out though. I do know how to sail - I used to take a boat up and down the Hudson River so maybe they would let me have one for a bit," he said thoughtfully. "So would you be interested in a trip out on the Aegean, Olivia?" he asked then.

She was surprised, but he was so casual about it that she felt herself nodding before she'd even thought about it properly.

"That would be fun, I think. Thanks for the invitation, when would you like to go?"

"I was thinking maybe once I've got some more words under my belt. How does the middle of next week sound? Though I don't want to take away from your plans..." he added then, a little more hesitant.

"Sure. The only thing I've got planned while here is sunrise yoga every morning and my hammock in the afternoon along with a few tourist trips here and there. Other than that, I would be only too happy to accompany you," she told him.

Their eyes met then and Olivia felt a frisson from Ben's appreciative glance, as well as a warmth from his respect and consideration, which she was not used to.

In hindsight, Derek the Dick had not been big on appreciation or respect.

CHAPTER THIRTEEN

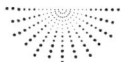

THE FOLLOWING THURSDAY MORNING, Olivia finished her last fifteen minutes of yoga, stretching and watching the boats in the lagoon Ben had mentioned.

She took deep breaths as they sailed by, or in the case of one colossal one, just stop and stare. It was a beautiful yacht, huge with a small skiff on the back.

As her last deep breathing exercises finished, the skiff was lowered and began making its way to the beach with people on board.

She said goodbye to her classmates and looked around for Ben who had said he would meet her after her class.

Today they were taking the boat trip he'd suggested, and she was looking forward to it more than she'd anticipated.

For the last week or so they'd pretty much kept themselves to themselves while Ben worked hard on his book, and Olivia worked hard on her tan.

They'd met up for the occasional coffee or drink on the veranda, but Ben was throwing himself into his writing and had no choice but to temporarily eschew Santorini's many attractions in favour of hard work.

Strangely, Olivia found she was missing his company and the cheerful camaraderie they'd shared in the early days of his arrival.

She was also more than a little bereft that her escape to this magnificent island would be coming to an end in little under a week.

The first ten days had flown by.

She drank some water as she looked down the beach for Ben. Then she heard his voice and turning, she saw him walk across the sand looking handsome in khaki board shorts and a white T-shirt.

"I hope I am not late. Did you have a good session?" he asked pleasantly.

"I did. It was blissful, and very relaxing. I decided I'm going to start a yoga routine when I get back to London. How has your week gone?" she asked as they walked down the beach a little way.

"Great actually - would you believe I got twenty-five-thousand words out? And I found the perfect boat, but they won't let me sail it." He frowned. "The open water is a little different from the Hudson River, though the Greeks obviously have never tried it," he added wryly. "So I got us a personal tour instead. Meals and a captain to show us around. Are you still game?"

Olivia nodded, encouraged by the idea until Ben pointed to a tiny little vessel on the shore about twenty-five yards away. She hesitated a little, seeing a man standing next to it in the clear waves.

"Meals too?" she repeated eyebrows raising, and he looked at the boat and then back at her before he got it.

Then he laughed out loud.

"No, no that is our taxi - to that," he said and pointed out to the big cruiser yacht she had been admiring earlier.

Immediately, Olivia felt herself blushing. "Oh crikey, sorry about that. You said a personal tour boat and pointed to the guy and the dinghy ..." she tried to explain, and Ben just shook his head chuckling.

"You should have seen the look on your face." He put his arm out to her and she took it. "Come, my friend. Let us check out the high seas," he added and they went and climbed into the little dinghy. "Breakfast is waiting,"

CHAPTER FOURTEEN

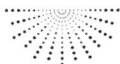

THE SAILOR SMILED and greeted her in Greek and Olivia realised he did not speak any English.

She managed a good morning in Greek but that was as good as it got as to her shame, she had not spent enough time learning the language.

The Greek man rowed them out to the big cruiser where a small platform and then short steps led them up to the main deck.

The captain who much to her relief introduced himself in perfect English as Captain Kastor, welcomed them on board. He then took Olivia on a tour while Ben trailed along, presumably having already seen it all before renting it.

Olivia was amazed at the luxuriousness of the vessel. The yacht had four guest cabins, several bathrooms, a fishing and sun deck, as well as a dining room and lounge. It was a small floating palace and she loved it.

She had seen pictures of boats like this in magazines but had never thought she would be on one.

She felt a bit like a celebrity - especially on the arm of a famous bestselling author! Wait until she told Aunt Carole...

When the captain left them on the lounge deck to get going, she turned to Ben.

"The management company paid for this?" she queried. The company had also offered them some tour options, but even for them this seemed a bit much.

Ben laughed. "I don't think it was included in the entertainment budget. Don't worry, I owe you not only for your remarkable patience and kindness in letting me share the cottage but also for your friendship. And I would have rented it anyway so you may as well come along. Don't worry about the cost," he said.

"What do you mean you owe me? I didn't do anything," she told him as the boat began moving through the water and heading out towards the open water, away from the coastline.

"You have been so positive and adventurous in your approach to this place that it inspired me to do the same, and now I am getting ideas left and right. So thank you. Like I said, I would have come out anyway so I am glad for the company," he told her, his dark eyes burning into hers.

Olivia blushed slightly but then the wind picked up and blew her ponytail around her face, breaking the moment. She laughed, gathered it back and tied it up better, then she pulled a wide-brimmed hat out of her big bag and put that on.

It almost blew off and she held it on with her hand.

"I think you may be fighting a losing battle there. Hungry?" Ben asked and she remembered the food.

They went back inside into a dining area where a tremendous spread had been laid out for them. Fruit, pieces of bread, juices and champagne. They were able to watch their progress out the wide windows while they ate.

"He's going to take us to what is supposed to be a good fishing spot. Do you mind?" Ben asked her.

Olivia finished the bagel she was eating and shook her head. "Not at all. It is your charter. And your research. Besides, I have never been sea fishing before. Should be fun," she replied with a grin.

The fishing deck was on the lower section of the boat and had rod holders and fishing chairs all setup. Olivia was more taken with the wide expanse of blue water than the fishing, but like she had told Ben, she was willing to give it a go.

The two sat companionably in the fishing chairs with the rods in holders which seemed a little bit like cheating. At least it did until Olivia realised deep sea poles were heavy and much longer than regular fishing rods. She would be lucky to hold one up for a few seconds, much less wrestle a fish with it. Unfortunately, they did not get a bite.

She and Ben hardly noticed though, pointing to distant isles or some of the bigger fish they could see in the water.

None of them went for the bait but at least they got to see some, she thought with amusement. Ben found it funny as well.

Occasionally another sailboat would pass by and everyone would wave excitedly to one another as if it was a huge deal to see someone out on the water.

"Why do you think that is?" Olivia asked. "I mean we don't know them, they don't know us and we are passing at a pretty good clip. That last boat was really moving, so why get so excited?"

Ben thought about it and chuckled.

"Good question. You always have an interesting way of coming at things. Let's see, maybe they are just showing off. The young guy holding the rudder looked like the type to want to brag, the women were having a good time and probably just waving for the hell of it. But it could also have come out of tradition originally, signalling passing boats for safety and respect. And modern man has transformed into a ritual of bragging," he finished.

She looked at him a long time, thinking about what he said, then raised her eyebrows in amusement.

"Did you just make that up off the top of your head - about the tradition?" she asked and he laughed.

"Well, yeah. It is what I do for a living you know," he joked, a twinkle in his eye.

When the captain came back down he said he did not know why people on passing boats got so excited. He did say older, more mature people, just waved politely, and did not jump up and down.

Olivia glanced amusedly at Ben who was listening closely.

He nudged her playfully. "I was right then. Young braggarts. You see Olivia, sometimes it pays to use your imagination," he teased, laughing at himself.

She smiled, enjoying herself immensely.

By lunch, they gave up on fishing and were more into sightseeing. By the end of the day, Olivia felt like she'd seen more of the islands than the Greeks themselves, and had done more laughing with Ben in a short few hours than she had over the last few months.

It truly was a perfect day.

CHAPTER FIFTEEN

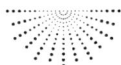

By the time they got back to the cottage, the sun was not more than half an hour from setting.

Olivia had been under the hot rays all day, had a wonderful time and had seen many wonderful things that had kept her mind busy, but she felt well and truly shattered.

Ben looked at her as he put the key in the door.

"I am going to go put on some coffee if you want the first shower. I'm exhausted, but I don't want to crash this early or I will be up at three am," he said.

She smiled tiredly and nodded as they entered the living room. She was not going to argue. A cool shower sounded fantastic and she gathered her clothes and proceeded to the bathroom.

Once in the water, she sighed. The cool water felt like heaven and she stretched out her muscles as the water ran over her. If it had not been for sunscreen she would have been toast.

It had been a fantastically enjoyable and fun-filled day, she had to say.

She and Ben had visited two smaller islands close to

Santorini and were able to take a look at an archaeological site. Nothing related to the Lost City of Atlantis, so Ben was a little disappointed about that.

She smiled. He was great company and was turning into a wonderful holiday companion.

When she felt refreshed and clean, she dried off and got dressed, putting on a long silk dress she'd bought especially for the holiday.

It was purple and white patterned, swirling around her body with a white and purple sash holding it in at her waist. She brushed out her hair and left it loose.

Tying it up on the boat had not helped, and her hair was in such a state so she might as well give up on it for the rest of the trip, she thought wryly.

"It is all yours, Ben," she said as she came out of the bathroom. Then she got a whiff of the coffee. "That smells heavenly."

He was sitting on the couch, writing by hand in a little book.

"It tastes even better if I do say so myself. How was the shower?" he asked without a break in his writing.

"Great. I left you some hot water, mostly because I didn't use much," she told him. He finished writing and closed his book.

"Boy am I looking forward to it. I will be out in a minute," he said standing and picking up a small stack of clothes he had ready.

He then went into the bathroom and she went for the coffee.

One sip and she was in heaven. The shower had been reinvigorating and the coffee was the perfect thing for the end of a busy day.

She went out on the veranda realising that it was not quite sundown yet. She leaned against the railing and just enjoyed the view. The waves were coming gently ashore, slow as if lazy from their busy day, and the fading light twinkled over the moving water making it appear almost solid, like a moving crystal sheet.

It was a lovely sight and she gasped, entranced.

She almost did not notice Ben joining her at the railing just as the sun was going down but felt her body instinctively flood with warmth as he appeared beside her.

"Good timing if I do say so myself," he said.

They both watched the sun lower into a red and orange flame that seemed for an instant to spring up from the horizon, bidding them a good night.

Then it faded and Olivia sighed. She wasn't sure it got much better than that.

After a moment they both went and sat down, putting their feet up. Enjoying their coffee and the magnificent view.

"So how are the ideas coming after today?" she asked.

"Good. I wrote a section I have been going over in my head since this afternoon. I will type it up in the morning. My hero still doesn't know what he is looking for. Maybe he will never find it. You know, the journey is supposed to be the worthier goal," he said whimsically, and she laughed.

"I didn't know you were a poet too."

"Sometimes, depends on the stimulus. And there has been plenty of stimuli so far. Did you enjoy the trip, Olivia?" he asked glancing sideways at her.

"I did. I must admit I have never been in that much luxury before. That boat had everything. Pity no fish were biting," she said. She knew he had been hoping for that.

"No big deal. I don't think I will be going for a yacht that big next time. A nice sailboat would be better. You're closer to the water that way. I had a great time too though. Those islands were amazing and some of those caves are astounding," he added with enthusiasm.

Both of them were gradually waking up with the addition of coffee to their system.

"So," Ben continued after a beat, "you said when we first met that you were here to lose something. May I ask what?"

Olivia hesitated a moment. She hadn't mentioned that to anyone. Then again, Ben was confiding plot points in his upcoming book and had just spent the day wining and dining her in incredible luxury.

She owed him a little trust.

"Heartbreak over losing my fiancé," she admitted ashamedly.

"Ouch, sorry to hear that. Was it bad?" he asked both concerned and curious.

"Bad enough. He slept with my best friend two weeks before the wedding," she told him in a rush and then took a sip of her coffee.

Ben looked astounded at her words.

"Damn Olivia, I am so sorry. I have had bad relationships but…damn. Not much of a best friend huh?" He said it with just the right touch of support and humour so that his remark did not bother her.

She smiled slightly, grateful for this response. "You're telling me. Anyway, my aunt suggested this - coming here I mean. I think she'd already booked it for me before she called and offered," she said, realising this just at that very moment.

Aunt Carole had always had the knack of knowing just what Olivia needed before she knew it herself.

"Ah family, they do come in handy some days don't they?" Ben joked. He had taken her hint and pivoted away from her fiancé, and she realised he really was a true friend. A lot of people would have just kept prying.

"Yes, Aunt Carole is great. She has looked out for me ever since my folks died when I was sixteen. I had no idea what to expect when she offered. I've never been to a timeshare, much less in the Greek Islands."

She and Ben sipped their coffee for a little longer and then they both decided to call it a night.

Yet Olivia guessed that her confession had moved their relationship on from casual roommates to true friends.

She said goodnight and went into her room. It was stiflingly warm in there so she opened the window and for the first time since Ben's arrival, left her door open too.

She'd guessed from the outset that she didn't need to worry about him but now she knew for sure; Ben Norton was a true gentleman.

In the bathroom, she changed into a vest top and shorts and then climbed into bed, just lying there for a while before drifting off.

She enjoyed the faint sound of people still on the beach and of course the hypnotic sound of the waves lapping the shoreline.

Olivia fell asleep dreaming of a moonlit beach with sparkling waves and laughter while she walked hand in hand with a handsome stranger.

CHAPTER SIXTEEN

BEN WOKE up in the early hours of the morning when it was still dark so he got up, made some coffee and began writing.

His mind was now well and truly bursting with his story and he had to get it down.

A couple of hours after he got up he could hear Olivia stirring in the other room. He registered it but kept going; they had talked the day before about meeting for breakfast after her yoga, so he had plenty of time, and just let the story come together on the screen.

When he felt he had enough written, he leaned back and sipped the remaining coffee in his cup. It was stone cold.

He got up, stretched and went out to the living room, hardly able to believe he'd written so much in a single week. The book was almost halfway done already. Kim would be ecstatic.

Olivia had already left for the morning and looking at the clock, Ben realised he had stopped just in time.

He got cleaned up quickly and by the time he was ready to go, he was starving.

He trotted down the steps to the beach and returned a wave

from the couple with the dog. The sun was bright and the water had that shimmering crystal sheen he enjoyed so much.

He could see sailboats out on the water and even saw the big yacht they had chartered the day before. He waved, knowing they probably could not see him. The wave was more for himself.

He approached Olivia's yoga class just as it was ending. His timing was good, he told himself. She saw him and smiled, then trotted down to the sand to meet him.

"Morning Ben. You were up early, get much done?" she asked, as they began walking side by side along the beach. He watched some kids splashing in the surf before looking down at her.

"I did, it was great actually. Something about this place is so invigorating when it comes to writing," he told her.

Of course, he told himself, this place wasn't the only thing that invigorated him - he'd realised that for sure on the boat yesterday when he and Olivia had shared a moment just before she'd struggled to keep her hair under that hat.

Today she was wearing a patterned blouse tied at the waist and a matching skirt and sparkly sandals. Her hair was loose and blowing in the breeze, her eyes sparkled and she was the perfect picture of vibrancy.

Ben wanted to strangle the idiot fiancé who'd abandoned her and hurt her so.

Still, perhaps the guy's loss ...

"So you mentioned a good breakfast place?" he asked conversationally.

"Yep, it is just up here. Any ideas what you want to do afterwards?" she replied.

"I do. I seem to recall you also mentioning a comfy hammock on the beach somewhere along here. After a whole night up writing, sounds like an experience I need. It has literally been years since I took a nap in the daytime," he laughed.

"Yes, after all the work you've done this week, I think you deserve it. And after yesterday I am looking forward to mine too. Especially after a big breakfast. This place is the best for those," she said and pointed up to the beach.

There was another open-air café just a few minutes away. Beyond that, Ben saw a stand of palm trees and guessed that was where the hammocks must be.

He had never slept in a hammock either, but no doubt it would be an experience.

Everything involving Olivia tended to be.

CHAPTER SEVENTEEN

HOURS LATER, Ben awoke from his slumber to the sounds of seagulls, lapping water, and the breeze through the leaves of the trees.

He stretched and yawned. It was an amazing way to get some sleep, he had to admit.

At first, he had thought there was no way he could sleep out in the open in public and in a hammock of all things.

Yet after the full breakfast Olivia mentioned, he had settled in and dozed off to the same sounds he awoke to.

He carefully got out of the hammock, having seen a tourist flip out of one when they had arrived. Olivia was already awake and sitting in hers.

She was fluffing out her hair and he realised how much he enjoyed watching her do that. She was graceful in everything she did.

They spent the day wandering around the area - Ben enjoying his first well-earned day off in some time.

They took a bus across the island to a historical site similar to one they had seen from the water the day before, in which they found the crystalline stone and volcanic rock to be an interesting beautiful contrast.

They were shown a cave that was rumoured to have once been a haven for pirates which Ben found fascinating. Not to mention fun as he and Olivia joked in pirate for the rest of the afternoon, uttering "shiver me timbers" and "ay matey" with huge abandon and much laughter.

Later, they enjoyed another fantastic dinner at Hali's and after picking up a nice Greek wine, they both decided to head back to their veranda for the sunset.

They had enjoyed it so much from up there the night before they wanted to see it again.

So Ben found himself, feet up with a glass of wine watching a spectacular sunset next to a beautiful woman who had so effortlessly become his friend.

Not a bad way to end the day, he thought, taking a sip of his wine.

As the sun dropped lower the light did something different to the previous night. Instead of shooting up like a brief laser blast, this sunset spread itself out across the horizon in brilliant hues of red and orange and then slowly faded, leaving Ben and Olivia to admire the sparkling stars and reflection of the moon on the water.

"I never get tired of that," she said in awe.

"Me neither. It is amazing how we humans can forget things as simple yet majestic as the sunset," he said and held out his glass to her.

They clinked them together in a toast.

"To three more Santorini sunsets," Olivia said mournfully, obviously thinking of her imminent departure.

They had both since showered and changed from their daytime clothes: he was now wearing cotton slacks and a shirt and she was wearing a white vest top and a simple sarong wrapped around her waist.

Quite lovely, he thought. Again, he remembered what she had said about her ex's behaviour and could not make sense of it.

What an idiot...

"Each one is different, like a snowflake or a fingerprint," Olivia was saying about the sunset.

He glanced at her and smiled. "They are. I never thought about it but you are right. I guess with the sunset it all depends on atmospheric conditions and things like that but I prefer to think of it as a daily gift from the earth and the sun to those of us trapped in the gravity, unable to fly to the heavens," he said. Sunsets made him whimsical. Olivia made him want to sound romantic.

"You just made that up, didn't you?" she grinned.

"Yep."

"Well it was beautiful, thank you," she said and sipped her wine looking back out at the water.

"You are welcome. Whimsy keeps the world turning I think. As does romance."

They sipped their wine in silence for a moment, appreciating the way the moonlight changed with the movement of the waves.

"So Ben, have you ever been in love?" Olivia asked out of nowhere, and then looked startled as if she'd been thinking out loud.

He laughed at the look on her face.

"Sorry. That was one of those; the mouth moves faster than the brain episodes," she admitted.

He laughed at this description. "It is a fair question. Would you believe I was married at the tender age of eighteen? We were so in love," he said truthfully.

"What happened?" she asked.

"After two years we weren't anymore. Fortunately, we knew it before we brought kids into it. I would have been a crappy father anyway," he added, without remorse or rancour in his tone.

Olivia appeared to think about this and then finished her glass of wine. He offered her the bottle and she poured another, topping his up too.

"You know, I think as bad as Derek the Dick was, I am glad it all happened before the wedding, not after the vows and paperwork and all that," she said sounding thoughtful.

"Derek the dick huh? Figures. I was thinking he must have been some kind of idiot to mess that up. You are better off without him, Olivia. Like you said, better to find that crap out before you got married." He was trying to keep a little bit of humour in his voice because he was sure it had been a heart-rending experience for her.

She just nodded. "I am trying to think about it that way - now. For a while, I thought I had to have done something wrong to have that happen to me. I just couldn't figure out what," she continued.

He shook his head, feeling incredibly protective of her. "No, it was nothing to do with you and everything to do with the guy, who really does sound like a dick. And also, it seems to me the one I might also be mad at in a situation like that would be your so-called best friend?"

She smiled slightly and nodded.

"I was for a while. She had been a friend since my early years and I will never understand what got into her. Nor do I care at this point. This whole trip is already working out better and better in that respect. Whatever her issue was, she is welcome to it. I don't want anything more to do with either of them," she finished.

"Good for you. I know it must be tough and I won't pretend to understand all that you went through. I do think you are going about it right, though. Keep busy and let time work its magic. It may not heal all wounds but it does do a good job of letting them scab over when you are not thinking about it."

Ben finished his wine and reached for the bottle again.

"That is an apt description. No wonder you are a writer. Do all writers speak so descriptively?" she asked and he could hear honest curiosity in her voice.

"Some do, some are a little leery about coming across as too bookish. For me though, I am a writer and don't feel like hiding it. People can take me or leave me. I am glad you seem to like it though. I would hate to think I was getting on your nerves all the time. It would make the lodging situation even more awkward," he said chuckling.

They both laughed in the comfortable way of people who both knew that their situation wasn't the least bit awkward at all.

Quite the opposite.

CHAPTER EIGHTEEN

EARLY THE FOLLOWING MORNING, Olivia came out of her bedroom, wrapping her robe around her.

She could hear Ben on the phone in his room and the door was shut. She could not hear what he was saying, but he did not sound happy about it.

She went along and got some coffee he had made earlier, then went out on the veranda, shutting the sliding doors behind her.

She sipped her coffee and watched the moonlight twinkling on the surf in the darkness before the sun came up. It was almost as pretty as the night before.

Mornings and evenings on the veranda were a blessing of the cottage and with only a couple of mornings left, Olivia did not want to waste these precious opportunities.

After a few minutes, the door opened behind her.

"Morning Olivia," Ben said.

"Morning. Early business?" she asked curious as to why he would be on the phone before daylight.

"My agent called. If I could reach through the phone and flip her off I would have. My Greek publisher heard I am here and they are clamouring for some PR plus a meet and greet. Seems it would go a long way to opening my books up to a new audience, at least that is what I was told," he said and took a drink of his coffee. She could see the annoyance in his eyes.

"How would that open up the market for your books?" she asked reasonably.

"My US publishers are hoping to have the new one translated into Greek also. If I do this and make a big deal of the fact that I've written it here, it may help in that direction," he explained.

"I see. I guess that makes sense. When do they want you?" she asked.

"Today apparently, I'm leaving for Athens in an hour. It is highly irritating in the middle of a perfect workflow," he said.

She shrugged. "Well, from what I have heard, part of being a writer is not only in the writing but also in other people reading it, yes?"

He nodded but still didn't look too happy.

"I guess I should go. I'm also sorry to be missing one of your last few days here too. Can I maybe meet you for dinner at Hali's around seven?" he asked hopefully and Olivia smiled, realising at once that he seemed genuinely disappointed they wouldn't get to spend more time together.

But was it more than that? Could Ben be… interested in her? Or was he just being a good friend?

Before she could think too much more about it, he rushed off to get ready and make sure she had enough time to shower before her yoga class.

Even in his haste, Ben was thinking of her. He was a good guy and again, so utterly different to Derek it was incredible.

But felt wonderful.

CHAPTER NINETEEN

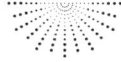

WHEN SHE FINISHED YOGA CLASS, Olivia went to breakfast and had a big plate of pancakes, Greek style. The meal was hugely filling and she felt like she was waddling to her hammock.

She decided to let it all settle a bit before lying back to snooze, so she checked the time in London and called her aunt.

"Hello darling, I hope everything is still working out OK with the double booking. Again, I am so sorry about that. I am milking it for everything I can from the management company though," Carole told her.

"All is well and we are milking it too. We have hardly had to pay for anything. It is working out great. Ben really is a nice guy - he just spends his days typing away while I am out and about. It works out fine. I just wanted to check in and see how you are doing," she told her.

"I am fine dear, and all the better now that I know all is working out. I thought it might be since I had not heard from you since. Are you having a good time otherwise?" Carole asked eagerly.

"I truly am and I owe you for this. This place is amazing, well you know that yourself. I am surprised you don't try and find a way to live here," she said, and Carole laughed.

"I thought about it but I would miss London too much. You might move there day, though," she said encouragingly.

"I am an accountant, Carole, I won't be buying a house on the cliffs of Santorini any time soon," Olivia joked and drank some lemon water.

"You never know, love. I am glad to hear you sound so good though. It sounds like the island is really working its magic on you and I am so happy about that. How are you feeling?" Olivia knew she was not asking if she had the flu.

"I am much better. Santorini is working its magic. Derek the Dick can go jump off a cliff for all I care. Actually, I am glad this whole thing happened when it did. As Ben pointed out, better before the wedding than after," she mumbled.

"You told your roommate about it?" Her aunt sounded surprised.

"Well, it is a small house. He is a nice guy, Carole. We're friends. He told me about his divorce if it helps any," she said and Carole laughed.

"I was just surprised I suppose. You can talk to whomever you want; you are a grown woman. I am glad you are making friends and it sounds like you are hooked on yoga too. Good for you, branching out. I am so proud of you and I hope the rest of your time there is as fun as it has been so far."

Olivia smiled, glad she had called her.

"Thanks and I hope all continues well with you. I have nap time scheduled on my hammock now and I don't want to keep you," she said.

"Okay darling, I will talk to you when you get back but until then, brilliant to hear from you," she said.

Olivia bid her beloved aunt goodbye and they both hung up.

Smiling she leaned back in her hammock and closed her eyes, feeling content.

It was not long before she fell asleep.

In her dreams she was rocking in a hammock with Ben laughing about something, she did not know what.

All Olivia knew was that she was incredibly happy and Derek the Dick was but a distant memory.

CHAPTER TWENTY

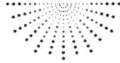

AFTER HER NAP, time seemed to drag.

She walked the beach but couldn't find anything that sounded fun to do. About mid-afternoon she realised if Ben was not getting back until late, Hali's might be full.

She moved further up the hill away from the sound of the surf and called the restaurant.

"Hi, I was wondering if you took reservations for tables?" she asked the man on the phone.

"Of course. When would you like it for," he asked.

"Great, I was thinking about seven-thirty this evening. The little table by the olive tree near the beach, would that one be available?" she asked hopefully.

"Ah of course. Your table will be ready for you at seven. Is there anything else I can help you with?" he asked politely.

"That will be it. Thank you for your help," she told him.

She was glad she'd thought of it. It would have been a pain to meet Ben there tonight and be unable to get a seat. She sighed and looked around the beach.

The sparkling blue water looked inviting and Olivia decided it was time for a swim.

Wading out into the water felt good and she swam around for a while, but all too quickly it seemed that too lost its excitement for her.

She trudged back up the beach, laid her towel out and stretched out on it to dry off and get some sun.

After about an hour she then got up and went to the little shower stands to shower off after swimming. She had not used them before and found them quite handy. She rinsed off the seawater and combed out her hair, letting her one-piece bathing suit dry in the sun while she put on jean shorts and a vest.

Olivia strolled back down the town, then stopped at a deli and got a Danish with a coffee. She sat under an awning and people watched for another hour before heading down the beach again.

She was feeling fretful and restless today and she did not know why.

It was weird and she wondered if she was coming down with something. She didn't feel sick, just out of sorts.

She sighed and found a bench higher up on the beach, pulled out a book and read for an hour, and found that she enjoyed just sitting and reading. Perhaps that was her problem.

She had been going non-stop since she got here, always exploring or looking for something to do other than the hammock nap, she hadn't really just idled around, doing nothing in particular.

It was about five o'clock then, and she walked up to the little bar down from Hali's, ordered wine and pulled out her book.

It was a historical mystery Ben had recommended that she was finding very engaging.

She read until almost six-thirty and then realised she should go down to Hali's to check on the reservation.

As she approached the taverna she saw the young man who had bumped into her chair that first night. He was leaving with two women on his arm and smiled mischievously at her as she passed. He was a busy boy, she thought humorously.

Then she saw Ben strolling up the beach and her smile widened. Olivia picked up the pace to meet him halfway. He was smiling too.

"Hey Ben, did you have a nice meet and greet, or whatever it was?" she asked and he laughed. He was looking a little tense, but now he seemed to visibly relax.

"It was okay. Thankfully most of the people I met spoke some English or it would have been all through translators. How has your day been?" he asked as they walked back towards Hali's.

"Good. I kept it a little slow today. Enjoyed just idling around. Missed you though."

And that was it, she realised suddenly, feeling a little embarrassed. That was why she'd been so unsettled today.

She'd been missing Ben.

He laughed and gave her a one-armed hug, obviously not in the least bit discomfited or embarrassed about her admission.

"Hungry?" he asked, as they entered the taverna and Ramone the waiter gestured them to the table. If she hadn't reserved it, they would not have had a table at all and she was doubly glad for the forethought.

They ordered some wine, and after the usual study of the menu, they ordered dinner and leaned back to relax.

Olivia immediately felt better and more relaxed than she'd been all day. Ben offered up a toast to a good evening and she returned it eagerly, lifting her glass to his, wondering how she was going to feel the day after tomorrow when her trip came to an end and she wouldn't see him ever again.

Was she falling for Ben?

CHAPTER TWENTY-ONE

JUST THEN, the food arrived and Olivia couldn't think about it any longer. She had chosen the broiled fish and he had gone with the lamb stew. They were both trying what the other had eaten the last time here. They laughed over that, as they did everything lately, and dug into the food.

It was the usual excellent quality they had become used to. She told him about swimming and walking the beach and he went over his day with her.

His sounded a lot more exciting, if a little frustrating.

"So after the short flight to Athens, I waited for two hours before seeing the publicity manager who had wanted me to come. Now as you know, I have certain ... tendencies when I don't eat. I can get a little cranky. I managed to hold it together for the guy, signed a few books and did some press, but by the time lunchtime came and went I was seriously thinking of letting my sarcasm loose on him. Fortunately, I had some time before the meet and greet with the publishers so I snuck off and went to a nearby café and ate the first thing on the menu. Would you believe it; it was a good old-fashioned American hamburger," he said with a laugh.

"A hamburger in a Greek café?" Olivia chuckled.

"I know, right? It didn't occur to me it was odd until I was halfway through. It was not jazzed up Greek style or anything. Just your typical bacon cheeseburger and it was delicious. After I stuffed my face I asked the waiter and he said it was on the menu for shy tourists who have not experienced the greatness of Greek cuisine. Or something like that. He did not speak English well and of course, I don't speak Greek at all. Anyway, after that I went back to the conference building and the handlers were freaking out. I guess I was supposed to stay out and they had lost me. I apologised and pointed out that no one had told me not to go anywhere, or even that I had handlers. They saw how that could create some confusion and accepted my apology. Then I met with about thirty people and took pictures and signed books for an hour or so. When I left everyone seemed happy. So overall it was a productive day in that sense. I would have preferred doing more exploring with you, but life does intrude sometimes," he finished and then forked up the last of his thick stew.

Olivia was laughing. "So I will keep in mind that if you ever get cranky with me, all I need to do is suggest a restaurant," she joked, and he chuckled and squeezed her hand, sending a flood of warmth from her head to the tips of her toes.

"Already you know me so well."

As they finished up and left the restaurant there was a commotion on the beach about a half mile down.

It looked like some people were setting up some kind of display, but as they got closer Olivia and Ben realised there was a group of hot air balloonists setting up multicoloured balloons with baskets for passengers.

"The experience of a lifetime!" the Greek hawker intoned. "Consider the views of the caldera and volcano at dusk from above. Consider the peace to be found in a higher elevation alongside with the birds," he continued.

A dubious-looking tourist stepped up. "Doesn't the wind off the water make it hard to fly the things?" he asked.

"Good question," Ben murmured and Olivia giggled.

"Ah my good man, you are most observant. You have no doubt also seen how once the sun goes down, the air currents cool and the wind dies off. That is why for a beach takeoff, we wait until dusk. The amazing coincidence is that it also makes for a much more romantic trip for you and your loved one, eh?" The persuasive Greek grinned as he said this along with a sweeping, grand gesture. He was going for the hard sell.

"Not a bad pitch actually. He may even be right about the breezes at night. They do calm down," Olivia commented to Ben.

"Yeah, I wouldn't mind trying it some night. I wonder if they are going to be around for long," he mused, then stepped forward to the eager balloon trip salesman. "Excuse me, sir. Will you be here tomorrow night?" he asked.

"Of course, we are here for five more nights to serve your romantic holiday needs," he said smiling at Olivia, who could not help laughing a little. The guy was pushing it.

"Thanks, I may be back some night," Ben told the man and stepped back alongside Olivia. "It could be fun, but not tonight? I would rather have a glass on our veranda."

She nodded, pleased at how easily he had referred to it as 'our veranda'.

"Sounds like a good end to the day. Besides, we will have a front-row seat for these taking off. See how well they do before risking it," she pointed out logically.

He grinned. "Nice thinking. Do we need to stop off to pick up some wine first?"

CHAPTER TWENTY-TWO

THEY HEADED off and by the time sunset had begun Ben and Olivia were back on the veranda with a glass and some cookies to munch on.

As usual, they stood together at the railing to watch the sunset.

Olivia noticed that again, this one was different from the previous nights. Instead of covering the horizon or a straight line downward, the glorious red and orange hues seemed to come off the water in majestic star patterns that took her breath away.

She and Ben watched in silence as the patterns brightened, glaring and beautiful and then slowly faded over several minutes until it was gone.

"Oh, look they are going to start filling the balloons. I am glad they waited, the flames would have been a distraction," he said pointing to the beach below and to the right twenty yards or so.

He was right. They watched men and women with flashlights setting up the furnaces that would fill the balloons and then fire them up. The whooshing sound of the furnace was powerful and seemed to echo up from the beach. It created a dramatic atmosphere as they watched, sipping their wine.

"I bet that is loud as hell in the basket when they are flying," Ben said.

"I hadn't thought of that, but you are right. Then again once you are up it is more a matter of them just blasting it now and then. I watched them fly out of Edinburgh once. It wasn't at night though, this should be good," she said.

Ben nodded in agreement then grabbed a few cookies and handed her one. She nibbled on the chocolate and sipped her wine as one by one, the balloons filled slowly, like the stirring of a long-sleeping dragon.

The breeze had died down to almost nothing, and sure enough, they got to watch each one take off with two passengers per ride.

It was an amazing sight and Olivia was glad they had not rushed to try it without watching it first. Each balloon was different and beautiful in its own way.

The first to go up was dark except for star-shaped patterns that were clear and let the light from the furnace shine through.

As it took off each burst of the furnace lit up the star patterns in the night sky and it floated up right in front of their balcony, then slowly took off down the beach from a few hundred feet in the air.

The second had a giant butterfly pattern, one on each side, so shaped that the wings looked like thinly veined delicate wings that again lit up with every burst of the balloon's furnace.

The crowd on the beach cheered and they could hear shouts from the balloon's passengers too. The last one was dark with pinpoints, like stars in the sky all over its surface. So it looked like a globe of stars as it rose and then followed the other two down the beach.

Olivia and Ben watched them all until they were out of sight and she sighed contentedly as they sat back down.

Ben poured them both another glass of wine.

"That was amazing. First the sunset, and then the majesty of the balloons. I am not sure if I want to take a ride and miss watching the take offs though. I have never seen balloons take flight before, it is amazing," he said, still memorised by the experience.

"I know what you mean. I did watch them in Scotland, but in daylight. They were still beautiful, but nothing like this. Santorini is still full of surprises, isn't it? I am glad we got to see it," she said.

But Olivia was especially glad she got to witness it with Ben. She thought briefly that Derek would have talked through the whole thing, as was his way, spoiling it.

Ben was head and shoulders a better man than her ex.

Neither of them had spoken while it was happening, but having a companion seemed to make the experience all the more special. That and the sunsets were something they'd shared together.

Indeed this whole trip was becoming a shared experience, and all the better for it, Olivia realised.

Ben's dark eyes glinted in the little lights they had on the table between them.

"Isn't this just the perfect spot to end a day?" he said as if reading her mind. "Two of us sharing our day's adventures with a glass of wine and an amazing view."

Olivia couldn't be sure, but she thought he was looking at her when he said the words 'amazing view'.

Then he cleared his throat and looked back out at the sea

and she felt herself blush. He seemed embarrassed by the comment now, and she looked away so as not to compound his discomfort.

She knew she was being ridiculous, considering she had just come off of a bad separation, but she was attracted to Ben.

Derek was so far out of her mind right then, that there was no way this could be a rebound situation.

Ben had looked at her with more than just friendship in his eyes - she was sure of it - and she felt the same way herself when she looked at him.

Maybe it was the wine, or maybe just the fact that she was on holiday, but there and then Olivia realised something important.

She was well and truly over Derek.

CHAPTER TWENTY-THREE

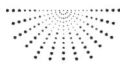

BEN WOKE EARLY and immediately began writing after his first cup of coffee. He had so many ideas that it flowed quickly.

He heard Olivia's usual soft steps as she got ready and then left for her sunrise yoga.

He had thought about going along with her one of the days but decided they both needed their personal time, and yoga was a spiritual thing.

She never spoke of it beyond how much she enjoyed it.

For his part, he was glad to get another early start to the day so he could spend some more time with Olivia. They had discussed their day's plans and had decided to go shopping, purely for the fun of it.

Ben had seen an open-air market yesterday on his ride from the house to the airport and wanted to see it on foot. She liked the idea so when the time came, he finished up the chapter he was on and got cleaned up for the day.

Today, he wore shorts and a loose shirt with sandals, unlike yesterday when he'd had to wear a suit, which he resented and made him feel like he was back in New York having boring meetings with his publishers and agent.

Santorini was amazing and he had begun to wonder if buying a place here might be a good idea. Sure, he would still have to spend some time in the Big Apple for work, but he would not mind spending the bulk of his time in such an enchanting place.

He was most definitely thinking of extending his time on Santorini in any case. Maybe even write his whole book here? With the success of his last few, it was not like he couldn't afford it. But of course, it wasn't just the island that held an attraction to him.

He realised for sure the previous day - when he'd had to spend time away from the island - that he was becoming very attached to Olivia. She was energetic, cheerful and more fun to be around than anyone he had ever met.

Not to mention that she was beautiful, funny and smart as well as compassionate.

He guessed that she had realised his attraction at one point the night before, and hoped she might feel the same, but due to her recent past with her ex, Derek the dick, he did not want to presume anything.

Still, tomorrow would be her last night and their time together was running out....

As he approached the yoga group he saw Olivia and waved.

No, he told himself, just wait and see what happens. Don't rush her.

He had no intention of destroying a perfectly good friendship.

"Breakfast and shopping then?" she smiled, coming up to him. She looked energetic and ready to go. Ben smiled back. He always smiled around her.

"Yep. I am looking forward to it. I can't imagine what sort of things the shops will have here, but I can't wait to find out."

They walked up the beach on the way for breakfast and she told him about the sunrise.

"It is a little different from our sunsets because the sun is rising behind us, over the island. It is kind of cool though, how the beach slowly lights up. Like slowly turning up the light controls in a room. Gradually getting stronger until it shines on the day," she said and he noticed that she had these cute little dimples that he had never spotted before.

They took an outside table in the shade at a nearby cafe.

"Now who is speaking like a writer?" he joked. "Lovely description, nice job."

"Thanks. Coming from a professional writer that is a compliment," she said, picking up the menu. "I must warn you, I tried the pancakes yesterday and I would advise against it unless you want to be weighed down for a few hours. I'm serious, they're great but would slow down a cheetah," she added.

"Good advice. My usual is heavy enough. I think I'll stick with the potatoes and veggie plate."

CHAPTER TWENTY-FOUR

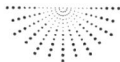

AFTER BREAKFAST, they skipped the hammock nap until after the shopping and soon found themselves walking down the streets through charming cobblestone courtyards.

Most of the houses and businesses looked identical: painted the same bright white with red brick edging and tumbling bougainvillaea.

The gardens were bright and colourful and when they came upon the market square it was even brighter with banners and wafting scents of cooking food.

Olivia and Ben looked at each other with anticipation, both obviously thinking: *This is going to be fun.* He liked the idea that they were so easily able to communicate without words.

He enjoyed watching her barter too. Coming from the States, he was used to the sticker price being what you paid for things.

Whereas Olivia had travelled enough around France and Spain to have picked up a talent for bartering. She was good, as far as he could tell, so he let her do the talking and she always brought the sellers down from their original asking price.

They mostly bought little keepsakes; Olivia picked up some things for her aunt and Ben found some wonderful hand-carved pens for his office.

He did very little handwriting anymore but he'd always preferred it to typing and had been wanting to get back into note-taking.

This trip was the first time he had done it in some time, and it was good for his creative juices, so maybe the pens would help him get even more motivated in that regard.

They finished up buying some fresh bread and a few bottles of some local wine that was recommended by a restauranteur at lunchtime. They were going to try it that evening on the veranda at their usual sunset-watching.

Walking back towards the beach with their packages in the afternoon was just as enjoyable. They greeted people they did not know and laughed at two little dogs playing in someone's garden.

Just a relaxing time with a person Ben was growing more and more to like and respect for her easy-going adventurous spirit.

He was also becoming more and more aware of her beauty. He had always been aware of Olivia's beauty of course; he wasn't blind, but now he was catching himself looking at her more in appreciation and attraction.

Her hair was wild, and during their walk back was constantly being pushed back from her eyes.

She was wearing shorts, a vest top and a little sweater over it. It was casual, yet she wore it like a princess in a modern-day fairy tale. She caught him looking at her and smiled slightly before blushing and looking away.

That was a good sign, wasn't it?

. . .

Eventually, they made it back to the hammock place along the beach and with a sigh settled in with cocktails and the sea in front of them.

Ben now understood how this shaded little piece of the paradise around them was so attractive to Olivia.

She put her hands behind her head and closed her eyes.

He lay back too, and for a while just watched the passing tourists down on the sand.

His eyes kept going back to Olivia though, relaxing in her hammock. Her heart-shaped face was smiling slightly and her breathing was deep and even. She was the picture of health and happiness, at least in his eyes.

Beautiful and relaxed.

Just taking the day as it came with no stress or mess. She was an admirable woman and he put his own hands behind his head and closed his eyes.

Ben could still see her as he drifted off into a pleasant dream of beach adventures with his friend.

Wondering if it was becoming more.

Hoping it would.

The two dozed on longer than anticipated and realised that getting a table for dinner may be difficult.

They also still had their packages to carry up to the cottage, as well as getting changed for dinner and that would take time.

It was a dilemma, but only for a moment.

"Olivia, I wonder if Hali's deliver?" Ben asked and she grinned widely.

"That is a brilliant idea. I think they do actually, because I've seen employees rushing out with orders. I hadn't thought about that. Genius." She began digging through her purse for her phone.

"If they are willing to take an order, I will have the same as last night," he told her. He had loved the broiled fish.

She gave him a thumbs-up as she held the phone to her ear. He listened to her talk to the staff at Hali's and order the food they wanted.

"Maybe an hour," she said into the phone, glancing at him for confirmation. He figured an hour would be good timing and nodded. They were almost back to the cottage as it was.

"Great, thanks," she finished up and then turned to Ben. "We will have it in an hour. Let's haul this stuff up and get organised," she said and picked up the pace to the path up the hill under their veranda.

Ben noticed then that she had a slight limp and wondered about it, but did not mention it. No doubt she would if it was important.

CHAPTER TWENTY-FIVE

"The shower is all yours," he said when they reached the cottage. "I will put some of this stuff away and keep an eye out in case the food is early."

Ben stored the bread, stacked Olivia's purchases by her bedroom door, and then put his stuff away.

Next, he opened the wine and let it breathe.

When Olivia came back out of the bathroom she was already dressed and sent him off to the shower in turn.

By the time dinner arrived, they were both more than ready for it and shared a glass of the most excellent wine, with a name Ben could not pronounce to save his life.

They had decided that trying to spread their feast out comfortably on the small patio table would not work, so they used the table in the cottage to eat on.

It was at the window so they still had a view and a light sea breeze.

They ate hungrily and finished just in time to go out on the patio to watch the sunset and the balloons.

He noticed as they went out that she was limping a little

more. He could not help but glance down at her bare foot as they stood at the balcony and Olivia noticed him looking.

"I think I twisted my ankle on a cobblestone along the market path," she told him grimacing. "The shower seemed to help, but after sitting for dinner it has begun aching. I am sure it is nothing though," she assured him.

"Are you sure? I had to spend time with a massage therapist for research once and learned all sorts of things. Apparently rubbing it and stretching the muscle helps to keep it from staying injured longer," he told her, a little nervously.

Though he did want to help, he hoped she wouldn't think the offer of a massage was weird or inappropriate.

She smiled. "Maybe I'll try it after the sunset, thanks," she said and as they turned away to watch the nightly theatre they both fell silent.

Watching the sunset together had very quickly become a pleasant, yet solemn occasion for them both. An important ritual in some way beyond the beauty of it.

Once again the display was different to the night before.

Ben watched and sipped his wine as the sun got lower and lower. He did not know if somewhere in the distance there was an atmospheric condition that was muting the usual brightness, but the red-orange color was duller, fading as the light did.

Then, just before it went out of sight it burst through in one bright brilliant blast of colour and they both gasped.

"Wow," Olivia sighed softly. He looked over at her, and she was still looking out at the water with an unreadable expression on her face.

Wow indeed, he thought, no longer thinking about the sunset.

CHAPTER TWENTY-SIX

As the sun faded, they sat down for the balloon launch. Olivia bent her leg up and massaged her ankle while sitting cross-legged in her chair.

"Just trying to get some circulation back," she told him and Ben realised having her legs folded up like that was probably awkward for her to work on her ankle herself.

"I can give it a go at massaging it for you now if you'd like?" he suggested.

Olivia swivelled in her seat slightly, swinging her leg over to him.

Trying his utmost not to react to this oddly intimate situation, Ben adjusted his position with her ankle on his knee and tried to remember what he had learned from the massage therapist.

Her skin felt so soft to the touch and he gulped a little, wondering what it would be like to run his hands all over her body.

Resisting the temptation to do just that, Ben tenderly

massaged Olivia's ankle and foot as the second balloon finished filling and rose up in front of them.

As he did, they munched on some of the cookies they had gotten the day before and were still fresh.

Ben had no idea why the food on Santorini was so good but he had stopped wondering about it and just accepted it. Like so many things on this trip, he was pleasantly surprised but did not need to analyse too closely.

He just wanted to enjoy it and take in all the wonderful stimuli he could.

"So did you enjoy the shopping trip?" Olivia asked when he'd finished. "That was brilliant, thank you."

"Watching you negotiate was an education," he chuckled. "I may write some of it down tonight for future reference. This whole island feels like a fairy tale coming to life. How does your ankle feel?" he asked, as she gently rotated it herself.

Then she stood up, took a few steps and turned back with a smile.

"It does not hurt at all now. I think you did it - you're a genius," she exclaimed happily and spun in place again, before reaching over for her wine glass.

He got up too and they stood at the railing shoulder to shoulder as the light faded, watching the people on the beach packing up their gear and going to wherever the balloons were going to land.

A little way down some people had started a beach fire.

"You know I think this book is going to be some of my best work," Ben said thoughtfully. "Something about this island, even with the summer tourists and crowds, there is something so *right* about the place that it tugs at me. Everything I have experienced has been amazing. Except maybe the lost luggage," he added and she laughed.

"I know exactly what you mean. And I'll be sorry to leave the day after tomorrow - for more reasons than one," she added, and after a beat turned to look at him.

Ben met her gaze then and out of the blue gently put his arm around her.

She did not resist, and they stood together quietly at the railing, drinking in the magnificent view and listening to the revelry on the beach.

Ben liked that it was far enough away to not be too loud, but close enough to enjoy it.

It was then that he realised that Olivia's eyes were glistening in the late evening sunlight, and she looked desperately sad.

"What is it?" he asked, dropping his arm quickly, worried now he'd come on too strong.

"It's nothing ... it's just, this trip really has been more incredible than I could ever have imagined."

"I know."

"And ... tomorrow is my last full day, and I don't want to say goodbye. To Santorini ... these wonderful sunsets ... you."

At this, she turned to face him directly, and Ben's heart soared.

Olivia had never been impulsive, not on this level but saying out loud what she was thinking just then felt so right she decided to just go with her instincts.

What she had said was true; she did not want to say goodbye to any of this, least of all Ben, whom she'd now well and truly fallen for.

"I was worried about how you were feeling, but then I felt well...maybe..." he murmured, stammering to a halt as he turned to face her and took both her hands in his.

They looked into each other's eyes and for Olivia, everything

313

around them seemed to fade into the distance - it was just them in that moment.

Ben had a soft smile on his face as he bent his head, and their lips finally met for a delicious first kiss that was filled with promise, while all around them Santorini was bathed in a golden glow.

"I think, much like the balloons, we should just take advantage of the atmospheric conditions and see what happens," Ben said, a gentle smile on his face. "It can't hurt, can it?"

"You're absolutely right," she said, beaming back at him. "Let's just see where the wind takes us."

But balloons aside, Olivia already felt like she was floating on air, and knew that no matter what the future held, this particular Santorini sunset was one she and Ben would treasure forever.

ABOUT THE AUTHOR

International #1 and USA Today bestselling author Melissa Hill lives in County Wicklow, Ireland.

Her page-turning emotional stories of family, friendship and romance have been translated into 25 different languages and are regular chart-toppers internationally.

A Reese Witherspoon x Hello Sunshine adaptation of her worldwide bestseller SOMETHING FROM TIFFANY'S is airing now on Amazon Prime Video worldwide.

THE CHARM BRACELET aired in 2020 as a holiday movie 'A Little Christmas Charm'. A GIFT TO REMEMBER (and a sequel) was also adapted for screen by Crown Media and multiple other titles by Melissa are currently in development for film and TV.

www.melissahill.info

Printed in Great Britain
by Amazon

POEMS FROM POOLE

POEMS FROM POOLE

Peter Phillips

Peter Phillips

First published in Great Britain in 2023 by

Peter Phillips

Salterns Road, Poole, Dorset, BH14 8BJ.

ISBN: 979-8-85392059-0

$$P_{eter} \; P_{hillips}$$

mail@peter-phillips.co.uk

https://peter-phillips.co.uk

*To Fiona, and to A, O, A and S,
with appreciation and thanks for your
love and encouragement.*

CONTENTS

vi

Introduction

Most of the poems in this volume are firmly rooted with a sense of place, often inspired by my observations while out walking. And the place that has inspired me the most is the place where I walk the most: Poole in Dorset, where I live and where my daily walk often takes me through Poole Park and alongside Poole Harbour at Whitecliff. So I've titled this volume *Poems from Poole*, although it also includes poems inspired by other places, and a few poems exploring Christian themes.

All the poems in this volume were composed between July 2022 and July 2023. Many of them reflect the season in which they were written, so I've presented them here in a seasonal journey from January to December. But you are free, of course, to dip in and out as you choose.

I hope you enjoy at least some of these poems. I welcome comments or feedback through my website at https://peter-phillips.co.uk/poems/

Peter Phillips,
Poole, July 2023.

New Year's Day (Observed)

Constitution Hill, Monday 2nd January 2023

See the Sea View
From Constitution Hill.
Poole spread below us,
Harbour, Park and Town:
Hamworthy, Longfleet,
Parkstone, Sandbanks.

Gaze to the distance
Beyond Brownsea,
Where Old Harry heads
The Purbeck Hills.
Corfe stands in the gap,
A castle in the mist.

Stir your soul,
Look beyond the view
To him who made
Earth and sea and sky,
The source of the light
That shines from the sun.

Greet the New Year,
Opportunity beckons.
He stands and knocks -

Who will open their door?
Whoever welcomes him
Will receive the crown
Of eternal life
On New Year's Day.

The Gull and the Ball

In the park, a herring gull
Found a purple plastic ball,
Pecked at it,
Picked it up in its beak,
Dropped it,
Pecked at it some more.

What did the gull think?
Was the ball edible?
Was it an egg, perhaps,
From a large purple goose?
Or was it just a plaything?
An interesting diversion
To liven up a dull morning?

The gull guarded the ball
Against all comers:
Other gulls, a crow,
All chased vigorously away.
'This is my ball.
I found it first.
Go away!'

An elderly couple
Stood next to me
Watching the gull.
We took photos.

We asked each other
What it might be thinking.
The gull ignored us,
Intent on its ball.

We parted without answers
And went on our ways.
The gull simply went on
Pecking and probing
Its purple plastic ball.

Apologies for the very-poor-quality photo!

Ask

"Ask," he said,
"Ask and you will receive.
Ask for anything; I will do it."

In the desert, in days of old,
They asked.
He gave them bread from heaven
In abundance,
Water gushed from the rock
Like a river.

He will supply every need,
From his riches in glory,
Pressed down,
Shaken together,
Running over,
Poured into your lap.

He came to serve,
To suffer,
To bear our sins,
To die.

To be raised
From the dead,
To ascend into heaven,
To return in glory.

He came to give life,
Abundant life,
Freedom life,
Eternal life.

You have not,
Because you ask not.
You ask and receive not,
Because you ask wrongly.

What shall I ask?
How shall I ask?
Delight in him,
Receive your heart's desire.

"Ask," he said,
"Ask, and you will receive.
Seek, and you will find,
Knock, and it will open."

"Ask," he said,
"Ask in my name."
Ask.

Poole Park in Early Spring

Sunday 19th February 2023

Mid-February. A sunny Sunday afternoon.
The first warm day of the year.
The people of Poole head to the Park,
Eager to take the air.

The playgrounds are full of young children
Joyfully running about,
Jumping, swinging, balancing, climbing,
With laughter and happy shouts.

Couples and families, young and old,
Promenade round the lagoon,
Walking, jogging, scootering, cycling,
Enjoying the afternoon.

A queue for the ice creams, a queue for the train,
All cheerfully waiting their turn,
Some sit on benches, with chips, coffee or tea,
And soak up the early spring sun.

After winter months of cold and grey
All of us agree:
When the first day of Spring arrives,
Poole Park is the place to be!

Tidal Crows

Whitecliff, March 2023

Crows at low tide, inventive and clever,
Black beaks probing the mud to find
Cockles, whelks, slipper limpets.
They seize the prize, then fly up high
To drop the poor mollusc
Onto the hard tarmac path,
Again and again,
Until the shell finally cracks,
And the crow can enjoy the tasty treasure therein.

Crows at high tide, irritable and listless,
Flapping about on the sea wall,
Croaking, quarrelling,
Brooding, bickering,
Watching the water,
Waiting for the tide to turn,
Envious of the gulls and waders,
Until the mud dries out enough
For the crows to return to their treasure hunt.

On the First Day of March, the Harbour sent to me...

Whitecliff, 1st March 2023

As I walked by the harbour on St David's Day,
Among the ubiquitous black-headed gulls,
I noticed some more unusual rarities.
I looked through my binoculars, and saw:

Five tufted ducks,
    With bright golden eyes,
    Diving soundlessly, then
    Swimming underwater
    For ten or fifteen seconds
    Before bobbing up again
    Without a splash.
    Two females, three males,
    One destined to be left,
    Disappointed.

Four redshanks,
    Paddling purposefully
    In the shallows.
    Long red shanks
    And a long red beak,
    Half-dipped in the water,
    Scanning from side to side
    As they wade on their way.

Three cormorants,
        Wings outstretched
        To dry in the sun?
        Or just to show off?
        Perched proudly on posts,
        Standing erect,
        Beaks held high,
        Like old men with pipes.

Two black-backed gulls,
        Sitting smugly
        On the breakwater,
        Resplendent in black,
        Plump and aloof,
        Looking down on
        Their numerous
        grey-winged cousins.

One Brent goose
        With a fine white collar,
        Floating on the water,
        All alone.
        Where's the flock?
        Has it been left behind
        In the migration north
        To the breeding grounds?

I walked home feeling thankful
For the variety of God's creation,
For the gifts: five, four, three, two, one,
That the harbour sent to me
On St David's Day.

DH Evans, Y Siopwr Mawr

Pontsian, Ceredigion, 18th March 2023

David Hugh Evans
Was famed throughout West Wales.
They called him 'Y Siopwr Mawr',
'The Grand Shopkeeper'.

He built in his image a model village,
With stores and industry and much more,
At a quiet spot in Ceredigion,
A hamlet called Pontsian.

In 1879, he knocked down the little shop
And built a bigger, better one.
And not just a shop, but a general store
And a post office
And a woollen mill
And a corn mill
All in a row,
With a nice house at the end
For Mr Evans to live in.

Soon he was selling anything and everything
From ovens to coffin nails,
Cloths, bicycles, animal feeds, dynamite,
Even Pontsian-branded tea.

One store was not enough for Y Siopwr Mawr.
He built a granary and seed store over the road,
And cottages and houses
For his workers and managers.

He added a generator to provide electricity
Thirty years before any other village nearby.
He had the only telephone for miles around;
He was king of his castle.

But we all are mortal,
And when his time came,
David Hugh Evans left Pontsian
To his granddaughter.

Over the years, the mills closed down,
The granary lay empty,
The cottages sold off
One by one.

Only the shop survived
Into the twenty-first century,
Before it too succumbed
To the inevitable.

But the buildings stand strong,
Built from good Welsh stone,
Now grade-II listed as
'Unusually interesting' -
'A Victorian industrial group in a rural setting.'

So the memory of Y Siopwr Mawr lives on
In the buildings he built,
Some restored as period dwellings,
And The Granary Cottage available
To rent from Airbnb.

Pontsian, Ceredigion was developed as a mini-model village by an ambitious young shopkeeper called David Hugh Evans. After an apprenticeship in what was then a new-fangled department store, he returned to Pontsian in 1876 with grand ambitions. Together with his father, a stonemason, he set about constructing a new village, knocking down the old shop and replacing it with a 200ft-long stone building housing a woollen mill, general store, corn mill and post office. He also built homes for managers and workers.

By the Twenties, the village had a generator, providing power for the inhabitants 30 years before most other places in the area, and the shop sold everything from coffin nails to ovens, cloth, feedstuffs, dynamite, Pontsian brand tea and bicycles. They delivered all round the region and had the only telephone for miles, so they controlled news of all types.

DH Evans was known locally as Y Siopwr Mawr, "the grand shopkeeper". Since his death, the properties in the village have gradually been sold and restored as period homes and holiday cottages. The shop itself continued to operate as a convenience store until it finally closed in 2022.

Pontsian in about 1890 and in 2023.
(1890 photo from http://pint-of-
history.wales/explore.php?func=showimage&id=1524)

Brimstones

Salterns Road, 4th April 2023

A flash of yellow golden wing,
In the April sun, dancing;
We welcome the good news they bring,
Heralding the spring.

Though they seem so delicate,
All winter long they hibernate,
Waiting for the right climate
To wake up, fly off and find a mate.

They emerge early every year,
Fluttering here, there, everywhere,
The first butterflies to appear,
Spreading to all their golden cheer.

Whitecliff in April

Breeze-blown clouds
Scud across the blue sky.
The view to Corfe crisp, clean,
Scoured by successive showers.

Bright white blossom
Adorns the black thorns.
Catkins dance
At the tips of leafless twigs.

Gulls and oyster-catchers
Wade in wind-washed wavelets.
Woolly-hatted walkers
Warmly wrapped in coat and gloves.

Then, all scurry for cover
As the next mighty shower cloud
Storms in from the sea
To lash the land with April rain, again.

Violets

Brockenhurst, 22nd April 2023

Tiny, intricate,
Fragile, delicate,
Precious purple petals
Pierce the dark forest floor
Like sparkling sapphires scattered
Among the leaf mould.

*(Apologies to those reading the printed version of this
book. The photo is more effective in colour!)*

Bird Haikus

Cheerful chirrup above my head,
Bright flashes of yellow and red -
Goldfinch.

Cormorant - perched on a pole,
Alert, erect,
Like a guardsman on duty.

Greylags, mallards, swans, moorhens
All paired-up in the park -
Mating season.

Two proud parents, dressed in white,
Six playful toddlers, fluffy and grey -
Swans and cygnets.

Dandelion Seeds

Salterns Road, 13th May 2023

In the breeze,
Flying, floating,
Dancing, drifting,
Tiny, downy,
tufts of fluff,
Mini-parachutes
Each bearing
A precious package,
A microscopic seed,
Dull, brown,
Insignificant,
Almost invisible,
Yet full of potential,
Packed with power
From our Creator
To reproduce
After its kind.
They come to rest
Unnoticed
In beds, in lawns,
In cracks between
Paving slabs.
They lie still,
Unnoticed,
Until woken

By sun and rain,
To send down roots,
To sprout up leaves,
To grow from nothing
Into strong plants,
Significant,
Noticeable,
Nearly impossible
To uproot.
We call it a weed
We wish it away
But why fight it?
Why not enjoy
The miracle of life
That God has packed
Into every tiny
Tuft of fluff
Blowing in the breeze?

Dartmoor Panorama

Gibbet Hill, Black Down, Mary Tavy. 1st May 2023.

First things first...
A patch of soft, springy turf,
Hot coffee from the flask,
A chocolate cake bar.

Then...
We spread out the map,
Consult Google on the phone,
Observe the 360-view,
Identifying landmarks.

Devon lies before us,
A patchwork of greens and browns,
Sun-dazzled and dappled by
Shape-shifting cloud-shadows.

Dartmoor dominates the scene,
Wild and desolate to the North,
Great Links Tor, Sharp Tor, Hare Tor,
Massive, steep, forbidding.

Next the deep, steep zig-zag of Tavy Cleave,
Wild and free near its source,
But tamed and domesticated
Through Peter and Mary to Tavistock.

The Southern Tors more welcoming,
Familiar from family holidays,
Three Staple Tors, Cox Tor,
Resplendent in sunlight and shade.

Heckford Tor and Pew Tor beyond,
More visible in memory than by eye;
Windy Cross, the Grimstone Leat,
Our old friend Vixen just out of sight.

Further South, the Tamar valley -
Harsh brown moors give way to
Lush, green fields and woods.
Beyond Plymouth we can even see the sea!

Looking West, a church balances
Incongruously, precariously
On the rocks of Brent Tor.
Bodmin and Exmoor loom beyond.

But now our eyes are drawn to
A white house closer by -
Our cottage at Was Tor,
Its welcome gleaming in the sun.

So we shoulder our rucksacks,
Head back down the hill,
Grateful to God for this
Delightful Dartmoor Panorama.

Looking West from Gibbet Hill, Black Down, Dartmoor.
Wastor Farm visible in the left middle distance.

Experimenting with Tetrameter

My son suggested I try out
A poem with even meter throughout,
So here am I a-sat in the sun
To see if the process can be fun!
I really ought to have a plan,
A subject even, rather than

Rambling vaguely line after line,
Waiting for some sort of sign,
Seeking inspiration for
Greater purpose rather more
Meaningful, not such a bore!
So far, I have tried to lick
Tetrameter iambic

In stanza one and then on to
A standard tetra in verse two
And back again for stanza three,
But do you care? Or do you see
That sad to say, this poem is
Almost completely meaningless?

A Windy Day in May

Wastor Farm, Lydford, Devon. 4th May 2023

Trees moan,
Gates creak,
Barns shudder,
Windows rattle.

The wind
Whistles through treetops,
Blasts through hedges,
Whines through wires,
Roars through the wood.

Hazel and birch
Whipped back and forth,
Even oaks and beech
Sway before the onslaught.

Sheep shelter,
Cows huddle,
Deer lie low,
Birds nestle,

Until,
eventually,
The wind subsides,
The din dies down,

The countryside quietens,
The meadows lie still.

Leaving
A debris of torn twigs and
Tender new leaves,
A few broken branches
Wrenched to the ground,

And
Blackthorn blossom
Scattered like confetti
among the bluebells.

We spotted 26 different birds this week!

Wastor Farm, Lydford, Devon. 6th May 2023

Eyes peeled, ears pricked, binoculars at the ready,
We spent a week at Wastor, on the edge of Dartmoor.
The woods were alive with birdsong, dawn till dusk,
So we took up the challenge (as all nature-lovers must) -
We made a list!

We spotted 26 different birds this week,
Not quite a full A-to-Z, but presented here in alphabet
order
(Not to offend any of them, or to be accused of bias).
We saw and we heard...

Blackbirds everywhere, some hopping in the grass,
Some in the trees singing melodies.

A bold bullfinch parading his pink plumage
From the top of his favourite tree.

A buzzard effortlessly soaring and hovering
With barely a flicker of its wing tips.

Two Canada geese flying in, honking,
Landing together on the pond.

Numerous chaffinches, black white and pink,
Cheerfully singing chaffinch songs.

Chiffchaffs, heard often, but seen only once,
Forever repeating their two-tone call.

Crows, big, black and ubiquitous,
On the ground, in the air, croaking everywhere.

Cuckoos calling, audible across the valley,
But never seen, or even heard close by.

Dunnocks, brown and boring and inconspicuous
Until they sing and call you to notice.

A goldfinch singing in a sycamore tree,
We saw its red head, but not its gold wings.

Great tits, perched proudly, easy to see,
Calling 'teacher, teacher', one and all.

Green woodpecker with a red head
Glimpsed briefly as it flashed across the wood.

Two greenfinches in a vicious street-fight,
Right in the middle of the tarmac lane.

A jackdaw nesting in a chimney pot,
Popping out like a rabbit from a burrow.

Magpies, strident in black and white,
Squabbling with each other in the trees.

Mallards on the river, swimming in pairs,
But no little ducklings hatched yet.

Pheasants in the fields, young and old,
Red-headed males at the alert in the long grass.

Robins galore, everyone's favourite,
And by far the least afraid of us.

Skylarks singing, singing high over the moor,
Not even put off by the mist and the rain.

Sparrows fluttering at our window,
They must be nesting in the eaves.

Stonechats perched on top of gorse bushes,
Their call sounds like two stones chinking.

Swallows swooping to and fro over the farm yard,
Occasionally resting on the wires to be admired.

Thrushes (mistle or song, who knows?)
Singing and showing off their speckled breast.

Wheatears on the moor, flitting from rock to rock,
Disappearing ahead in a flash of black and white.

Wood pigeons in the wood (where else?)
Repeating their name, 'wood-pigeon-pigeon'.

Tiny wrens, hopping in the undergrowth,
Singing amazingly loud for such a small bird.

So there we have it, the amateur Dartmoor birders' list -
We spotted 26 different birds this week!

Unrest on the Railway Embankment

Salterns Road, May 2023

Screaming, snarling, yelping, yowling,
Crashing and lashing in the undergrowth -
Fox-fight.

Life of a Fly

Salterns Road, 28th May 2023

On a Sunday afternoon,
Behold the little fly
Buzzing to and fro,
Who knows where, who knows why,
Sadly oblivious to
The chicken's beady eye.
Suddenly, snap!
Fly becomes snack!
Such is the short life of a fly!

The Dorset Shepherd

Dorchester, 30 May 2023
(With apologies to William Barnes)

Cast in bronze, a-standen strong,
On his crook a-leanen,
There he do bide all day among
The busy shoppers passen.

Across the street, zee en stare,
His wold groun' wrap'd in tarmac bare.
Will'm Barnes woonce kept school there,
Nwone knoow 'zackly where.

His dog, quiet at his veet a-lies
At rest, head down, but not a-zleep,
Allus alert to's master's cries,
Ready to roun' up strayen sheep.

But where now the vlock, where the vwold,
When come the sheades of evenen?
No shepherds now, nor young, nor wold,
No sheep now heard a-bleaten.

"This sculpture is a tribute to the quiet heroism and wisdom of pastoralists and cultivators who provide inspiration for the literary tradition associated with Dorchester." Sculptor: John Doubleday, 2000.

Brambles in June

North Road Field, 25th June 2023

A thicket of thrusting thorns,
A tumult of tangled tentacles,
Spiky stems snarling,
Vigorous, vicious,
Like serpents of Medusa,
Eager to ensnare the unwary.

But from a distance, disguised
With a display of beautiful blossom,
Soft white and pale pink,
Like a delicate wild rose,
A visual feast for the eyes,
A nectar feast for the bees.

And each flower a promise
Of a real feast to come,
Blackberries galore
For crumbles and jam,
A rich harvest of ripe fruit,
Free for everyone.

Love is Patient

A meditation on 1 Corinthians 13:4

Love is patient,
Love is kind.
God is patient,
I am not.

Why am I irritated
By queues, by traffic,
By other people doing just
What I want to do?

Why do I care
About those few seconds
I might be able to save?
What would I do with them?

Can I see each moment
As an opportunity?
To practice patience,
To learn to love?

Will I let God ripen in me
The fruit of his Spirit:
Love, joy, peace,
… and patience?

Can I wait patiently for him,
Not relying on myself,
Not rushing ahead
Impatiently?

Will I live in his love,
In the riches of his grace?
Will I show love to others,
In the peace of his patience?

Can I let him turn my
Selfishness into love,
My brooding into joy,
Frustration into patience?

Or will I go on being
Impatient with God
When he doesn't do
What I want?

Love is patient,
Love is kind,
God is patient
With me.

Parkrun

Dedicated to the 713 runners and 55 volunteers who took part in Poole Parkrun on 1ˢᵗ July 2023

They gather in a crowd at nine,
Every Saturday morning,
Come rain or shine.
The regulars greet each other,
A community run,
Like sister and brother.

Assemble on West Field, then go!
Round the cricket pitch and
Round the lake and so
Once more round the cricket ground,
Back to West Field,
Exactly 5k the whole way round.

Young or old, big or small,
None need be ashamed,
There's a welcome to all,
Weak or strong, fit or not,
Everyone joins in,
It's a friendly trot!

Some run alone, some run in pairs,
Some with dogs on leads, or
Babies in pushchairs,
Some proclaim past participation,

Wearing numbered
T-shirts in celebration.

The thundering thump of hundreds of feet
Pound the path like
A Serengeti stampede.
Huffing, puffing, groaning, grunting,
A few cheerfully chatting,
The rest grimly concentrating.

Volunteers in pink hi-vis jackets
Shout encouragement,
Applauding, enthusiastic.
Many runners politely say
"Thank you, marshals"
As they run by.

Ahead of the pack, the properly fit,
Strong and straining,
Eyes forward, face set,
Hoping for a Personal Best.
The stragglers finish at a gentle walk
But cheered on just as much as the rest.

At the finish, everyone
Congratulates each other
On completing the run.
This is community, not competition,
This run is not a race,
This is the Poole Parkrun.

The Pottery Cottages

Pottery Road, July 2023

Cream, grey, blue, yellow
Blue, turquoise, pink, green.
The pottery cottages stand in a row,
Pastel-painted and pristine.

Desirable Victorian houses now,
Workers' cottages no more,
Comfortable middle-class families now,
Where potterymen lived before.

The pottery itself just a memory
Of Poole's past industrial day,
A massive business last century
Making money from ordinary clay.

But gone now the kilns and the ovens,
The pits where they dug out the clay,
Gone are the barrows and wagons
The tank-engine and the tramway.

George Jennings achieved great fame
He made a fortune in his day
Now memorialised in street names:
Jennings Road, Potters Way.

Older houses still show his style
In architectural window mouldings,
Decorative details, fine ridge tiles,
Terracotta plaques on public buildings.

History can seem so long ago
If we rush about too fast
But the pottery cottages stand in a row,
Offering a reminder of our past.

These cottages are on Pottery Road, Parkstone. Next to these used to be the site of George Jennings' Southwestern Pottery, which operated from 1855 to 1967. Products were exported all over the world, and at its height, the pottery had 12 kilns and 6 chimneys. The site was developed for housing in the early 1970s. See https://poolemuseumsociety.wordpress.com/2014/06/1 4/george-jennings-and-the-growth-of-parkstone/

Hottest Day of the Year

Poole Park, 19th July 2022

Hottest day of the year
Poole Park almost people-less
A warm breeze blows over the quiet playground
Swans sail serenely
Ducks doze on one leg
Gatekeepers galore fly to and fro
Fluttering from flower to flower
Revelling in the peace and the hot sun.

An Evening Garden Vignette

Salterns Road, July 2022

Three guinea pigs are in the run.

Caramel and Nutmeg are eating grass
        as if they know it will be
        out of stock tomorrow.
Cinnamon is running in circles
        through one tunnel,
        then the other tunnel,
        then back to the first tunnel again.

Our friendly young robin arrives
        and perches on the edge of the run.
Then it flies down to catch an insect,
        landing a few inches from
        Caramel and Nutmeg.

How do they react?
They carry on munching grass
        as if they haven't been fed for a week.
Cinnamon carries on with her running circles.

The robin flies back up to the edge of the run,
        perches a while,
        then nonchalantly flies on
        to find the next insect.

Summer Haikus

Summer sun on the apple tree,
Speckled Wood
rests a while, basking.

Yellow leaves fluttering down
from the still-green silver birch.
The fading of a long hot summer.

Scratched wrists,
Juice-stained fingers -
Blackberry harvest.

Summer's End

Salterns Road, September 2022

One fat caterpillar
wriggling its way across the patio
replete with weeks of continuous eating,
searching for a suitable spot
to rest and pupate and hibernate,
hoping to emerge in Spring
as a handsome hawk moth.

Two cheerful chickens
roaming the garden, clucking, pecking.
Rocky spots the juicy caterpillar, pecks.
Devon rushes over, grabs.
Both squabbling, chasing, squawking,
hoping to enjoy the prize
as a tasty afternoon treat.

September Saturday Morning Stroll

Poole Park, 10th September 2022

Bright blue sky after the rain,
The water still, clear, like a mirror
Reflecting the low early-morning sun.
Suddenly, in the corner of my eye,
A plop, a splash, a stream of ripples
And bubbles disturbing the reflected sky.
Some sort of speedy-swimming fish?
No - a cormorant! Its head breaks the surface,
Sharp eyes look keenly from side to side
Before diving again to continue the hunt for breakfast.

Among the rushes, a pair of swans
Grazing voraciously with their five cygnets
Still drab, grey, ugly-ducklings,
But full-grown, plump with summer's bounty,
Now as big as the parents that have cared for them.

Across the lake, hundreds of Park Runners
Setting off for their weekly circuit
Round the cricket pitch, round the lake,
Then round again a second time,
Some fit and well-trained, many puffing and wheezing,
But all feeling virtuous every Saturday morning.

High-tide flood through the Keyhole Bridge.
An elderly couple balance precariously
On the narrow pavement, hoping that
No insensitive car-driver comes through to drench them.
Beyond, the harbour lies clear and peaceful,
Brownsea, Corfe, the hills in the distance.
On the rocks a black-headed gull,
Now white-headed, ready for winter.

Dogs large and small, running, barking,
Owners throwing tennis balls and pausing to chat.
Children at football club, running with enthusiasm,
Coaches shouting encouragements,
Parents on the sidelines, wrapped up in coats.
Joggers wearing ear-buds lost in their own world,
Cyclists casual, cyclists serious,
Pedalling with purpose or pleasure.
The distant roar of a jet overhead,
Travellers off to Alicante or Madeira
To get away from it all.

I sit awhile on a friendly bench,
Thankful for the place I call home.

Seend

Manor Cottage, Seend, September 2022

Mansion houses for the Georgian gentry,
Grown wealthy from Wiltshire wool,
Sit proudly on the ridge
On the south side of The Street,
Secluded behind high walls and hedges
But open to the miles of views
Over the vale to Salisbury Plain.

Today's residents recline repletely,
Enjoying their grade-II listed glory
And their immaculate gardens
Tended by an army of local groundsmen.
They worry (a little) about inheritance tax
And the cost of restoration and repairs,
Then share a G&T or two, and play tennis.

Oak and Chestnut

September 2022

Beneath the mighty oak, acorns fall by thousands,
To lie on the ground, unwanted.
No more cottagers lead their pigs to gorge on the feast,
The ancient rights of pannage a distant memory.
The traditional backyard family pig replaced by
Convenient shrink-wrapped sausages from Sainsbury's.

Beneath the chestnut, conkers lie peeping out
From their split spiny cases, unwanted.
No more schoolboys gather to fill their pockets,
Their fathers' playground battles a distant memory,
The quest for the champion conker replaced by
Media streaming, TikTok and screen-scrolling Snapchat.

The trees look down, indifferent to man's fickle fashions.
Oak and chestnut stand tall, year by year, season by
             season,
Acorns and conkers, mini miracles every autumn,
Bear witness to God's unending abundance.

Autumn at Anderwood

Anderwood, New Forest, 6th October 2022

We sit in the still-warm October sunshine
With Sainsbury's sandwiches and a flask of coffee,
Watching the bright white clouds in the bright blue sky,
Listening to the ever-changing sound of the breeze in the
trees.

Silver birches swaying, shimmering, sighing,
Sweet chestnuts bright green, but turning yellow,
Oaks now dark green, fading slowly with the season,
Bracken below in technicolour, green, yellow, orange,
brown.

Brimstones, floating yellow like the falling leaves,
Then fluttering up and away with purpose.
Red Admirals pause, soaking up the sun,
Speckled Woods fly through the speckled wood.

We are buzzed by a Southern Hawker,
Iridescent green, wings flashing in the sun,
Hovering at eye level, checking us out,
Then hawking back and forth catching its prey.

Robins perch expectantly, on fence posts, on the litter
        bin,
Then suddenly the unexpected star of the day -
A nuthatch, grey back, orange breast, black eye stripe,
And long sharp beak finding food under the next picnic
        bench.

Anderwood is a favourite place
To pause for an hour, to watch and wait
And drink in the sights and sounds of the Forest
As we sit in the still-warm October sunshine.

To the Memory of the Brendon Hills Miners

Treborough, Exmoor, October 2022

High on the moor, deep underground,
Hundreds of men work six days a week.
They hack at the seam with shovel and pick,
Hewing the ore from the depth of the earth,
Working by candlelight, always alert
For fear of the sound of danger or fall.

The nuggets of ore are collected in buckets,
Weighty with iron, twice as heavy as rock,
Drawn to the surface like water from a well,
Tipped into wagons ready for transport,
Hauled by steam engine along the high tramway
Through Exmoor mist, and Exmoor gales.

Then down the Incline, one wagon at a time,
Slowly, slowly, slowly, down the 1 in 4 slope
Carved out of the mountainside, even and straight.
Two thirds of a mile takes quarter of an hour,
The winding house brakesman lets out the cable
Inch by inch to the valley eight hundred feet below.

From Comberow six miles beside the River Washford,
Pulled by a saddle-tank named 'Pontypool'
To the harbour at Watchet, onto the West pier,

Horse-drawn the last leg out to the wharf,
Filling the freighter, then setting the sails
Across the Channel to the ports of South Wales.

From pit to port, to foundry and steelworks,
From ore to cast iron, the heat of industry,
Hewn by miners, smelted by furnacemen,
Company owners profit from workers' sweat.
Iron, the heart of industrial revolution,
All comes from underground, high on the moor.

The West Somerset Mineral Railway ran from the mines in the Brendon Hills 13 miles to the harbour at Watchet, transporting wagons of iron ore, which was then shipped across the Bristol Channel to the iron foundries of South Wales. The Incline from the hills to the valley level is a spectacular example of Victorian engineering, constructed between 1857 and 1861. It was a uniform gradient of 1 in 4 and was just over one kilometre long. The Winding House at the top of the Incline contained two winding drums which lowered wagons of iron ore down the slope, at the same time hauling empty wagons (or even passengers 'at their own risk') back to the top. Each cast iron drum was 1 metre wide and 5 metres diameter, and the cables wound on to them were 1000 metres long and weighed 3 tonnes. The mines closed in 1883, but the railway continued to operate until 1898.

Brendon Hill Incline. Photo from https://www.visit-watchet.co.uk/Guide_Request/WSML-Incline.pdf

Walking across Treborough Common

Treborough, Exmoor, October 2022

Flurries of pheasants fly from thickets,
Scatter before me at every stride,
Wings whirring into the mist.

Wait

Wait upon the Lord,
Wait, for he is God,
Wait, for I am not.

I wait for the Lord,
My soul waits,
In his word I hope.

My soul waits in silence,
Waits for God alone,
From him comes my salvation.

I wait patiently for the Lord,
He puts a new song in my mouth,
The joy of the Lord is my strength.

The Lord is good to those who wait for him,
His steadfast love never ceases,
It is good to wait quietly for his salvation.

Be still and know that he is God,
He is my refuge and strength,
In him I live in hope.

God works for those who wait for him,
Trust in him and he will act,
Don't lean on my own understanding.

Wait on the Lord, be strong,
The Lord is my stronghold,
Whom shall I fear?

Fear not, stand firm, and see,
The Lord will fight for you today,
And you have only to be silent.

All who wait for the Lord shall renew their strength,
I will rise with wings like eagles,
I will run and not be weary.

Rejoice in hope, be constant in prayer,
In this hope I was saved,
I wait for it with patience.

Be still before the Lord,
Wait patiently for him,
The meek shall inherit the earth.

The Lord waits to be gracious,
He abounds in steadfast love,
Blessed are all who wait for him.

Wait upon the Lord,
Wait, for he is God,
Wait, for I am not,
Wait.

Bible references in this poem:

> *Exodus 14, 34*
> *Nehemiah 8*
> *Psalms 25, 27, 37, 40, 46, 62, 130*
> *Proverbs 3*
> *Lamentations 3*
> *Isaiah 30, 40, 64*
> *Matthew 5*
> *Romans 8, 12*

War Memorial, Poole Park

Sunday 13th November 2022

Raucous white gulls on sun-glinted lagoon;
Poppy red wreaths round silent grey stone:
Remembrance Sunday afternoon.

Photo from IWM War Memorials Register
© Keith King (WMR-26372)

Silence and Solitude (Upton Heath)

Upton Heath, 12th November 2022

Be still and know that he is God
He is my shepherd, I shall not want
He restores my soul.

I sit in silence on soft springy heather
Low November sun warm in my face
The breeze gentle in my ears
Dry bracken rustles, heather shimmers
Silver birches sway gracefully,
Leaves golden beneath the blue sky
Two pines stand tall, firm, straight.

The earth is the Lord's and everything in it
I lift up my eyes to the hills
From where does my help come?
My help comes from the Lord,
The maker of heaven and earth.

Across the valley, on the next hillside
A fellow wanderer also sits in solitude.
She wraps her arms around her knees,
Contemplating.
Is she thinking the same thoughts as me?

Delight yourself in the Lord
And he will give you the desires of your heart.
Be still before the Lord,
wait patiently for him,
Trust in him, and he will act.

Brief Encounters

Late November, Black Hill, Bere Regis.

Bright blue sky, green meadows in the valley,
Woodland gold and brown, but still tinged dark green,
Dead bracken quietly collapsing into leaf mould.

Solitude here, but not silence.
Traffic thunders by on the A35
Unseen, but a continuous assault on the ears.

A glimpse of movement just twenty yards ahead:
Four Sika deer, strolling, browsing,
silent among the bracken and gorse.

Three move quickly out of sight into the trees
But the buck stands firm on the brow of the hill
A moment, his eyes on me, my eyes on him.

Then he turns and follows his family,
Walking away, unworried, unhurried,
Grey, white and black rump, tail held high.

Later, on the open Heath,
Another sika, a solitary fawn
Looks up, eyes wide, startled.

It moves, a few short leaps, then stops
And looks again, then with a single bark
Bounds away, dancing lightly over the heather.

Autumn landscape glows in the slanting sun,
The sika at home here in woods and heath
And I return to my own home and family

With precious memories of brief encounters.

Chilly Haiku

Blake Hill, 10th December 2022

Frosty morning in December -
Crisp white grass, crystalised leaves,
Breath-clouds hang in icy air.

A Robin in a Holly Tree

Friday, 23rd December 2022

Perched proudly among the prickles,
Bright red breast glowing,
A flash of fire in the dark green.

Sharp eyes alert, piercing,
Beak open as wide as it will go,
Warming the winter with cheerful song.

The notes vary with every verse,
Endlessly inventive,
Loudly carolling a Christmas call.

About the Author

Peter Phillips worked as a competitive intelligence analyst in the telecommunications industry before retiring from full-time employment in 2022. He now focuses on writing (family history and poetry) and on voluntary work. He is an enthusiastic advocate for families with special educational needs and disabilities and he is an elder in a local church. He lives with his wife in Poole, Dorset. They have three grown-up children.

This is his first published volume of poetry. Most of the poems in this book are also published at https://peter-phillips.co.uk/poems/ where forthcoming poems will be published too as they are written.

Peter Phillips has also published a biography of two of his great-great-grandfathers:

Thomas Phillips and Richard Laybourne
Two Victorian industrialists who prospered in the boom years of Newport, South Wales

Printed in Great Britain
by Amazon